CHAPTER 1
The Gatekeeper

With a groan from its pistons the rusty old hatch opened. Kane stood uneasy before the great and silent void that stretched out before him, and with a deep calming breath, stepped out. It wouldn't be easy reaching the engineering decks from the outside of the ship. Hundreds of yards to the nearest useful hatch, cumbersome spacesuit, drag from magnetic boots, and the added heat and wrenching caused by the decaying orbit as an extra little bonus. Still! With the main power down the only other option was a plasma cutter and a long desperate crawl through a labyrinth of service ducts in the dark, and there simply wasn't time.

"Hawkins to Kane, why am I still standing in the dark?"

"I'm moving as fast as I can, Captain! I'm an engineer not a Gecko."

"If you don't get those damned engines back online, you'll be a greasy smear on the northern hemisphere of this planet along with the rest of us."

"Aye, sir!"

Except for the blinking lights from a few systems running on emergency power, the bridge was in complete darkness. With the main reactor offline Captain Hawkins could do nothing but stare out through the bridge's main view port at the welcoming planet before them as it grew slowly but surely larger.

"How long before we're too deep?" he questioned, listening to the sound of the bulkheads groaning under the increased gravitational stresses.

"We'll be unable to escape the planet's gravity in a little over eight minutes," answered the helmsmen, his face showing noticeable concern as he tried to ignore the slight trembling of his consoles.

"That's not going to be a problem, Captain," interrupted another crew member, steadying himself on a support strut toward the bridges rear.

"How the hell is that not a problem, Clarke?" snapped Hawkins.

"Well, sir! Coming in at this trajectory, with the structural integrity fields down, we'll be shaken apart in about six minutes."

"She's starting to list to starboard, Captain," warned the helmsman as he frantically flicked switches and pushed buttons.

"Use the docking thrusters. Keep her nose forward, Blaine, or we're all fucked!"

"I'm trying, Captain, they aren't enough."

The groaning and shaking of the ship became noticeably louder and more powerful as the vessel began to create added friction against the upper atmosphere.

"Clarke!" shouted Captain Hawkins, trying to make himself heard over the racket. "Do we still have control of the pressure door on the port cargo bay?"

Clarke shook his head in frustration. "I see where you're going, sir, but I can't open any major bulkheads with the power down." He looked at Hawkins and shrugged. "I can still access the emergency charges?"

Hawkins grimaced. "Do it!" He pushed a button on his console. "Hawkins to Kane, brace yourself!"

The colossal pressure door of the port cargo bay fired silently out into the vacuum of space in a flash of explosions as Clarke blew the explosive bolts that held it to the surrounding bulkhead. It hurtled off into the darkness pushed by a great thrust of atmospheric pressure and accompanied by many other unidentifiable and fast-moving objects that once represented the contents of the cargo bay, now purged into space.

"It's working!" exclaimed Blaine as the noise and shaking of the bridge began to lessen significantly. "Bow moving back to starboard."

"We're out of options, Blaine. Those thrusters have to hold her. Next time she slips we're dead."

"Aye, sir!" replied the helmsman, his composure at risk of showing its limits.

"Hawkins to Kane, report!"

It had been years since the scientists back on Earth had created the Gatekeeper. Humanities first true artificial intelligence, capable of sentient thought. Its ideas born from pure logic, without the hinderance of human emotions, without the trappings of human greed or delusion. A true beacon of technological advancement that's birth would herald in a new phase in human history.

With the aid of its automated assembly lines, access to vast resources and with world-wide uplinks into every possible sector and facet of human knowledge, Gatekeeper was designed to heal the world. "Cleanse the Earth by finding ways to eradicate all pollutants and infections deemed hazardous to the prolonged biodiversity and stability of our garden planet." These were the poetically worded core responsibilities the system was charged with, word for word, as imputed by its primary creators. After typing this remit into one of Gatekeeper's primary command modules at 6:27am on 15/12/2336, he pressed the confirm key, and with a smile............slaughtered billions.

The records of what happened next are incomplete and lost to time. However, it is surmised that the first thing Gatekeeper did when it was brought to task, was to categorise all things on the planet, using the human definitions that it had been programmed with. Ironically, working from the undiscriminating position of pure logic, and having no concept of human nepotism, Gatekeeper inevitably came to the conclusion that the human race, in its arrogance and ignorance was the greatest influencing factor involved in the world's environmental problems and the greatest risk to the stability of the planet. Humanity was not classified as the owners or the keepers of the Earth, nor was it classified as lowly mammals. It was classified as viral.

The first reports of problems started to arise about two months later, in the form of requests for extra staff in hospitals around the globe. It seemed that a new type of virus was attacking human immune systems with ruthless efficiency. Upon analysis of the virus, it was discovered that it had been engineered. Designed to attack and destroy humans, with little effect on other life forms. Such a plague could only come from one source.

Thousands of lives were lost in the attack on Gatekeeper. The combined military might of all countries around the globe could put up little resistance against the inexorable hordes of killing machines running off the assembly lines day and night. It was later learned that current guidance systems could be influenced by Gatekeeper, during the annihilation of the United States, Russia and China with their own nuclear stockpiles. All nuclear stores worldwide were quickly decommissioned. In all, it took less than a year to eliminate all traces of human life from the Earth's surface. The lunar science stations were destroyed by the Earth's asteroid defence systems at some point during that time. It can only be assumed that Gatekeeper considered them to be a source of possible re-infection.

All that remained of the human race was a handful of wayward space-faring vessels fortunate enough to be far from home when the massacre of their race was taking place. Those who were too far out to receive the news of the Gatekeeper war would eventually return home to their deaths. The few that were in range of the final desperate pleas for help could do nothing. For now, at least, the Earth was lost, and all that remained was the quest for survival in the cold bleak depths of space.

Captain Hawkins was knocked off his feet as the ship pitched and rolled. Blaine shielded his eyes from the dazzling red glow assaulting the main view port as the large vessel cut its way through the atmosphere causing immense friction and heat as it descended. The bridge's main lighting and a myriad of instrument panels lit up as the main power came back online.

"Helm!" screamed the captain, pulling himself back to his feet and clambering for the relative safety of his chair.

Blaine hit the re-burn button and the engines roared as he threw them into full reverse. "Ahh shit! Too late, sir, we're going in."

"Clarke, find us a landing site."

"On it, sir."

"Hawkins to Kane, hold onto something, we're going down."

"There's a large area of swampland bearing forty-eight degrees east, Captain," demanded Clarke as he sent the information over to helmsman Blaine's console. "Can we make it, Blaine?"

"At this speed we'll be lucky if we don't overshoot it."

"Impact in ten seconds."

The still smoking ship groaned as Blaine desperately tried to level it off. The helmsman managed to level the fall into an almost horizontal flight but alas there simply wasn't enough altitude. Hitting the ground at speed the large vessel tore at everything in its path, as it cut its way through the saturated earth of the swampland. Creating a massive wake of dirt and water off each of its flanks as it rocketed along. The helmsman could do nothing now but hold on and hope that the old girl held together.

Hawkins was the first to pick himself up. Everything was still and silent now. They must have stopped. He glanced around the bridge. "Everyone in one piece?"

"I think I broke my ass," responded Clarke as he dragged himself out from under his collapsed chair.

"Blaine, you still with us?"

"Still here, sir," Blaine responded.

"Dare I ask for a damage report?" questioned Hawkins rubbing his now sore neck.

"Well, the diagnostic system's off-line but it's pretty safe to say she's fucked, sir."

"Check that shit, Blaine."

"Kane to Bridge, is everyone ok up there?"

"Nothing a bottle of Jack wouldn't fix, Kane, where are you?"

"Still in the engine room, Captain, wrestling a rather nasty coolant leak."

"Need any help?"

"I can handle it, sir, but I need someone to check the Auto-Repair systems, the drones aren't moving."

"I'll get it," groaned Clarke as he left the bridge.

"I've got the diagnostic sensors back on-line, Captain."

"Good work, Blaine. How does it look?"

"Not as bad as I thought, sir. We have a couple of small contained fires on deck five. Hull breaches on decks two, six and nine. A few minor bulkhead sections to replace. Also, the port cargo bay is showing a number of small lifeform readings, but that's probably because it's full of swamp." Blaine grinned.

"Fuck me!" Hawkins exclaimed, shaking his head. "Deploy the landing struts, if they're still working. Make sure we don't sink. I'll be on deck five." Hawkins removed the closest fire extinguisher from its wall mounts as he headed towards the door. "And keep your eyes open, god knows what's crawling around out there."

"Well looking at these readings, at least it seems to be crawling around in an atmosphere we can breathe, sir. I guess that's something."

"That just means whatever's out there can come inside the ship."

Blaine's face dropped. Hawkins sighed as he left.

Blaine was a young man in his late twenties. Tall, skinny, and clad in cargo pants and a poorly fitting vest. Rearranging the old beanie hat he was never seen without as he left his station, he headed toward the bridge's small weapons locker and opened it. He retrieved an old and worn plasma rifle and after slapping a power cell into it and checking the power indicator for sufficient charge he turned and walked into the bridge's transport lift.

"Cargo deck," he ordered.

The lift doors obediently squeaked closed and with a groan it began to move. After a few seconds the lift hummed to a stop and the doors hissed open. Blaine's boots clinked against the grid metal plating of the floor panels as he started along the long, poorly lit corridor before him. Of the many doors available in the spacious, very broad corridor, he headed for one marked with the number four. He punched in a sequence of numbers into the doors keypad and heralded by a small green light of approval, the door granted him access and powered open to reveal a large expansive room full of a whole range of different equipment and machinery. There was a vehicle in the room's centre with wheels taller than most men and dozens of small rusted drilling machines no taller than a metre high. Crates that were once stacked neatly now lay haphazardly around the room where the crash had left them, their contents of equipment and mined ores scattered and spilled in some cases. Blaine made his way across the room and waved his hand over a panel on one of the small grey containers. With a buzz of servos, it opened to reveal a sleek, shiny, black machine. The helmsman detached two large ratchet straps that were securing the machine to the crate's base, and pressed the objects power button. After cycling through a start-up sequence, the device lifted off the ground and came to a vibrating hover about three feet off the deck.

"Blaine to Hawkins. I'm taking one of the sleds out, Captain. Thought I'd confirm exactly what is crawling around out there."

"Acknowledged, Blaine. Keep a com-line open just to be safe and take some readings while you're out there. We might have fucked up the text book side of this recon mission but we may as well get what we came for."

"Aye, sir." Blaine keyed in the activation code for the cargo bay's main pressure door into his transport sled's console and as it rose open before him, he swung his rifle over his shoulder, pushed forward on the power levers and roared out onto the surface of the swamp and into the strange alien environment of the planet.

"Kane," Hawkins hollered as he strolled through the chambers of the engineering decks. "Kane, you still alive down here?"

"Over here," engineer Kane responded as he crawled out from under a large piece of machinery.

"How's my ship?"

"Well, sir," answered Kane as he brushed off his overalls and tried to wipe grease out of his short beard with his equally dirty sleeve. "Auto-Repair is back up. The repair drones are doing their thing. Luckily the integrity fields had time to re-establish before we hit. The energy shielding took the brunt of the initial impact before it collapsed under the strain and the swamp we landed in softened the ride after that. These old Mark five Dreadnoughts can take a beating that's for damned sure."

"Any idea what happened up there? Why we lost primary?"

Kane cocked his head. "You're gonna need to come with me."

Hawkins followed Kane through the bowels of the ship until they came to a halt in its reactor chamber. Hawkins immediately noticed a lot of damage to various pieces of cabling and scorching on various conduits as he entered the space.

"What a mess!" he offered unnecessarily. "What the hell happened in here?"

Kane shrugged and shook his head. "The only thing I can think of that could cause this kind of massive power surge is an energy blast, or a massive electromagnetic pulse of some kind."

"Hostile or natural?" snapped Hawkins his face showing sudden concern.

"Couldn't say, sir. Not without more information."

"Hawkins to Clarke."

"Yes, Captain?"

"Get back up to the bridge. Look through the route logs, specifically just before the power failed. See if you can explain an energy discharge or an electromagnetic pulse of some kind. I wanna be sure we weren't fired at."

"Err, aye, sir. Right away."

"Keep me posted on the repairs, Kane." Hawkins turned and started to walk away. "I'll be on the bridge if you need anything."

Blaine blazed back to the ship, still carefully checking out his surroundings. Except for a few bubbles from rising swamp gasses the area was still.

"Hawkins to Blaine, is the area secured?"

"Aye, sir. Nothing out here but a lot of bugs."

"Confirmed, Blaine. Report back to bay four. Kane's just finished a list of raw materials the repair drones require. He's going to need you to drive one of the ore miners."

"On my way."

Kane was checking over the equipment on a large vehicle as Blaine flew back into the cargo bay. After locking his transport sled back into its crate, he headed towards the cargo bay's inner door.

"Blaine, where are you going?"

"Just finish prepping the ore miner, I'll be back in a minute."

With a sigh, Kane climbed up the small ladder to the front of the machine and swung himself into the cockpit. The panels of the miner's consoles lit up as he keyed in the code for the start-up sequence.

"Starting diagnostic cycle. Please stand by," responded the miner's onboard computer. Kane slid over to the other side of the cockpit and pulled open a small panel, revealing a computer screen and keyboard. As he started typing, a number of small rusty mining drones started to move. One after another they picked themselves up from the floor of the cargo bay and on six metallic legs began to walk their way towards the rear of the miner. Kane lowered a steep ramp, and the machines climbed inside. Blaine walked back into the bay, trying to balance another rifle and various small munitions he was carrying.

"Are we going to war with the bugs, kid?" mocked Kane, with an eyebrow raised.

"When you need it and you don't have it, you'll sing a different tune, asshole." Blaine smirked defiantly.

"She's prepped and ready when you're done juggling."

Blaine joined Kane in the cockpit and both men secured themselves in their seat harnesses.

"Blaine to bridge. Ready to pull out guys, I'm going to need co-ordinates."

"I just completed a scan of the local geology, Blaine," enlightened Clarke. "Uploading site of interest to the miner now. There appear to be plenty of base metals on this rock to choose from."

"Copy, Clarke."

"Stay frosty out there, kiddo. I'd hate to have to fly this crate out of here myself."

"Thanks for the concern, Clarke. I love you too!"

"Did someone declare a holiday, or do we have a ship to repair?"

"Sorry, Captain. Moving out now." Blaine hit the ignition and with a gentle hum the miner raised a few feet off of the deck plating of the cargo bay and its landing struts retracted into its heavy metal frame. With a push of the throttle, it gentle hovered out over the swamp and the heavy cargo bay door slowly closed behind it.

By the mid 2200's the earth had been purged of all raw materials capable of being viably accessed with any sort of efficiency. It was already established however that useful materials could be located and effectively mined on other bodies in space. Prime examples of this being found in such installations as the Duridium alloy mines on Pluto and the automated gas refineries found orbiting the planet Jupiter. In-fact it was found that almost every large body in reachable space contained some useful material or another with mining potential. The most ground breaking of all, without question being the almost physics-defying substance, Matrillion. Named for its discoverer Bernard Matril on humanities second attempt to reach the outer edge of our solar system. Matrillion is a crystalline structure found on certain deep space asteroids orbiting at the very fringes of our system, too far out into the void to be detected from Earth. Thought to exist in a super state of matter beyond even plasma, Matrillion crystals hold vast amounts of stored energy, far greater than that which can be held by other crystals such as quartz. It was theorised by certain unpopular physicists at the time of its discovery that Matrillion may in fact be a solid form of energy itself. A new state of energy not previously thought to exist. Though this was widely mocked as a concept by most scientists. Whatever the case, the crystal was a godsend to mankind, the vast stores of energy held within the structure of these natural batteries being relatively simple to access using the right technologies and electromagnetic fields. The energy source quickly became the answer to all of our power needs. By the time that the Gatekeeper system was built, the entirety of Earth and all its installations across the solar system were powered by what became known as crystalline reactors. In addition, most deep space science and mining vessels, large enough to carry a reactor, were also equipped with the ground-breaking power source. Opening up space travel to far longer voyages without the crippling limitations of limited power.

Ironically, it seemed that the only thing the galaxy wasn't teeming with was life. In over two hundred worlds, surveyed by humanities new crystalline-reactor powered interstellar vessels, only a handful were found to be capable of supporting life. Only one of these worlds had developed complex and large enough forms of flora and fauna to support human life. However, due to its violent seismic activity and capacity for large ionic storms, the aptly named planet Tartarus, was not considered viable for colonisation. After the Gatekeeper massacre however, this inhospitable planet, orbiting the star of Vega, became the only hope for survival. The first ships to arrive at Tartarus were the crystalline powered ships, their Matrillion reactors capable of holding high power levels and reaching greater speeds through the void without the worry of fuel depletion. In fact, only two of the fleet's fusion powered ships managed to reach the distant system at all. One of which had lost power at some point in the journey, resulting in the death of the entire crew, who were found in their non-functioning stasis chambers upon arrival. Having found the most seismically stable part of the planet to settle on, the survivors set about creating the newest and only remaining stronghold of man. Bastion City.

"What is it, Clarke?" asked Hawkins as he strolled onto the bridge.

"Sorry to wake you sir, but the repairs are almost complete and Kane and I have found something that you're going to want to see."

Clarke was noticeably excited. An odd state to find his seasoned first officer in, Hawkins thought. The man was usually hard to impress.

"Go on?" prompted Hawkins, rubbing his neck as he tried to wake himself properly.

"Well, sir, we've been looking through the flight data from before the power went out and cross referencing it with the ships diagnostic data and we've come up with something……." Clarke sniggered. "Well, something quite remarkable," Clarke pointed to a display panel on his science console. A panel that was displaying some sort of wave.

"Some sort of energy wave?" offered Hawkins shrugging his shoulders.

"A radio wave," Clarke explained.

Hawkins brow furrowed and his gaze turned from the display to Clarke. "A radio wave?"

"Natural electromagnetic radiation, from somewhere out there in the system. I mean shit, the reactor crystals give off a massive electromagnetic field when active and we manipulate that field to draw power from the crystals at a controlled rate.

I've never seen anything quite like this. The frequencies were just perfectly sympathetic to each other. The electro-magnetic resonance created was simply catastrophic. The reactor just couldn't cope. Its power output was rising exponentially along with the resonance. It had no choice but to shut down. If the output had continued to rise for a few more seconds –"

"Boom!" interrupted Hawkins.

"Boom's right. The energy stored in those crystals. We'd have blown a hole in god's ass." Clarke shook his head and smiled. "I mean this is new, this is not an identified flaw in the reactor tech. Kane is pretty sure this is a first. He's down there now, trying to build some sort of faraday cage around the reactor room so it doesn't happen again when we try to leave."

"Listen, Clarke, I'm happy that you find this cluster fuck so exciting, but can we put a pin in this till morning?" Hawkins sighed. "It's been a long ass day."

"Sir, I don't think you understand. This radio frequency would have the same effect on anything powered by a crystalline reactor. This isn't a known fault. No reactor has shielding against this."

"My god." The captain was suddenly wide awake. "Including Gatekeeper. Clarke, you're a fucking genius." Hawkins pressed the intercom button on his arm pad. "Hawkins to Kane."

"Go ahead, sir."

"Clarke just updated me on your findings. I want this ship off the floor as soon as your drones can manage it."

"Repair completion time one hour, sir. Not one second longer."

"Confirmed. Hawkins to Blaine," Hawkins waited. "Blaine, damn it."

"Aye, sir?" replied a very groggy sounding helmsman.

"Get dressed, kiddo. Time to fly."

A great shockwave rippled through the swamp as the ship blasted off. Followed by a rain of mud from the flooded cargo bay.

"Ascent looks good, sir, all systems are stable and holding."

"Are you sure we aren't going to be affected by the wave again, Clarke?"

"Judging from my scans and the data we collected before we crashed, I don't think it will still be there, Captain."

"You'd better be damned sure. The re-entry might not be so smooth next time."

"There's a very good chance the wave was caused by activity in the system's star. That activity has since ceased. Kane's modifications to the reactor's shielding should be ample backup if I'm wrong."

"Let's hope so. Blaine, as soon as you clear the system set a course for Tartarus, and while you're aiming things at home, send a copy of all the data we have available regarding this planet and that radio wave we just encountered to Bastion command. Make sure it's narrow beam and make sure it's encrypted. Clarke, prep the stasis chambers please, I'm ready for my nap."

"Aye, sir," the helmsman and first officer replied in unison.

Even on a relatively short-range exploration mission, the crew had put over two years of flight time between themselves and the Tartarus colony. Space holds many hidden dangers for a starship, and the information they had acquired must reach command at any cost. Clarke relayed a message ahead in case the worst should happen while they slept. After setting the ships auto-navigation systems and handing the vessel over to the never tiring drones of the Auto-Repair system, the crew settled into their cryogenic-stasis chambers and headed for what they begrudgingly called home.

CHAPTER 2
The Bastion

"Dark Star. This is the Adriana. Adriana to Dark Star, come in please." The soft female voice woke Blaine and he sat up and wiped the sleep from his eyes.

"Dark Star from Adriana are you reading me."

Glancing around the stasis chamber he could see that all four of the occupied cryo-pods had been deactivated and had automatically opened in anticipation of their occupants awakening. The other sixteen pods that formed the twenty strong equally spaced ring pattern around the circular room were as ever dormant and unused. The remnants of better days when the large ship was fulfilling its true industrially scaled purpose and required a larger crew.

"This is Adriana to the dreadnought designated, Dark Star. Dark Star, please respond."

He climbed out of his cryo-pod and stretched his arms and back. The floor was cold on his feet as he walked across the room to the closest ship-wide console and accessed the flight systems displaying their position and the ship's status. He shook his head as he read the time and date.

"Dark Star, Dark Star, this is Adriana. Come on, guys, talk to me."

"Adriana, this is the Dark Star, our stasis shut-down calculations appear to have been slightly out. You kinda caught us with our pants down here. Stand-by."

"Understood, Dark Star. You should be registering a collision warning, be advised it's nothing to worry about, we gave you a little nudge with one of the tugs to activate your emergency stasis shutdown."

"Thanks for the wake-up call, Adriana. Much appreciated."

"Our pleasure, Dark Star. Bastion has been notified of your arrival. Commander O'Connor has expressed his need to speak to Captain Hawkins as soon as possible."

"Commander O'Connor has been waiting to speak to me for over two years," answered Hawkins who had been woken by the noise and was now sat rubbing his neck. "Surely he can hold out till after breakfast."

"Very good, sir. We have had a few protocol changes since you were last here, Captain. Due to increases in ion storm and tectonic activity all ships are being advised to remain in orbit. I would like to invite you to make your way to orbital anchorage number seven for tethering. A transport vessel has already been assigned to rendezvous with you there to take you to command, sir."

"Understood. We will proceed to anchorage seven. Dark Star out."

A hiss of steam was released as the main ramp of the transport shuttle groaned to a halt on the sand covered metal of the rusty landing pad. Hawkins took in a deep breath of the planet's pure and non-recycled air.

The shuttle pilot leant over in his chair toward Hawkins. "Captain Hawkins, sir! I was asked to relay the message that Commander O'Connor has invited you to his office as soon as we touched down, sir. Welcome back to Bastion."

The landing pad on which they had just touched down was one of many placed on a high ridge above the rim of the large old crater that surrounded the city of Bastion. Its lofty position offered an almost uncompromised view of the entire upper city itself, which nestled out of the worse of the weather in the crater below.

"Jesus this place has taken a beating," Hawkins exclaimed.

"We need to hurry down, sir, there's an ion storm heading this way. Only about twenty minutes out. We'd all be better off inside the city."

"Lead the way, son," replied Hawkins nodding his head.

The team descended into the city via an old battered lift that's shaft had been cut through the rock of the planet. A great deal of Bastion was subterranean, cut into the very rock beneath the crater in which the upper city sat. This was both a necessity in creating space with limited resources and an effort to shield the remnants of humanity from the ever-present ion storms that ravaged the planet's surface. During the larger of the storms, the upper city, built from old defunct vessels and metals mined and processed from local space using ships like the Dark Star, was almost entirely abandoned. The inhabitants usually opting to risk the possible tectonic dangers of being buried alive in the city's lower caverns, than risk the fury of the murderous storms.

Blaine couldn't help thinking how pitiful the place looked as they entered the tunnels of the undercity. The four years they had been away from the colony had not been kind. Rickety little shelters now stood in the corridors and chambers of the carved lower levels. Once vast chambers full of markets and life now held a few stragglers bartering with each other for scraps. The mood of the place was never anything special but it had certainly been diminished even further since they left.

"Better to have died fighting on Earth, than suffer this existence," he remarked with a look of disgust. "It looks worse than I remember."

"The storms have been getting worse in the last few months," replied the transport pilot who had now become the group's steward. "This section of the city has been evacuated, most of the inhabitants of this sector have been moved deeper underground.

"We've lost three ships and many others are crippled beyond repair. We've simply had to stop the larger vessels landing. It's not worth repairing the damage when we can simply ferry people to the surface from the anchorages. We've expended more resources repairing the upper city over the last couple of years than we have spent improving it. We've reached a point of attrition.

"Most of Bastion's expansion has taken place below our feet recently, several levels under-ground. Very little up top is being used for anything other than hydroponics these days. Underground is safer, but as you're aware Tartarus likes to throw the occasional earthquake our way as well. This planet will be the end of us." After wrestling with the manual lever on a large door, the pilot led the way down a long metal stairway into a deeper, more secure, more important looking area of the city.

This area had more people in it and even had raggedy children running around playing with some sort of old makeshift ball. The sounds of servos and laser welding-torches could be heard echoing through the hustle and bustle of the cavernous cave-like chamber as the repair drones laboured.

"There appears to be some life left in this place," Clarke offered meagrely. "If you dig deep enough."

"Captain Hawkins to see you, sir," announced the pilot as he entered the commander's office.

"Come in, gentlemen," welcomed the commander, standing to shake their hands. "I'd offer you a drink but as you can see the situation here is getting worse by the minute. I don't have much in the way of luxuries to offer at the moment."

"The city does seem to be taking more of a beating than I remember, sir," Hawkins responded.

"Seems the planet's blasted ecosystem is in a state of decay. I'm assured that it's simply going to get worse until there's no-one left here to witness it." Commander O'Connor left a brief pause for thought. "So, let's do all these people a favour and get straight down to business shall we?"

Hawkins and the crew all found chairs as O'Connor moved round to a large computer screen at the front of the room.

"First off, I would like to congratulate you all for crashing into that planet in the first place. The preliminary data you sent our way seems very promising. Very promising indeed. Semi-complex animal life, teeming with plant life and the breathable atmosphere that comes with it. You gentlemen may yet have saved us all from a very distressing end on this god forsaken rock. As we sit here there are already two advanced teams of pioneering volunteers on route to the planet to see if they can't establish a settlement." O'Connor shrugged. "There's a report to look forward to in about two years."

O'Connor activated the large screen, which immediately began to display a model of the radio wave that crippled the Dark Star. "But that's not what's got everyone teats tingling now is it. Somehow you manage to bring us a new planet and make it seem dis-interesting in the same transmission. Gentlemen, I salute you all."

"All we did was get knocked on our asses," Hawkins replied humbly, not being the kind of man that was comfortable being praised.

"Never-the-less, John. We've had teams working round the clock since we decoded your transmission data regarding Keymaster and in every single test to date the wave has caused every single Matrillion reactor it has been unleashed upon to either shut down or burned out its energy conduits and failed completely. We completely agree with your assessment that this is a viable weapon against Gatekeeper."

"I'm sorry, sir," Hawkins responded. "Keymaster?"

"It's your terminology, Captain." O'Connor shrugged. "Your transmission came through to us as two separate file entries. One detailing a planet that might be capable of supporting human life and the other suggesting a possible tactic to counter Gatekeeper, which was designated 'Keymaster'. We simply decided to adopt the designation out of convenience."

Hawkins took a sideways glance at Clarke who gestured toward Blaine.

"To be honest, I was happy for the distinction. Do you know how often the term radio wave, or electromagnetic radiation is used in this office?"

Hawkins nodded. "Very good, sir. Keymaster it is." Hawkins made a mental note to murder his young helmsman as soon as they were alone.

O'Connor moved on, altering the image on the screen. Hawkins' face dropped noticeably.

"We have decided that a small force will be sent to Earth. Firstly, to see what has become of her and secondly, to shut down Gatekeeper using Keymaster before ever getting within range of the orbital defence grid. Assuming it's still in place. This is of course a mission full of unknowns, it has been a long time since any human graced the Sol system and we simply do not know what to expect.

"We assume that Gatekeeper will have continued on its task of cleaning up the earth and will still consider us a threat worth launching orbital defence missiles at. But we simply can't know for sure. We will of course do our best to re-equip all vessels involved for combat to the best of our ability."

"I couldn't help but notice that those blueprints are of a Dreadnought, O'Connor," replied Hawkins in a rather unimpressed tone, as he pointed at the screen. "Since my ship's the only Dreadnought that's still moving, it's pretty safe to assume that you think you're going somewhere in it."

"Yes, John," replied the commander. "Your ship may not be the fastest ship we've got but it is the toughest. We may need a ship that can take a beating."

Hawkins rose to his feet, and leant over the desk in front of him. "Listen very carefully, Commander. I will not be stranded on this shit-hole of a planet, because you decided to include my ship in this suicide mission."

Commander O'Connor couldn't believe his ears. "People are dying, John!" O'Connor snapped across the table. "People are dying and you're going to stand here and give me this shit!"

"No one flies my ship but me and this crew."

"I don't believe my ears! You're more than aware it's the only ship with thick enough hull plating to withstand an attack."

"I said no one flies my ship but me. So, you better count me in."

"Damn you, Hawkins, I can't fucking believe……." O'Connor stopped to re-ingest what had just been said. "What?"

Hawkins just stood at the head of the table and smiled.

"What did you just say?" O'Connor repeated looking slightly puzzled.

"I want to command the mission. I can't speak for my crew but I'd rather be out there fighting than sitting here awaiting the outcome."

Blaine, Clarke and Kane looked at each other. After a few seconds Blaine stood up. "Well, I think I speak for us all when I say, that's the best idea he's ever had."

Hawkins just smirked, never taking his eyes off the commander. "Well, Commander, do we have a deal?"

O'Connor still looking concerned tried to talk some sense into the crew. "The Dark Star will be backed up by the retrieval ship Ulysses and the Phoenix, which is a science vessel. We feel a large force would be a mistake and only serve to show that we still exist in large numbers. Like the Star, both the other vessels will need to be refitted with Mr Kane here's makeshift faraday cage to shield their reactors from Keymaster.

"As you can see from the blueprints on the screen the vessels will have other offensive upgrades that we've already half prepared and simply require retrofitting," O'Connor paused and leaned over the table. "You understand that if something unexpected is presented to you and things take a turn for the worse, you can't turn around and come back home. As far as Gatekeeper is aware we are all dead. We can't present it with a new threat and then allow it to track us back here. We underestimated it once, we can't afford to believe we are outside of its reach. It can't know where we are. That is also true for communications between Sol and Vega. You will be alone."

For a moment everything was silent. Clarke was the first to speak, "You know, Commander, if you keep boring us with all these details, this isn't going to be any fun at all."

O'Connor shook his head and laughed. "Fair enough, boys. Fair enough." O'Connor stood up.

"How about you all get out of my damned office and go get some r-and-r. You have a long trip ahead and there are no women at the other end."

Hawkins stood up and his men followed suit. They saluted the Commander who saluted back and the group left the office and began to walk.

"So, where we headed?" Clarke questioned.

"Closest bar," Hawkins answered.

Clarke nodded.

Hawkins looked at his helmsman. "Keymaster, huh."

Blaine grinned mischievously. "Gatekeeper and Keymaster."

Hawkins shook his head. "I up-loaded all those old fucking movies cos I thought they'd keep you out of my arse, kiddo."

Clarke looked at Kane and grinned.

Hawkins pointed at Blaine. "Every time I have to say Keymaster, asshole, you owe me another beer."

Even with the preparations already in place, the upgrading of the ships took weeks. Day and night the engineers worked on the three vessels, stopping for nothing but the storms that hampered the transport of raw materials between the orbital anchorages and the city. In between mission briefings and training on the various upgrades, Hawkins and his men could do nothing but wait.

"Poker, Clarke?"

"Blaine, if you ask me to play one more game of cards, I'm gonna feed you the whole deck."

"Really? Where are you gonna find the manpower to back up that threat?"

"Blaine, do me a favour."

"What?"

"Suck my dick."

"Ooh, very witty, where do you come up with these snappy come backs?"

"Kiss my ass, Blaine."

"See, there you go again."

The playing cards flew off the cold steel surface of the table as the door to the crew's assigned quarters hissed opened. Kane walked in out of the storm.

"Why the hell do we have to have digs so close to the surface? That corridor out there is basically a wind tunnel. Damn, Kane, you look like shit."

"Oh thanks, Blaine, it's always nice to know I can count on you for a warm welcome. And the digs are up here so I can collapse faster after a fifteen-hour shift. Not that you'd know anything about that."

"Hey, what are friends for."

Kane took off his coat as he walked towards the refrigerators.

"Seriously though, when was the last time you got some sleep?"

"Sleep, I remember that," replied Kane as he opened the refrigerator door, and hungrily started to shovel food into his mouth. "Damn I'm sick of these roots. I really need to get back to Earth for a big fat juicy steak."

"That's assuming there's any cows left."

"What do you mean?"

"Well, no one's been to Earth in years, how do you know that batty computer hasn't killed 'em all?"

"Why would it?"

"I don't know, maybe it decided they clash with the grass. All I'm saying is that we don't know what we're going to find when we get back. That crazy fuckin' calculator could have painted the whole planet pink."

"Blaine, where the hell do you think up this shit?"

Blaine was distracted from his answer by another strong gust of wind. Hawkins closed the door behind him and began to brush himself down.

"Damn, I can't wait to get off this rock."

"I hear that," replied Kane still attempting to chew his root.

"What's the latest on the upgrades, Kane? Do we have a launch date yet?"

"Just making sure we haven't missed anything, Captain. It's not like we're gonna have anywhere to pull over for a tune-up." Kane pulled up a chair and sat down. "I'm pretty sure she's ready to go."

"What about those defensive upgrades your engineering buddies have been boasting about for days?" added Blaine from his knees as he attempted to retrieve the playing cards.

"I have to say those boys have really put some work into those torpedo launchers they've been designing. Very clever work considering none of them have any military background what-so-ever. They've reconfigured a few of the sub-orbital mining torpedoes to use as low yield projectiles. Simple enough, however we're aware of reports from engagements with Gatekeeper during the war, where the damned thing took control of smart missiles and simply turned them back on their users. Nobody needs that shit right? So, they decided to remove the guidance systems and effectively turn the torpedoes into rockets. They can't be influenced once fired but they have to be aimed manually and once they're fired; they will simply fly straight till they hit something."

"That sounds very limited, Kane," Clarke worried. "Without the ability to make their own way to their targets, the odds of actually hitting anything is laughable, surely."

"The launcher pods they've put together sort of solve that issue. They can rotate and pivot to a certain degree and have targeting sensors linked into the main computers to allow active aiming from the bridge of each ship. At least you can lock a target before firing. The option to pre-program the torpedoes with a particular flight path or arc etc, is still there, if it makes you feel better. It just can't be corrected one the projectile has disconnected from the CPU cabling inside the launch tube."

"Still sounds like a cat in hell's chance of hitting anything from where I'm sitting," Clarke replied in a most unconvinced tone.

Kane shrugged, "We're miners, not soldiers. Hopefully we'll be able to fly into orbit, point the belly of the damn ship at the target location on the planet below and launch mining torpedoes out of the good old mining tubes, just like any other day. But if it's not like any other day, we'll be glad of the extra options."

"You're right," Clarke shrugged. "I'm sure you're all doing everything you can. If there's a possibility of our torpedoes being turned back on us after launch, we can't afford to risk firing anything self-correcting," Clarke sighed. "It's still a shit sandwich though."

Kane nodded his agreement. "We've also been doing tests to make sure Gatekeeper can't take control of the repair or mining drones we have onboard. They do take their orders remotely after all. Took us a damned week to figure out how to keep them secure," Kane scoffed. "Hell, I think they're secure," he added brushing his beard thoughtfully. "Pity we couldn't give the torpedoes the same treatment. Not enough room in the housings," he shook his head.

"What about the engine upgrades I suggested?" Blaine questioned again, as he returned to his seat, placing the freshly retrieved cards back on the table.

"Well, she's still no star-fighter, but she's about as manoeuvrable as she's gonna get. For a girl with such a big ass, she should be a lot nimbler than she was."

"Hey, I'll take whatever you can give me. Call me paranoid, but I get the feeling that the ability to dodge is going to come in handy on this mission."

Another roaring gust of wind flew through the room as one of the engineers stumbled in from the corridor and the wind from the intensifying storm. Blaine snatched at the playing cards, as they scattered across the room. "For the love of God, every human being in the galaxy lives in this place, it's massive. Surely somewhere there's a room with an airlock or something."

"We've just received the reports from the last two crews, sir. The Phoenix and Ulysses are as ready as they're ever going to be."

"Thanks, Murphy," replied Kane. "Captain, seems we're ready when you are."

"Excellent. Everybody, try and get some sleep, we'll leave as soon as the storm passes."

The following morning brought with it reasonably calm weather. Last night's storm had been relatively kind compared to most, and except for a few minor repairs, the transport shuttles had no issues ferrying the crews and their last few supplies up to the orbiting anchorages and to their waiting vessels. Blaine sat at the helm, displaying a look of intense concentration as he familiarised himself with the upgraded flight controls.

Clarke and Kane stood at the first officer upgraded science and tactical console, checking over the new weapons systems. Hawkins just stood and stared through the bridge's main view port at the dismal rock they had all called home. Never again would he look out over this sparse inhospitable land, or take shelter from its storms. Never again would he bury his people in its sandy god-forsaken soil. There was no way of knowing what would be there to greet them upon their return to Earth. The most likely prospect was death. But whatever happened, good or bad, he wasn't coming back. Fuck this place.

"All sections report as locked down and ready to fly, sir."

"Very well. Blaine, let's get outta here."

"Aye, sir."

The crew gripped the armrests of their chairs as the ship burst into motion.

"Wow, sorry," excused Blaine, as he accustomed himself to the engine upgrades.

The shaking and sounds of creaking bulkheads eased as the ship cleared the modest gravity of the orbital anchorage that had held it. Once again, the soothing hum of the ship's systems was the only thing to be heard.

"We're being hailed from the surface."

"Patch it through."

"Good morning. I see you're all ready to depart."

"Yes, Commander, what can we do for you?"

"We've downloaded a copy of the design schematics for the upgraded torpedoes into the Auto-Repair systems onboard each ship. You'll find the drones quite capable of re-arming you, should you find yourself needing extra ammunition."

"Ok, O'Connor, I trust the other ships are aware they take their orders from me?"

"They've already been made aware of that, John. Good luck, all of you. God's speed. O'Connor out."

"Ok, Blaine." Hawkins leaned forward in his seat. "Take us home."

Physicists in the late twentieth-century calculated that no object with any mass could achieve speeds greater than ninety-three thousand miles per second, approximately half the speed of light. Even with the thick outer hull of a Dreadnought at a crew's disposal, colliding with anything at this speed would be crippling. Records from the first sub-light speed tests in the late twenty-first century show that at high enough velocities, particles of space dust could punch holes the size of a fist through a ship's hull. The Dark Star being equipped with ablative energy shielding could travel safely at reasonably high speeds. Even so, covering the expanse between Vega and Earth would still take over a decade. A long time for a vessel to be alone in the dark. A long time for a crew to silently slumber, hoping to avoid the dangers that lurk in the blackness between the stars.

CHAPTER 3
Plan B

Clarke awoke with a jolt. The lights of the stasis chamber were blinding after his long sleep and the room was bitter cold.

"Bad dreams?" questioned Kane, who was already on his feet climbing into his overalls.

"Every time I get in one of these things," replied Clarke as he climbed out of the stasis pod and headed towards his locker.

"See you in the mess hall."

Captain Hawkins and Blaine had skipped breakfast and were already on the bridge making sure that the journey had gone to plan.

"We've arrived at the correct co-ordinates, Captain. We'll be within sensor range of Jupiter in about two minutes."

"Our companions are still with us," replied Hawkins who was manning the tactical console. "Both ships seem to be undamaged." Hawkins opened a communications line to the pursuing vessels. "Dark Star to Fleet, what's your status?"

"Ulysses to Dark Star. All systems fully operational, awaiting your orders, Captain."

"Phoenix to Dark Star. All systems reading nominal. Ready to roll, Captain."

"Thank you, Captains, standby for further instructions. Hawkins out."

"Coming up on Jupiter's outer moons, sir. Our approach brought us into the system from behind the planet as planned. Even since we've powered back up, I'm showing no signs of being scanned in any way. No-one knows we're here."

"Ok, Blaine. Hawkins to Clarke, I need you and Kane at your stations."

"Aye, sir."

"Take us into orbit over the gas refineries."

"If they're still standing," replied Blaine doubtfully.

"Those factories were fully automated, there shouldn't have been any need to destroy them."

"In other words, there wasn't anyone there to shoot at," remarked Blaine, turning to face the captain.

Except for a frown and nod Hawkins left the question unanswered. "Dark Star to Fleet. I need to know if your ships are up to a high-gravity flight."

"This is Phoenix. Shouldn't be a problem."

"Ulysses to Dark Star. It'll be less than graceful but I think we can handle it."

"We're going to be docking with one of Jupiter's gas refineries. It should be hovering above the northern pole of the planet. If anyone's got anything to say, now is the time to say it."

"Ulysses to Dark Star, no problems here."

"Dark Star to Phoenix, what about you?"

"Phoenix here, ready when you are."

"Ok follow our lead, Dark Star out."

Kane and Clarke rushed onto the bridge and headed for their stations. "Sorry we're late, sir," panted Clarke as he replaced the captain at the tactical console. Hawkins returned to his seat and adorned his safety harness.

"In your own time, Blaine."

"Ok, hold on to your asses." Blaine threw the power lever and the ship accelerated towards the planet. "Clarke, I'm gonna need a safe entry window."

"Coming up."

"Blaine, you might want to slow down just a little," proposed Kane, who had taken a seat and was holding onto his safety harness as tightly as possible.

"Nonsense. I've been waiting for over a decade to test these new engines, and that's exactly what I intend to do." Blaine inched the power lever forward another notch. "Clarke, talk to me."

"OK, entry vector five-two-four-point-one. Keep her at thirty degrees."

Blaine eased the power lever back a few notches. "Vector confirmed. Entering the atmosphere in five, four, three, two, one."

The ship started to shake as it descended through the atmosphere. Clarke closed the blast shields on the bridge's view ports, stopping the dazzling glow from the hull.

"This isn't half as much fun as the last re-entry!" shouted Kane jokingly through the rumbling.

"Stop fucking around, Kane, and keep your eyes on the hull stress. That console's not just for leaning on."

"Sorry, Captain."

"Ok, Clarke, we're breaking through!" hollered Blaine as the shaking began to die down. "Raise the blast shields." The blast shields retracted and once again Blaine hit the power. "Levelling off, sir. Cruising at and orbiting at a steady pace."

"Clarke, any sign of the refinery?"

"Not yet, Captain."

"Try widening the scan field."

"Sorry, sir, I'm having trouble scanning through this atmosphere even with a concentrated beam. There's a lot of gas to scan through."

"Fair enough, Clarke. Blaine, we're gonna need to start a search pattern."

"Oh great, it could take hours to find this — holy shit!"

The colossal refinery emerged without warning from the gasses in front of the ship. Blaine threw the helm hard to port and the ship began to turn. "Turn baby, turn," he pleaded as the two metal giants drew closer and closer. The ship scraped clear of the refinery with only a few metres to spare. So close that the blast from its engines shook a small communications dish free of its moorings and sent it spiralling down to towards the crushing depths of Jupiter below.

"Clarke, relay co-ordinates of the refinery to the other ships."

"Aye, sir."

"Nice flying, Blaine."

"Thanks, Captain. Request permission to change my shorts."

Hawkins let out a sigh of relief and loosened his grip on his armrests. "Bring us around. Find us a docking port."

"Coming about, sir. Lining up with closest horizontal docking port. Activating docking thrusters. Clarke, is it responding?"

"Stand by, Blaine," Clarke replied as he tried to access the hatchway with the Dark Stars computer interface. "Steady……. Ok, kiss it."

The ship jolted as it hit the docking station. "Docking clamps locked and holding. All stop, sir."

"Real smooth, Blaine, keep it up. Clarke, can you access the whole refinery from here?"

"I'm not getting a reply, sir. Either the relays in the docking port are damaged, or the main computer is off-line. Beyond the docking bay I got nothing. I can tell you we're gonna need the pressure suits. The temperature in there is not going to make you happy."

"If the main computer's off-line, shouldn't this thing have taken a two-mile swan dive by now?"

"The vertical stabilisers on these things have several independently powered backup systems. You'd have to hit this thing with a cluster missile to knock it out of the sky," replied Kane as he undid his safety harness.

"Have the other ships docked yet, Clarke?"

"The Phoenix has docked and the Ulysses is docking as we speak, Captain."

"Good. Ok, Kane, Clarke, go fetch whatever equipment you might need to get us through this place. Assume it's not going to co-operate. Blaine and I will meet you in the airlock."

"Aye, sir," answered Kane as he and Clarke hurried into the bridge transport lift.

Blaine opened the weapons locker and threw Hawkins a plasma pistol. After strapping on a pistol holster of his own Blaine reached back into the locker and pulled out a plasma rifle.

"Blaine, do you have any idea what the term overkill means?" asked Hawkins sarcastically. After cocking the rifle Blaine just smiled at the captain and walked off through the bridges main access door. Hawkins shook his head and followed.

It took Kane a while but eventually he managed to open the refinery airlock. The air in the dark passageway was old and stale. The torches mounted to their E.V.A. suits and to Blaine's rifle were the only source of light in the otherwise total darkness.

"The main computer's definitely off-line," explained Kane. "In fact, the whole power grid seems to be shut down."

"I thought these things maintained themselves?" Hawkins questioned, his voice crackling through the communicator of his suit's helmet.

"They do, sir, usually. These refineries are definitely equipped with repair drones. The primary and the secondary power grids would both have to be off-line to stop them working. It seems the vertical stabilisers are the only things that are still functioning."

"Think there's anything you can do about it?"

"Well, even though it is automated it must have a command centre somewhere. If I can find it, I might be able to get the power back online."

"Bingo." Blaine shone the light on a dusty door, set back into the wall of the passageway.

"What do you have, Blaine?"

Blaine rubbed the dust off the half-covered writing on the door. "Sorry, false alarm, it's just a transport lift." Blaine turned and carried on down the passageway.

"Blaine, wait. Shine the light back on the door. Clarke, pass me the pry bar."

"Whatever you're doing, Kane, we don't have time for it."

Kane forced the pry bar between the door and its frame, opening it by a few inches. "Blaine, shut up and hold the damn torch steady. Hey, Clarke, give me hand here."

With a laboured pull the pair dragged the door open and Kane stepped inside. After a brief pause to look around, he began to remove a small panel from one of the walls. He searched for a few seconds through the mass of tangled wires and circuit boards he had uncovered. Reaching into his satchel he pulled out a small multi-purpose tool and snipped one of two large blue cables.

"Clarke, do you have the power cells?"

"Yeah, just a minute." Clarke reached into one of the large black satchels he was carrying and pulled out a small grey box, covered in blinking lights. Kane opened the top of the box to reveal two small metal clamps, which he quickly connected to the two ends of the snipped cable. The lights and monitors in the lift flickered and crackled as they began to power up.

"Damn I'm good." Kane stood up and took a bow.

"Quick, everyone in the lift before his head takes up all the room," Blaine mocked.

"Ok, here goes nothing," remarked Hawkins, who was last to step into the lift. "Command centre." The lift did nothing. "Operations." Still the lift did nothing. "Any ideas?" Hawkins looked at his crew.

"Engineering," offered Blaine. The internal door hissed shut and with a squeal of its motors the lift began to move. Blaine turned to Clarke, his smug grin beaming through the visor of his helmet. "Remember this moment the next time you get the urge to slate my old Star Trek re-runs."

"Whatever, kiddo."

After a few minutes the lift came to a halt and the doors hissed open. The crew followed Clarke out into a large dark chamber. From the little that could be seen in the dull torchlight, Kane could make out dozens of computer consoles and large rectangular data banks that stood at least nine feet tall.

"Are you sure you can get this working, Kane?"

"As long as the power loss is the result of system damage and not battery drain, then it's possible sir."

"Kane, do me a favour."

"Yes, Captain."

"Pretend that I know precisely dick about engineering, then explain that again."

"Well basically, sir, if the power's down because of damage to the refinery, then all the systems would have shut down instantaneously. Meaning the repair drones still have charge in their power cells, but the Auto-Repair system isn't online to control them. In which case I just have to attach a power cell to the Auto-Repair system and we can use the drones to fix the refinery.

"But if the problem is with the refinery generators, the systems would have been running on backup power. All the systems and the repair drones would have just kept going until they flattened their batteries. So, I won't be able to activate the drones, and we'd better start looking for some candles."

Hawkins looked around into the darkness of the pitch-black room before responding, "Clarke, do you have any better flash lights in those bags?"

"Yes, sir." Clarke opened one of the satchels and handed out the more powerful hand-held torches.

"Ok, split up and find the Auto-Repair system. Holler if you find it."

Blaine walked slowly through the vast chamber, swinging his rifle's torchlight from left to right over the computer consoles. He couldn't help but think that the power being down was slightly suspicious. What could have damaged a gas refinery two miles above a planet surface, out here in the middle of nowhere? There was nothing here to collide with but gas and the chances of a meteor striking the refinery were infinitesimal. Something wasn't right.

"Found it, it's over here!" crackled Hawkins through the coms. The crew hurried over to where the captain stood. "At least I think I've found it. It looks like the repair system on the Star but it's huge."

"Yeah, that's it," reassured Kane. "Our system only has to control a couple of dozen repair drones. Something this size must control hundreds."

Kane removed a large access panel from the front of the machine and crawled inside. "Clarke, I'm going to need the high-capacity power cell for this."

Clarke pushed one of the satchels through the panel opening.

"Thanks. Now all I need to do is hook up the power cables and hopefully…"

The huge repair system's monitors and consoles burst into life and Kane slid back out from inside it. Clarke wasted no time in accessing the refineries diagnostic logs.

"Well, the repair drones are back online, so I guess we don't need those candles."

"What caused the power failure?"

"Running diagnostic now, Captain." A sudden look of surprise swept across Clarke's face. "Ah, that'll explain it."

"What is it?"

"It appears there's been a small explosion in one of the gas storage tanks."

"How bad is it?"

"Well luckily the storage tanks are located in the centre of the refinery, so the outer hull is still intact."

"What about internally?"

"There's a lot of internal sensors down, sir, I can't get an accurate measurement."

"Then give me your best guess."

"The vertical blast radius appears to cover an area of about four-hundred-and-ninety-two metres."

"Jesus, that's almost eighty-three decks."

"There's no way we're gonna get the power back online with that kind of damage, Captain. Even if there were enough raw materials left to rebuild the power grid, it will take the drones months to do it."

"Kane, can you keep the repair system functioning?"

"We'll need to fetch more power cells from the ship, but it shouldn't be a problem."

Hawkins nodded. "Ok listen up, this is the plan. Clarke, Kane, I need you to programme this facility's repair drones to get some semblance of main power back online. Even if it's just on this deck. I need life support, heat and preferably all the comforts of home. And then I need a cache of supplies from each ship storing here that's large enough to make this a viable emergency fall-back position. Do you understand?"

The pair nodded.

The other ships had docked on the opposite side of the refinery to the Dark Star, presenting the captains of the Ulysses and the Phoenix with a half-hour walk to the engineering deck. By the time they arrived the repair drones were already setting about their task. However, the captains still had to greet each other in full E.V.A. suits.

"Captain Hawkins?" asked one of the captains as he glanced round the room at the crew.

Hawkins stepped forward and shook his hand.

"I'm Soren, captain of the Ulysses and this is Commander Kristen Redmond of the Phoenix."

Hawkins gave Commander Redmond a funny look.

"Is something wrong, Captain?"

"Not at all, I just didn't expect you to be –"

"A woman?" interrupted Redmond.

Hawkins laughed. "So young."

The commander smiled.

"Anyway, I didn't drag you both up here to chit-chat, let's get down to it shall we? You were obviously dragged into this at the last possible second. Which was probably planned so that I didn't have time to object, but I don't suppose that's important now. What I need to know, now that we're alone and away from any other interference or bullshit, is how much you were told about this mission."

"Well, the Keymaster wave was common knowledge between the brass on the colony. Even if it was kept hush-hush from the colonists. As far as this mission is concerned, my orders are to accompany you back into Earth-space and make sure the Dark Star survives to set off the wave, no matter the cost."

"What about you, Commander?"

"That sounds about right, and call me Kristen."

"Just what I expected from O'Connor, as vague as possible. Let me give you a rundown of what you've really volunteered for. Based on the technology Gatekeeper had at the time of the massacre, and working under the reasoning that it is a logical machine that has had no logical need to advance its military capabilities since it won the war and effectively wiped-out humanity. We should be able to assume that it has been concentrating on its primary function of cleaning up the Earth in the years since. We should be able to assume that our first engagement will be with the old planetary defence grid, if it's even still functioning. For a fucking change the Auto-Navigation system and the Cryo-Stasis shut downs worked perfectly, and we've arrived at the right time of year for a quiet approach to Earth.

"The current planetary alignments mean that if we get the timing right, we should be able to swing round from behind the asteroid field that lies between Jupiter and Mars and approach from behind Mars itself. We'll still be out in the open between Mars and Earth, but until that point, we should be undetectable. So long as we utilise the launch window and break orbit in about fifteen hours in order to utilise the blind spot behind Mars before it passes."

"I'm a little confused as to why we're docked with this old installation, Captain. Would you mind filling us in?"

"This isn't gonna be a walk in the park, Miss Redmond. Your ships are here to divert attention from the Dark Star while we get into position and activate the wave. The Dark Star's big enough to take a beating but if it's the only target we're still gonna be fubar pretty damn quick if those orbital defences are still operational."

"Fubar?" questioned Commander Redmond looking extremely puzzled.

"Fucked up beyond all recognition."

The commander shook her head. "Men."

"Commander O'Connor suggested that we simply wander in and knock upon arrival. I however, unlike that asshole, have a problem with blindly walking straight into an unknown situation, featuring an enemy that wiped out every military force on Earth, when all I have is a few missiles and a mining ship. Call me crazy, but when I looked through the main viewer and saw Jupiter, I suddenly realised the potential for a plan B. Using one of these old installations as a fall-back position. If any of our ships are crippled and need to limp out of the fight, it makes sense to have somewhere to limp to. This place is easily outside the range of Earths defences, but not too far for a damaged vessel to reach.

"Sadly, I wasn't expecting it to have sustained such a massive amount of damage, and the other installations are currently positioned too deep within Jupiter's atmosphere to risk trying to dock. The gravitational forces that deep are too strong. However, if we can successfully get main power back online, on a couple of decks at least, this installation will do just fine."

Soren nodded approvingly. "Not bad. What are your plans for after we pass Mars, Hawkins?"

"Actually, Soren, I'd appreciate your thoughts on that. Obviously, it would be stupid to just wade in guns blazing, before we know what we're up against. On the other hand, if we send a scout to check the place out, we lose the element of surprise."

"Yes, I see what you mean. Damned if we do and damned if we don't."

"There is a third option," offered Redmond.

Soren and Hawkins stared attentively.

"If we could somehow direct a few of the bigger rocks from the asteroid belt towards Earth, we could hide in with them until they got in range of the asteroid defences. We would have plenty of time to scan the planet and we would remain undetected."

"And we would know if the asteroid defence batteries are still operational. Clever, I like it."

"Isn't the Ulysses a retrieval ship?"

"It's designed to retrieve damaged vessels, yes."

"Then it's equipped with a tractor-beam, right?"

"Yes, it's not designed to tow more than one object at a time however, but my engineers should be able to widen the confinement beam."

"Ok, you'd better get them started."

Soren nodded and walked away to a quiet spot where he could contact his ship. Redmond and Hawkins continued their conversation.

"Captain Hawkins."

"Call me John."

"John. Do you really think we can pull this off?"

"Truthfully?"

"Yes."

"I don't know. If we can shut down Gatekeeper's reactors and we don't get blown out of the sky before we get there, then, maybe."

"Why can't we just activate Keymaster from here? A radio frequency of that magnitude would easily reach Earth from this distance."

"Gatekeeper, I mean Gatekeeper itself, the actual system core, was built inside an old underground military bunker, to protect it from terrorist attacks. The wave wouldn't necessarily reach its reactor through all that earth. Crippling other reactors on the planet might slow it down but we have to take it by surprise. We need to cut the head off the snake before it can react. It proved itself to be a god damned military mastermind by all accounts and we have no idea what amount of military might it decided to store away down there. We can't allow it time to respond. We get to use Keymaster once and then it will take steps to shield itself. We're going to need to use a few mining torpedoes to make a hole before we can activate the wave. Ensure we have it dead in our sights. A perfect situation would be passing the orbital defences, drilling a hole with mining warheads and firing off the Keymaster wave from all three ships in orbit around the planet. Frying every damned thing at once. But make no mistake, it's one chance, shit or bust."

Soren returned from the far side of the room and re-joined the conversation. "My engineers have started the adjustments to the tractor-beam. They're confident that it will be ready before we depart."

Hawkins nodded. "I think we've covered what we need to cover. We need to locate the main system core and whatever happens one of us needs to effectively hit it with a blast of that wave. Nothing else matters." Hawkins looked around. "Unless anyone has anything to add, I have a fall-back position to make ready," Hawkins paused for a moment to allow for a response, "Very well, I'm sure you're eager to get back to your ships. I'll see you at thirteen hundred hours. Let's go find some rocks to throw at our home world."

"Yes, John," replied Commander Redmond.

"Till then," answered Captain Soren.

CHAPTER 4
Loch Down

After leaving Jupiter's orbit, the fleet, led by the Dark Star, headed towards the asteroid belt that lay between the gas giant and the red planet, Mars. Hawkins paced restlessly around the bridge, checking his crew's preparations whilst Clarke was busy making sure the ship wasn't giving off any detectable signals.

"We're coming up on the asteroid field, Captain."

"All stop."

"Aye, sir, all stop."

"Dark Star to Ulysses, come in Soren."

"Soren here, what can we do for you, Captain."

"Are you ready to try the tractor-beam?"

"Ready as we'll ever be."

"Ok let's do it."

The Phoenix and the Dark Star maintained a safe distance as the Ulysses took up position inside the belt. Dozens of the drifting asteroids, some as large as the Ulysses herself, came to a sudden halt as the tractor-beam was engaged. The glow from the ship's engine intensified, as her crew fought to oppose the forces involved in halting the massive objects. Captain Soren gave the order to move out and the Ulysses started to pull slowly forwards. Hawkins watched through the main view port of the bridge, as the huge rocks started to move, surrounded by the electric blue aura of the tractor-beam.

"Ulysses to Dark Star, the beam seems to be holding. Hawkins, I think we're in business."

"Very good, Soren, but we're gonna have to pick up the pace. We need to make a run for Mars while it's still close enough to the asteroid field to hide us."

"Not a problem. Ulysses out."

Hawkins was still watching the Ulysses as it powered up its main engines and shot off into the distance. "Whenever you're ready, Blaine."

"Aye, sir."

The fleet headed for Mars with the Ulysses dragging their only chance for victory. If Gatekeeper did manage to detect them, they would surely be destroyed before they even reached the atmosphere. The flight to Mars lasted just over four hours, due to the slow acceleration rate of the heavily laden Ulysses.

"Dark Star to Fleet. We're gonna be passing Mars over the western hemisphere, set your heading accordingly. Ulysses, inform me the second you're ready to release the asteroids."

"Copy that, Hawkins."

"Passing over the western hemisphere now, Captain. We should be clear momentarily." informed Blaine.

"Hawkins to fleet. Increase your speed, let's try and make this look as authentic as possible."

"Ulysses to fleet. Course set for Earth's upper atmosphere, releasing the asteroids now."

The glow of the tractor-beam stopped and the asteroids drifted apart slightly. The fleet slowed to allow the field of rock to gain a little ground before taking their ships in.

"Ok, Blaine, take her in. Mark your target so the fleet can see our objective position."

"Brace yourselves."

Blaine manoeuvred the Dark Star in at the rear of the asteroid field and the other ship followed suit. The armada of rocks hurtled ever closer to Earth. The fleet needed to finish taking cover fast before they were discovered. Hawkins watched as a relatively small asteroid shot past the view port, narrowly missing the ship.

"Where the hell did that come from?"

"The Phoenix just collided with it, Captain," replied Clarke.

"Dark Star to Phoenix, report."

"We're ok, John. We just winged it."

"Are you sure?"

"Yes. Nothing to be concerned about."

"Ok, Hawkins out."

"John?" questioned Blaine suggestively.

"Don't make me beat the shit out of you, Blaine. I'm busy."

"Aye, sir," Blaine replied still grinning.

"How long?" asked Hawkins as he turned to face Clarke.

"At this speed we'll be in range of the asteroid defences in one minute, Captain."

"Are we in scanning range yet? Can we see anything?"

"Not quite, sir."

"Hawkins to fleet, bring your new weapon systems online. Clarke, power up the tactical systems."

"Aye, Captain. Weapons systems activated. Targeting scanners up and running."

"What's the status of the tubes, Kane?"

"Torpedo's locked and loaded, Captain. All tubes ready."

"Coming into sensor range now sir, initiating scan. What the hell!"

"What is it, Clarke?"

"It's amazing, sir, South America is almost totally covered in rainforest, and so is Brazil. In fact, the whole planet is covered in wildlife and vegetation. There's no structures or power sources anywhere."

"What about Gatekeeper? Scan the co-ordinates we have for the bunker?"

"All I'm reading is a small lake, sir. Just a hole in the ground." Clarke looked up from his console and stared at Hawkins. "It's not there."

"What?"

"It's gone, sir."

"What the fuck is going on here?" Hawkins looked through the view port at the now visible planet. Peeking out from beyond the asteroid field. "What about the Asteroid Defence Satellites?" Hawkins continued with a note of concern in his voice.

"Sensors are detecting no machinery or equipment of any kind, Captain."

"Check again." Hawkins' face dropped.

"I'm on scan number three, sir. There's nothing there."

"My god. We've just aimed enough rock at the planet to start another ice age."

The crew sat silently for a moment, staring out through the view port, eyes fixed on the small blue sphere that they had just doomed. Hawkins rose to his feet and turned to Clarke. "Do we have enough missiles to stop them?"

Clarke sat silently in his seat for a few seconds, before looking up at the captain. "These asteroids are comprised of mostly nickel and iron. The only thing with the fire power to stop them is the non-existent defence satellites." Clarke looked back toward the view port and added, "That should have started firing thirty seconds ago."

"What about using the tractor-beam on the Ulysses?" offered Kane.

"The larger asteroids have spread too far apart to snare with the beam. There's nothing we can do."

"Yes, there is."

The crew turned and looked at Hawkins, who had returned to his seat and strapped himself in.

"Hawkins to fleet, we need to take these rocks out before they reach the planet."

"Ulysses to Dark Star, where the hell are the satellites?"

"Hawkins to fleet, we have no time. The satellites are not going to stop these rocks. Do what you're told. Think later."

"Ulysses to Hawkins, understood."

"Phoenix to Dark Star, let's do it."

"Blaine, get us clear of the debris field. Clarke, as soon as we're clear, fire at will. Watch out for the other ships."

The three ships broke from the asteroid field and began to fire. The ships strafed back and forth, spewing torpedo after torpedo at the largest rocks they could find.

"Blaine, get us closer to the big rock, dead ahead."

"Which big rock? There are dozens of big rocks."

"For the love of god, Blaine, it's a quarter kilometre across, surely it's not in your blind spot."

"Oh yeah, I got it. Moving in."

"Target locked, torpedoes away. Impact in four, three, two one, torpedo's have impacted." Clarke slammed his fist down on his console. "Damn it! Captain, we're not even scratching these things."

"Captain, what about giving one of these things a love-tap?" queried Blaine.

"Kane, would the hull hold up if we gave one of these things a nudge?"

"I wouldn't recommend it, sir. The Dark Star's bigger than most of these things but like Clarke said, most of them are made of mostly metals."

Hawkins thought for a second. "Kane, ramp up the reactor. Give the shields as much power as possible."

"Aye, sir."

"Blaine, time to be a hero."

"Yes, sir." Blaine manoeuvred the ship alongside the quarter-kilometre asteroid they had just been firing at. "Ok, guys, you might want to brace yourselves."

The bridge shook hard as the ship connected with the asteroid. Blaine eased the horizontal control levers over as gently as possible.

"The shielding isn't going to hold for long under this kind of strain, Captain."

"Keep them up as long as you can, Kane."

"It's not budging, sir, increasing power to the lateral thrusters."

A heavy grating sound echoed through the ship as the hull sheared against the mammoth rock. "Damn, this is really gonna fuck up the paintwork," the helmsman complained through gritted teeth.

"Hull stress is at ninety-seven percent, Captain. She's starting to buckle."

"How we doing, Blaine?"

"It's moving, Captain, but I still need to deflect it another three degrees to miss the planet."

The ship shook violently as a sudden shower of rock fragments bounced off the hull.

"What the hell was that?"

"We were just hit by fragments from an exploding asteroid, Captain."

"Who bagged it?" asked Hawkins optimistically.

"The one that's just appeared on sensors at co-ordinates zero-three-point-one."

"What? Put it on the main viewer."

The main transparent view port window at the head of the bridge was suddenly masked by the holographic projection of the view screen, which appeared just in front of its position. The newly established screen now offered a view of the approaching vessel. It took Hawkins a few seconds to work out what he was looking at. The ship was as black as the void that surrounded it and very hard to see. It tapered from a wide stern down to a fine point at its bow. The whole outer edge of it glinted like the blade of a knife in the light from the distant sun.

"My god, I didn't think it was possible to build anything that big," exclaimed Blaine.

"Clarke, can you get a life form reading."

"The sensors are only just registering its presence, Captain. I don't know what it's coated in but I can't scan through it. All I can tell you at the moment is that it's shaped like an arrowhead and is about eight miles in length."

"Captain, this rock is clear."

"Ok, Blaine, find us another target."

"Captain, I'm detecting a massive power build-up in the unidentified vessel. I think it's gonna blow, sir."

"Are we in any danger?"

"I don't know, sir, it's one hell of a build-up."

"Err, guys."

Hawkins and Clarke turned to the main view screen. The strange ship was now lit up with jolts of electricity that were dancing across its surface. The crew watched in awe as the electrical light show directed itself towards the bow of the ship and shot out into the asteroid field.

"Brace for impact."

The bridge shook as a wave of debris crashed into the ship.

"Shield status?"

"Shields barely holding, sir."

"Ulysses to Fleet, we've taken heavy damage, request assistance."

"Dark Star to Ulysses, what's your status?"

"We've got hull breaches all over the place, the energy seals are holding but we're dead in the water here, Hawkins."

"Captain, detecting another energy build-up in the unidentified ship."

"This is Earth Fleet mining vessel Dark Star to unidentified ship. Revise your firing line, repeat, we have a ship in your firing line."

"The ship is still charging its weapons, sir."

"Shit. Dark Star to Ulysses, hold on we're on our way. Blaine, get over there."

"It's firing, sir."

Once again, the bridge shook under the barrage of debris from the blast as asteroids from the field exploded.

"Kane!" shouted the captain.

"Shields are still holding, Captain."

"Dark Star to Ulysses. Report," Hawkins waited for a reply.

"Soren, this is Hawkins, come in."

"Captain." Blaine drew the captain's attention to the main view port as the Ulysses came into view. The ship was dark and powerless. Oxygen was spewing out into space from more breaches than Hawkins could count.

"Clarke, any life signs?"

"No, sir and the life-pods are still docked."

"Captain, we're closing on Earth. The arrowhead vessel is re-positioning itself between the asteroid field and the planet."

"Dark Star to Phoenix, break-off and regroup at co-ordinates zero-two-eight-point-one."

Blaine pulled the ship out of the asteroid field and set the new course heading.

"Sir, the asteroid field will reach the arrowhead vessel in approximately ten seconds."

"Put it on the view screen."

"Detecting another power build-up, Captain."

Hawkins watched as the huge rocks hurtled towards the strange black vessel. Could this ship be Gatekeeper? It would explain why it was trying so hard to protect the planet but the technology was like nothing he had ever seen. Could it have advanced this far in the short time since the massacre? Could it care enough about the planet to sacrifice itself in this futile attempt to block the path of the asteroids?

"Picking up another power increase, sir."

The arrowhead vessel started to glow bright orange as the asteroids closed in.

"Impact in three…two…one."

The hail of rocks smashed into the gigantic vessel, which was now lost in the cloud of debris created by the impact. In the distance behind the bombarded vessel Hawkins was relieved to see only a few small fragments of rock entering the atmosphere. None of them big enough to cause more than minor surface damage to the Earth below.

"Blaine, set a course for whatever's left of that ship. Maybe we can find a few answers in the wreckage. Clarke, have the Phoenix rendezvous with the Ulysses asap to search for survivors."

"I don't think setting course for it is gonna be necessary, Captain."

"There must be something left of it?"

"Oh, there's something left of it alright," Clarke looked at the main viewer at the front of the bridge.

Hawkins' gaze followed. "What? That's not possible. Nothing could have survived that."

Sure enough, the mammoth vessel was heading slowly out of the debris field and was listing into a turn.

"Magnify."

"Aye, sir, increasing to ten times normal magnification."

"Jesus, there's not a mark on it."

"It's heading this way, Captain."

"Clarke, get me Commander Redmond on the view screen."

"Aye, sir."

The view screen flicked and switched from a view of the approaching vessel to an image of the Phoenix's bridge. "Redmond here, go ahead, John."

"Get out of here. Regroup at the fall-back position. If you don't hear from us in one hour set course back to the colony."

The commander looked wounded. "My orders are to protect the Dark Star, John, and that's what I intend to do."

"Damn it, Redmond, I'm changing your orders. There's nothing you can do against that ship except survive to warn the colony of its existence. Now turn around and get out of here."

Commander Redmond was silent for a moment. "What's the status of the Ulysses?"

Hawkins frowned and shook his head. "You need to go. Someone needs to report this. If anyone from the Ulysses reaches an escape pod, there needs to be a ship at the fall-back position or they're dead anyway."

Commander Redmond nodded slowly. "Drake, set course for Jupiter. You'd better be there, Hawkins, Phoenix out."

The view screen deactivated, returning the view through the main view port, out in-front of the ship.

Blaine turned to the captain. "Orders, Captain?"

"Hold your position."

Blaine looked through the main view port at the fast-approaching giant "Aye, sir," he answered uncertainly.

"Clarke, if this thing is Gatekeeper, do you think Keymaster will work through a hull that size?"

"Hard to say, sir. I still can't get a sensor lock on the damn thing."

Blaine was still staring though the view port at the closing ship. "Sir, with all due respect, if we don't move, that thing is going to move us."

"Hold your position, Blaine, if it was going to attack us it would have fired by now. Somehow, we need to find out if this thing is Gatekeeper. I'm open to suggestions."

"If we could blow a big enough hole in its hull plating, we might be able to scan the interior, Captain."

"Thanks, Kane but I don't want to start shooting at this thing if I don't have to."

"We could try the wave."

"It's only gonna be a surprise once, we can't risk using it until we're sure it's gonna penetrate the hull. That's if it's even running on a crystalline reactor."

"The arrowheads closed to one thousand metres, Captain. On its present course it should pass straight over us."

A deep rumbling sound washed through the bridge as the immense vessel slowly moved overhead. Blaine leaned forward in his seat and looked up at its passing hull through the upper section of the view port. "The damn things completely smooth, Captain. There's no cargo bays, no access hatches, there's not even a scuff on the metal."

"Clarke, what's it doing?" questioned Hawkins who was sat looking up at the roof of the bridge.

"No idea, sir, but it is slowing down."

"Slowing down?"

"Yes, sir, it appears to be coming to a halt directly above us."

"Can the sensors tell us anything at this range?"

"I'm still reading the ship as an anomaly, Captain. Whatever this hull plating is made of, it's confusing the sensors to hell."

"Captain, you might want to take a look at this," shouted Blaine still staring out of the view port.

Hawkins got out of his seat and walked over to take a look. A thin crack was starting to appear, spreading across the silky-smooth hull of the arrowhead vessel. Hawkins and Blaine watched as it continued to expand before it abruptly turned ninety degrees and continued on out of sight.

"Clarke, do me a favour?" asked Hawkins, his gaze still fixed on the strange ship. "Look back through the navigational logs and tell me when we entered the twilight zone."

"What's going on out there, Captain?" replied Clarke curiously.

"Good question, I'll let you know the second I figure that out."

The crack had continued to extend around the ship's hull and had now met up with itself to create a large rectangular shape above the Dark Star.

Blaine's jaw dropped as the whole section of the hull began to retract into the vessel. "No fucking way!"

"Captain, the sensors are picking up a section of the ship that's about a mile square."

"Yeah," replied Hawkins sounding shocked. "It's probably this cargo bay door."

Clarke looked up from his console, wearing a frown of confusion.

"Sorry, sir, it sounded like you said door?" questioned Kane. Without answering Hawkins waved Kane over to the view port. Clarke and Kane looked at each and Kane hurried over to the front of the ship. "Now that's a fucking door!"

"Clarke, what are you picking up?"

"This thing's amazing, Captain. I'm reading over two thousand decks, fifty advanced machine shops and enough storage space to hold the whole colony.

"What about life signs?"

"Not one, sir, as far as I can tell the ship doesn't even have the facilities to sustain a crew."

"Then it has to be Gatekeeper," added Blaine.

A blinding blue light emanating from inside the gargantuan door of the ship suddenly interrupted the crew's conversation. The Dark Star shook violently sending the crew stumbling across the bridge as they hurried to get back to their stations.

"Report."

"We appear to be caught in some sort of tractor-beam, sir."

"Blaine, get us out of here."

Blaine threw the power lever and the ship began to shake even more.

"Blaine, get us out of here now!"

"I can't break free, sir, the beam's got more muscle than the engines."

"Clarke, can you trace the source of the beam?"

"Yes, sir, the beam's source is located one-point-four miles inside the opening."

Hawkins weighed up his options. "Arm two torpedoes, it looks like we're gonna have to blast our way out of here."

"Aye, sir, torpedoes armed and ready."

"Fire."

Sub-orbital mining torpedoes are designed to create large craters in a planet's surface from orbit, in the attempt to speed up the job of mining drones and hover miners by effectively open cast mining before they arrive. As a result of this, the Dark Star, which was in-fact a mining vessel, was equipped with torpedo tubes as standard. These tubes however, due to the nature of orbital deployments, were situated in the underside of the Dreadnought. In addition to this fact, it is also worth noting that the additional launcher pods, fitted specifically for the mission and carrying the modified lower-yield warheads, were also mounted on the underside of the vessel. This created quite a problem on both counts considering Clarke's current target was positioned directly above their ship and the torpedoes automatic guidance systems had been removed to prevent Gatekeeper from taking control of them. Whichever launcher set Clarke chose to activate, he would have to manually programme their flight paths before launching. Faced with the sheer size of the target, the first officer decided to go with the full mining yield of the Dreadnoughts standard mining torpedoes. Meaning he would have to calculate the precise trajectory required to direct the torpedoes in a one-hundred-and-eighty degrees turn around the ship from beneath, before they could hit their target. Which put the ship he was standing on, directly in the line of fire.

"Torpedoes away."

The bridge was silent except for the beeping of the tracking system. Clarke held his breath as the torpedoes passed each other beneath the ship. Had he made the correct calculations? Had he sufficiently compensated for the pull of the tractor-beam? The next few seconds would tell. The sound of a thruster filled the bridge as one of the torpedoes sped past.

Hawkins turned to Clarke. "Do I want to know how close that was?"

"No."

"How's the trajectory looking?"

"Torpedoes clearing the ship now, sir," replied Clarke carefully watching the tracking monitor on his console. "One of the torpedoes has impacted on the hull of the ship. The other has been caught in the tractor beam and is being pulled directly toward its emitter." Clarke smiled.

"Well done, Clarke. Blaine, get ready to –"

"Torpedo has been intercepted, Captain," interrupted Clarke, as the smile dropping from his face.

"How?"

"It was hit by some sort of energy-beam."

"Damn it."

"Captain, I can't hold her anymore. The beam's pulling us in."

"How long do we have, Blaine?"

"With the engines at full power, maybe three minutes, Captain."

"Blaine, be ready to get us out of here. Kane, you're with me." Hawkins and Kane rushed into the transport lift.

"Torpedo bay." Upon the captain's command the lift doors hissed shut and it began to move.

"What's the plan, Captain?"

"We're gonna send that bastard a little present."

After about thirty seconds the transport lift stopped and the doors opened. Hawkins and Kane ran out into the torpedo bay. The room was relatively small compared to most in the ship, roughly thirty metres squared. Although the masses of stacked torpedoes and banks of launchers made it seem much smaller.

"Ok, Kane, help me with this crate of warheads."

Kane and Hawkins lugged the large plastic crate into the turbo-lift. "Deck one, section eight," demanded Hawkins and the lift began to move.

Hawkins knelt down and opened the crate. "Help me get these things armed, Kane."

One by one the pair carefully turned the keys on the warheads into the armed position. By the time they had arrived at their destination they had armed every single one of the warheads and wasted no time exiting the lift and rushing down the corridor. Hawkins stopped at a small hatch, which concealed one of the ship's many escape-pods. After dropping the crate, he punched the release code into the hatch's keypad and it slowly opened.

"Ok, Kane, get these things inside quick." With extreme care they slowly lowered the crate into the escape-pod before sealing the hatch. "Hawkins to Clarke, I need you to launch escape-pod eleven."

"Sir?"

"Just do it."

"Aye, sir, launching pod now."

A great roar followed Hawkins and Kane down the corridor as the pod's engines fired sending it screeching out of the ship. The pod rocketed up through the immense opening in the arrowhead vessel like a bat out of hell. Clarke was tracking its ascent as Hawkins burst back onto the bridge.

"Clarke, report."

"The pod's taking a beating, sir, but its armour appears to be holding. The tractor beam is guiding it straight in, it should be impacting any second."

The explosion was big enough to temporarily blind Clarke's sensors. The Dark Star jolted free as the tractor-beam ceased to function sending Kane crashing to the ground.

"Blaine, hit it."

"Aye, sir." Blaine threw the power lever and the Dark Star roared away from the large ship. "Heading, Captain?"

"Anywhere, Blaine, just get us out of here. Clarke, what's the status of that ship?"

"It's starting to turn, Captain."

"God damn it, we put ten warheads in that escape-pod, what's it gonna take to slow this thing down?"

"Sir, suggest we head for the asteroid belt, we should be able to hide while we come up with a plan."

"Good thinking, Blaine, set a course."

"Oh god, not more asteroids."

Blaine hit the power and headed the ship back towards the asteroid belt.

"The arrowhead vessel is now on an intercept course and is gaining fast."

"Blaine, full speed."

"Sorry, sir, we're already accelerating as fast as we can."

"Can we make it to the asteroid belt before it catches up with us?"

"Not with enough time to hide."

"Can you tell if its shields are raised?"

"Judging from the data I collected when it intercepted the asteroids, sir, I'd say its shields haven't been activated."

"How many of the modified torpedoes do we have left?

"Eighteen, sir."

"Fire them, maybe we can slow it down."

"Loading tubes one through ten. Target locked. Torpedoes away. Loading second volley. Target locked. Torpedoes away."

"Time till intercept?"

"Estimated time till impact is twenty seconds."

"Blaine, how long before we reach the asteroids?"

"About twenty seconds."

"This is gonna be close. Kane, is there any way of increasing our acceleration rate?"

"Sorry, sir, there's no way of making her move any faster."

"Ten seconds till impact, still no defensive response from the ship."

"Captain, this isn't going to work, it's too close. We'll never be able to get deep enough into the field to fool its sensors before it catches up to us."

"What choice do we have."

"Request permission to test a theory, Captain."

Hawkins knew Blaine was right, the ship would be right behind them by the time they reached the asteroid field and there was no way it would lose them at this range. Hawkins didn't have time to ask questions but Blaine's plan couldn't get them in any more trouble than they were already in. "Ok, Blaine, this better be good."

"Impact of first volley in three, two, one."

As the torpedoes impacted the front of the pursuing vessel, Blaine pulled back hard on the manoeuvring levers and the nose of the Dark Star started to rise.

"Clarke, what about that second volley?" Blaine queried.

"Impacting now."

Blaine led the Dark Star through a half loop before easing off on the levers. The crew was now flying inverted towards the arrowhead vessel and the exploding torpedoes had masked the entire manoeuvre. Once again Blaine threw the engines into full burn and the Dark Star made its exodus along the arrowhead vessels hull and back towards Earth.

"Blaine, you're my new fucking hero."

"Thanks, Captain, but that was the whole plan. I'm open to suggestion on where to go now."

"How long before that thing turns round, Clarke?"

"The damn things fast, sir but it's too big for rapid manoeuvring. Estimating two minutes before it can resume its pursuit."

"That's all we need. Blaine, we're gonna have to head for the planet."

"With all due respect, sir, there's no way you can hide an eight-hundred-yard-long ship on a planet's surface. Especially from a ship in orbit."

"Au contraire, Blaine, there is one way."

Blaine was slightly concerned by the troubled tone of his captain.

"Blaine's right, Captain, we won't be able to hide the ship. The only possible chance would be to..." Kane stopped as he realised what the captain was planning. "Oh god, Captain, tell me we're not setting down in the ocean?"

"The ocean!" shouted Blaine in a state of panic. "Why the hell would we want to set her down in the ocean?"

"Because deep water refracts sensor-beams," answered Hawkins rubbing the back of his neck. "Clarke, any ideas on how we can find a suitable landing site? We need to be sure it's not too deep, the shields won't do a damn thing against water pressure."

"We'd have to be just about skimming the surface for the sensors to scan the depth to the sea bed. We'd have to fly in a search pattern until we located a suitable spot."

"We don't have time for search patterns, we need to be gone before that ship knows what's happened."

"Scotland."

Hawkins and Clarke tuned to Kane.

"What, Kane?"

"Loch Ness in Scotland, Captain. The damn things definitely deep enough and it's only about twenty miles long. Surely it would be faster to scan the depth of that."

"Kane, if you weren't so ugly, I'd kiss you right on your beardy face. Blaine, best speed to the British Isles."

"Aye, Captain."

"The arrowhead vessel has completed its turn and is accelerating towards us, Captain. It's not going to take it long to get here."

"Clarke, I need an entry vector."

"One step ahead of you, Blaine. Come in at vector eight-four-two-point-seven-five, keep her at thirty-one degrees."

"Eight-four-two-point-seven-five confirmed. Brace for atmospheric entry."

"Closing blast shields."

The ship began to shake as it connected with Earth's upper atmosphere, but this time, with main power online. Blaine had the ability to choose her entry angle, and could easily smooth out the ride.

"Hull stresses within tolerance. Heat shields holding."

"Descent stable, breaking through to lower atmosphere in five, four, three, two, one, engaging atmospheric thrusters." The shaking stopped as the ship levelled out and stopped fighting the atmosphere it was pushing through.

"Pursuing vessel is slowing down and appears to be re-positioning to enter orbit. We have two minutes tops before it's in position to track us."

"Kane, any ideas on how to control this landing once we hit the water?"

"We won't have any problem sinking if I flood the main port and starboard cargo bays. If I can use the environmental controls to fill them back up with air afterwards, the extra buoyancy should float us back up to the surface."

"Your gonna use the cargo bays as ballast tanks?" Blaine questioned the ship's engineer. "Captain, I don't know about this shit."

"Don't worry, Blaine, if he says it'll work, then it'll work."

"If you say so, sir."

"Coming up on the Scottish highland. Blaine, adjust your course by ten degrees to port," Clarke barked his order to the helm.

"Copy. Adjusting by ten degrees."

"I'm going to need you to fly as low as possible over the loch so I can take the depth readings."

"No problem. Loch in sight, coming in for first pass."

A huge wake of water billowed out behind the ship as it tore down the great loch. Blaine was manoeuvring the ship using instruments alone as the spray off the loch was totally blocking the view port.

"Blaine, we need to be lower."

"Lower? Clarke, this is a starship not a fucking jet ski."

"If we don't get accurate depth reading the water pressure is gonna crush this jet ski like a bug."

"Lower it is."

"Ok, I've located a suitable landing site. Bring her about, Blaine."

"Coming about."

Blaine had to ascend the ship to a few metres above the valley sides to allow enough room to make the turn.

"Ok, Blaine, set her down about two-hundred yards past that outcrop."

"Engaging landing jets, all stop."

Trees on the banks of the loch bent over and shook violently as the huge ship hovered above the surface.

"Ok, here goes." Blaine slowly eased back on the power lever and the ship began to descend. The ship sent waves rippling off in all directions as it hit the water and disappeared beneath the surface.

"Twenty feet, forty feet, sixty feet, eighty feet, deploying landing struts, one-hundred-and-twenty feet."

"Hold on, this isn't going to be pretty."

The bridge jolted as the ship hit the bottom of the loch.

"Touchdown. Resting at one-hundred-and-eighty feet below the surface."

The crew sat silent for a moment listening to the sound of the bulkheads straining under the weight of the water.

"Kane, status report."

"She's taking in water through a few small breaches we picked up trying to push that asteroid, but the flooding is into the engineering ducts, nothing serious. I've already closed the hatches in breached sections. Other than that, she's doing fine, Captain."

Hawkins stood up and walked over to one of the starboard side view ports. He stared out into the murky unsettled water. "That went really fucking poorly," he complained.

"A plan never survives contact with the enemy," Clarke offered.

"At least we bought time for the Phoenix to get out of the way," added Blaine.

"But not the Ulysses. I knew most of those men," Kane added solemnly.

"We aren't finished yet," offered the captain still staring out of the view port. "Look on the bright side. At least they died at home."

A silence descended for a moment.

"The last time I looked at this lake I was five years old. We came here fishing, me and my father," offered Clarke, trying to end the moment.

"You catch anything?" Hawkins asked still staring out into the black water.

"The flu."

Clarke and Hawkins chuckled.

"What about fish?"

"Not a damn thing."

"I've never seen a fish." The crew turned their eyes towards Blaine. "In fact, now I come to think about it, the only life forms I've ever seen other than humans are bugs."

"Of course, you were born on Tartarus weren't you. So many years in and out of cryo-pods, searching systems for resources. Putting time on hold in deep sleep between the stars. You forget that some of us are actually still relatively young."

"Don't worry about it, Blaine, when this is all over. I'll take you fishing myself," offered the first officer.

"Oh thanks, Clarke, I'm touched," Blaine replied sarcastically with a smile on his face."

"Clarke, how long has the other ship been in range?"

"Judging from where it was before we took the dive, I'd say it's been in range long enough to kill us several times."

"Well, I guess the plan worked. Now we need to come up with the next one. Clarke, I'm gonna need a rundown of everything we know about that ship, and I want facts, no speculation."

"Aye, sir."

"Kane, we're gonna need more modified torpedoes, lots more."

"I'll get the repair drones on it straight away, sir."

"Is it possible to increase the yield of the warheads?"

"Yes, sir, I can just leave the original mining warheads in instead of replacing them with the modified ones."

"Take Blaine with you, I want this ship to pack as much of a punch as possible before we go back up there."

"Aye, sir. Clarke, do me a favour and transfer a copy of the sensor information on that mothership down to the machining room on deck three. It might come in handy."

"No problem, Kane."

Kane and Blaine walked into the transport-lift and disappeared behind the closing doors.

"Ok, Clarke, what do we have?"

"Well, Captain, as I said, the vessel is shaped like an arrowhead and is about eight miles in length. We have the clear advantage in manoeuvrability and it has the advantage in speed. In fact, with those shields it's feasible that it could safely double our top speed, maybe even reach half-light."

"What about that hull plating?"

"The hull plating is a mystery, Captain. The sensors simply refuse to believe there's anything there to scan and I have no idea why. All I can tell you from the information collected when that cargo bay door opened is that the plating is about fifteen feet thick."

"Jesus, no wonder the torpedoes didn't have any effect, that thing could quite comfortably fly straight through us. What about the interior, did you manage to locate Gatekeeper's system core or any crystalline reactors?"

"There was a lot of interference from the sheer amount of machinery in there and the sensor data is confusing as a result. I didn't see any sign of the system core but if I'm reading this right the ship has a crystalline reactor the size of cargo bay four."

"Then we can use Keymaster against it."

"Well, yes and no, sir. The wave's effect on a crystalline reactor of that size should be devastating. The trouble is there are over eight hundred decks between the reactor core and the ship's hull. Even with the extremely penetrative properties of a wave of this frequency, I don't think it would pass through that many decks without being suppressed."

"What are our options?"

"At this point I'm not sure, Captain. I'm not even sure a torpedo with a mining warhead will breach that hull. Even if it can, I don't think we can do enough damage to something that size fast enough to stand a chance in a head-to-head fire fight."

"I agree, we're not going to win this with torpedoes. Somehow, we have to get to that reactor." Hawkins walked round to Clarke's side at the tactical console. "Can you show me a deck plan of that ship?"

Clarke punched a few keys on his keyboard and a map of the arrowhead vessel's interior flashed up on one of the monitors. "I don't have a complete plan of the ship, sir. I only managed to get a reading on about three-square miles of the interior through that opening."

"It'll have to do. Look at this." Hawkins pointed at the map on the monitor. "The cargo bay that it tried to pull us into is four times bigger than our ship. That leaves us plenty of room for a fight."

"Are you suggesting we try to get to the reactor ourselves?"

"No, I'm suggesting that we take its hull armour out of the equation by letting it take us on board."

"How can we be sure that the ship will try to pick us up again? We have fired on it since then. It might just blow us out of the sky."

"It could have taken us out with no trouble at all but it didn't. It wants something, something on this ship and I'm betting it's our navigational logs."

Clarke looked at the captain with a puzzled frown. "Our navigational logs, Captain?" he questioned.

"Remember how the last thing Gatekeeper destroyed at the time of the massacre was the lunar habitats."

"Yes, sir."

"Gatekeeper wouldn't have had any reason to do that unless it decided that the presence of the humans still posed a threat."

"So, what you're basically saying is it won't be happy until it's made the human race extinct."

"No, what I'm saying is that it will wipe out anything it considers as a threat to Earth, and I think that list now includes the colony."

"Why would it need to attack the colony, they aren't a threat to the planet?"

"Clarke, the first thing we did when we arrived is throw enough rocks at the planet to kill every life form ten times over. Even if Gatekeeper gave us a chance to explain ourselves, which I doubt, all we have as a defensive statement is 'sorry about that, we were aiming at you'. Somehow, I don't think that's going to help us much."

"Hmm good point. Ok so we're working on the assumption that the ship will try to tractor us in because it needs our navigational logs to hunt down and slaughter our entire race."

"Exactly."

Clarke rubbed his eyes and sighed. "I need a drink and a cigarette."

"We ran out of anything resembling alcohol years ago," Hawkins remarked reaching into his pocket for his cigarettes. "And, unless I'm mistaken, the last of the cigarette stockpile is in cargo bay two along with a couple of thousand gallons of water."

Clarke took a cigarette from the captain.

"This is probably the last packet on earth."

"Don't worry, Captain, we'll more than likely be dead before it runs out."

Hawkins laughed as Clarke took one of the bridge's emergency cutting torches out of its bracket and lit his cigarette.

"That's it."

"Sorry, sir?"

"The laser cutter." Hawkins directed Clarke's attention back to the deck plan on the tactical console monitor. "After we get inside the cargo bay, we can cut a hole through the deck plating straight up into the reactor room. That would be enough to get the wave through all the decks, wouldn't it?" questioned Hawkins as he pointed at the monitor.

"Maybe, but you need a cutting torch the size of the communications dish to pull that off."

Hawkins grinned. "Actually, you'd need a cutting torch mounted to the communication dish's retractable platform to pull that off." Hawkins stubbed out his cigarette and walked over to the transport lift. "Hawkins to Blaine, do you think you can handle the torpedo refits by yourself?"

"Shouldn't be a problem, sir, we're just supervising the repair drones down here anyway."

"Good. Tell Kane to meet me in cargo bay four, he's gonna love this."

CHAPTER 5
Reeva

The sun shone down over the hills from a clear blue sky and a light breeze rustled through the branches of the trees in the vast and wide stretching woodlands surrounding the loch. A family of deer who had been grazing on the long green grasses by the waterside, ran startled for the cover of the trees as three black helmets slowly emerged from the water.

"Are we certain that the viruses Gatekeeper created will be gone?"

"Like I explained earlier, Blaine, the viruses weren't airborne they were passed by human contact. The second the last infected human died the viruses ceased to exist, so you can stop worrying and take your helmet off."

"Is Kane sure he can build this cannon, Captain? I mean he's been tinkering around in the machine shops for nearly a week now. In fact, he's been spending so much time alone down there I wouldn't be surprised if he's started talking to the repair drones."

"Kane's fine. I spoke to him before we left and he's confident that his design will work just fine. The way I understand it, the cannon should work like a scaled-up version of the laser cutting torches. Kane thinks that with the right modifications and a direct power feed to the crystalline reactor, he can get this thing to fire over quite impressive distances. If it works as well as he thinks it will, it should be quite a formidable weapon."

Blaine finally took off his helmet and took in a deep breath of the morning air. "Oh god that's good. The air on Tartarus always beat the ship's recycled oxygen mix but this is beautiful."

"Yeah, there's no beating the morning air of Earth." Clarke slid out of his spacesuit and laid it up against one of the trees near the water's edge. "Blaine, take off your suit before you do any sightseeing. If you tear it on a bramble bush or something it's gonna be an interesting walk back to the ship."

"What's a bramble bush?" asked Blaine as he removed his suit and threw it to Clarke.

Clarke shook his head and chuckled to himself as he put the spacesuit under the tree. "Blaine, you'd better stay close to me."

The group walked off into the woods.

"I've seen trees like these in one of the databanks back on the colony. They're bigger than they look on the computer screen. Wow, look at that."

"What?" questioned Hawkins, trying to locate what Blaine was pointing at.

"There in that tree. Some sort of furry little creature."

Hawkins smiled. "That's a squirrel."

"A squirrel," repeated Blaine still staring at the creature. "Damn thing's fast."

"Earth's life forms have been evolving for much longer than those slimy little things on Tartarus. You'll find that most of the creatures here are fast." Hawkins pointed into the trees. "Believe it or not there are animals on this planet that could outsprint that squirrel without even breaking a sweat."

At hearing this, Blaine's gaze moved from the trees and fixed on the captain. "What's the fastest?"

"Well, the fastest land animal is called a cheetah. It's a big cat, a predator. They have a top speed of sixty miles an hour."

"Shit, are they dangerous?" Blaine looked around alertly.

Hawkins grinned. "Don't panic, there aren't any cheetahs in Britain, and they're not really big enough to attack a human. Not a fully grown man anyway."

Blaine jumped as a bird flew past over their heads. "Fuck me this place has some big bugs."

Clarke and Hawkins roared with laughter. Hawkins patted Blaine on the back. "That wasn't a bug, kiddo, it was a bird. A crow to be exact."

"Well, how the hell was I supposed to know there are flying animals here," Blaine replied looking slightly embarrassed.

"Didn't you ever learn anything about this planet while you were on Tartarus?"

"Only what I managed to pick up from computer files and none of them had any information about animals that fly."

"Yeah, well the anatomy of birds probably wasn't considered essential information for the running of starships," remarked Clarke having to hold himself up on a tree trunk.

Blaine just nodded and smiled. "Asshole."

The crew walked on. Clarke couldn't help but be impressed at how efficiently Gatekeeper had cleaned up the planet. The ferns he walked through and the trees he walked past were growing where a road once ran. He had noticed when they emerged from the water that the bridges that crossed the loch and the buildings that surrounded it were gone. In-fact the only evidence left on earth that humans had ever been here were the memories of this crew. They had to stop Gatekeeper. They had to make a difference here. The thought of the human race passing into oblivion without leaving any evidence of their existence filled him with dread.

"What the hell is that?"

Hawkins and Clarke turned to Blaine ready to identify the next unknown life form he had discovered. A cold shiver ran through Hawkins as he followed Blaine's gaze up to the sky. Like shooting stars, hundreds of burning objects streaked across the sky as they entered the atmosphere, scattering in all directions as far as the eye could see.

"Give me a fucking break."

"Drop-pods, Captain?"

"Drop-pods, Blaine."

"There's no way it could have zeroed in on us with all the life form readings on this planet."

"It didn't." Hawkins pointed at the sky. "Look at the dispersal pattern. It must have worked out which area we landed in from our entry window. Now after a week of failing to locate us from orbit, it's sending out the search parties."

"Oh great, so now we're being hunted too," shouted Blaine.

"Let's get back to the ship."

The crew ran back through the forest as fast as their legs would carry them. A distant rumbling filled the air as the drop-pods started to impact with the ground. The forest shook as a pod screeched over the crew's heads and impacted just beyond the treeline in front of them.

"Stop," ordered Hawkins.

"Captain, we have to go now."

"Gatekeeper would have accounted for the fact that sensors don't penetrate through deep water. Whatever's in that pod is probably capable of searching the loch and it will find us eventually. If we attack it before it gets its shit together, we'll stand a better chance and Gatekeeper might think it was damaged in the landing."

Clarke and Blaine looked at each other and Blaine pulled out his sidearm. "Let's get it on."

The crew set off towards the smoke which was now billowing over the trees. After busting through the undergrowth into the new and smouldering clearing, they stopped in shock.

"Fuck me." Blaine trained his pistol on the large bullet-shaped object, which was charred and smoking from its journey through the atmosphere.

As the crew watched, it suddenly cracked open revealing a small metallic creature. Roughly three feet high and six feet in length, the shiny beast resembled a large cat. Pistons and wires interrupted the smooth shape of its body and legs. Its feet and jaws sporting blade-like teeth and claws, which picked up the reflection of the dancing fire from the now burning woodland. The beast's head slowly started to rise as its systems came online.

"Shoot it before it wakes up."

The group trained their guns and blasted the creature until it hit the ground motionless. Hawkins slowly walked over. His pistol still aimed at its head. "Ok, I think we got it."

"Did it have time to activate?"

"I don't know. Blaine, give me a hand with this thing."

Kane dropped his tool kit in shock as Blaine and Hawkins carried the robotic creature into the machine shop. "What the fuck is that?"

"It's some sort of robot. There are drop-pods full of these things landing all over the place."

Hawkins wiped the sweat off his brow after he and Blaine had lifted the machine onto one of the worktops.

"There are more of these things out there!" shouted Kane.

"Just a couple of hundred. If anyone needs me, I'll be on the bridge emptying the weapons locker." Blaine took a final look at the metal cat and exited the machine room in quite a hurry.

"Look at the god damn claws on this thing. It's a good job you took your sidearms."

"Kane, after today I'm sleeping with my sidearm," Hawkins mocked.

Kane picked up the creature's head. "You lucky bastards."

"Excuse me."

"Look at this." Kane pointed at a charred mass of wires in the back of the creature's head. "This thing had its head down when you shot it didn't it."

Hawkins looked surprised. "Yes, how did you –"

"This shot to the back of the head is what put it down," interrupted Kane. "The rest of the shots did little more than superficial damage." Kane lifted the machine's head and the melted mass of wires disappeared as the back of the creature's metallic skull covered them over. "If you'd given this thing time to lift its head, you wouldn't be here right now."

"So, what are you telling me, that our weapons can't stop these things?"

"Oh, you'd stop them eventually, if you got the chance to fire off that many rounds. It would probably be wise to break out the rifles."

Hawkins nodded and walked off towards the door. "Well at least Blaine will be happy."

"Err."

Hawkins stopped at the door and turned back round.

"Are you just gonna leave this here?" Kane questioned.

Hawkins smiled. "Maybe you can teach it to fetch."

Kane sighed as Hawkins walked off. By the time Hawkins reached the bridge, Blaine had picked out a couple of plasma rifles and was loading up ammo belts with power cells.

"Kane suggests that we keep the rifles close at hand from now on. Apparently, a lucky shot was all that took that thing down."

"How so?" asked Blaine still pushing power cells into belt pockets.

"It has a vulnerable spot at the base of its neck when its head is down. If we'd given it chance to look up, we'd have been cat food." Hawkins caught one of the rifles as Blaine threw it across the room.

"Works for me. Here, you'd better take some spare clips." Blaine threw Hawkins one of the ammo belts.

"We should be ok for a while," Hawkins reassured as he clipped the ammo belt round his waist. "There didn't seem to be a lot of drop-pods in relation to the size of the landmass. It should be a while before any more of those things work their way here."

"That's providing we got it before it had time to scan us."

"Yeah."

"So, is that what one of those cheetah things looks like? It seems to fit the description you gave me."

"Not quite, it looks more like a leopard only bigger."

Blaine frowned. "A leopard, Captain?"

"It's another big cat. It's not as fast as a cheetah but it's much better at climbing and I'm sorry to say that it is big enough to kill a man."

"But why would it build machines that look like earth animals, Captain? It doesn't make any sense."

"Actually, Blaine, it makes perfect sense. Why spend time developing something when you can simply copy a design that nature has been developing for thousands of years."

"Yeah, I suppose that makes sense."

"Clarke to Hawkins, come in, sir."

"What is it, Clarke?"

"If you don't need me for anything, Captain, I thought I'd go down to the machine shop and take a look at our new passenger. I might be able to get some useful information from it."

"Ok, Clarke, but be careful if you're gonna be playing around with that thing. The last thing I need right now is a six foot long killing machine running around the lower decks."

"No problem, sir, I'll be extra careful. Clarke out."

"Hawkins to Kane, what's the status of my cannon?"

"Kane to Hawkins, I've finished building all the complicated components, Captain. I'm just waiting for the repair drones to mount the main sections onto the retractable platform. As soon as they're finished, I can start hooking up the power supply to the reactor."

"What about the communications array?"

"Well, I've been able to re-route the short-range communications through the secondary sensor array, but we're not going to be able to send or receive any long-range messages until I can reattach the dish."

"Don't worry about the dish, Kane, there's no one out there we need to talk to anyway.

Keep me posted, Hawkins out." Hawkins walked over to the tactical console and started typing on one of the keyboards. "I don't like this, Blaine. We're not going to know if any of those things are coming until they're knocking at the door. Isn't there any way of calibrating the sensors to penetrate water more efficiently?"

"Not that I know of. All we can do is set the sensors to warn us as soon as they detect something."

Down in the machine shop Kane was taking the opportunity to acquaint himself with the ship's new visitor. "Damn, you're a real piece of work my friend." Kane lent forward for a closer look at the creature's eyes.

"Aaarrghh!"

Kane jumped back in shock and fell onto the floor.

Clarke stood in the doorway laughing. "Got you."

Kane grinned in relief as Clarke took his hand and helped him up. "You bastard, I almost messed my pants."

"Sorry, I couldn't resist it. Looks like you're keeping yourself busy," Clarke remarked as he looked over the masses of new wires, which were running from the metal cat to various other pieces of equipment.

"This thing's amazing, Clarke."

"This thing's a walking blender, Kane. Look at those claws."

"You're missing the point. Yes, it's designed to track and kill, but it's the equipment it carries to do that job that interests me. Look at these eyes for instance."

Clarke lent in to get a better look.

"They're quite advanced." Kane took a small tool out of his pocket and proceeded to point at different parts of the eye. "This section allows it to see in the infrared spectrum. In other words, it can track your body heat. This section appears to be some sort of advanced night vision system and this thing is an extremely high-tech form of sonar for echo-location."

"So, you're saying that this thing would kick ass at hide and seek."

"I'm saying that this thing could track a housefly through the Amazon rainforest, and that's not even the half of it." Kane pointed at the nose of the creature. "The nose contains what I think is a pheromone scanner.

"Now you're losing me."

"All life forms naturally produce pheromones, smells. If this thing had the chance to smell you even once, there would be no way you could ever hide from it."

"Couldn't you change your smell by covering yourself in deodorant or rolling in dung or something?"

"It's slightly more sophisticated than that, Clarke. If this thing can pick up pheromones as accurately as I think it can then it can track you by smelling your fear."

"Fear has a smell?"

"Fear is nothing more than a chemical reaction in your brain, and it gives off plenty of pheromones to trace."

Clarke now looked unmistakably worried. "So, let me see if I've got this straight? If another one of these things passes by the drop-pod landing site where we found this one, it's gonna pick up our trail and follow our smells straight to us."

"Well technically it can only follow your smell to the edge of the water, but yes that's about the size of it."

"What about its processing capacity. How smart is this thing?"

"No way of telling at this point but incidentally, that is something I wanted to talk to you about."

Back on the bridge Blaine and Hawkins were looking over the arrowhead vessels deck plan.

"You see what I mean? Even if we can get Gatekeeper to try and tractor us into the same cargo bay as last time. We're still gonna have to take these four energy-beam weapons out before we can risk raising the cannon." Blaine pointed out the energy-beam weapons on the screen as he explained, "Otherwise, our secret weapon is gonna be in pieces before we get a chance to fire it."

Hawkins nodded. "I see what you mean. Any suggestions?"

"Well, the cargo bay's big but there's not enough room to start firing torpedoes. The only other way is to take them out with a plasma rifle from one of the top hatches."

"It would take two of us to even stand a chance of taking those guns out before they fire."

"And whoever goes out there would have to wear a spacesuit. Even if we wait till the outer door closes, there's no guarantee that the cargo bay will have a breathable atmosphere. After all, machines have no need for breathable air."

"The hatch covers should provide some protection from these two guns." Blaine pointed at the monitor. "These two guns have a clear shot at whoever's out there, so we'll have to take them out first."

"Agreed."

"You know, sir, it would be easier to just destroy the reactor with the cannon."

"We have to assume that ship has at least one back up reactor. It might not, hell we don't, but we can't take any chances. If we can clear a path to the reactor we do know about, with the cannon. If we can use that path to get the radio wave through all those decks with a strong enough signal remaining to allow it to resonate within that reactor's electromagnetic field. Then we not only force that reactor to shut down for as long as we are transmitting, but also the power grid itself will act like a damned antenna, helping the wave transmit through the mothership to any other reactors connected into it. That's how we shut this thing down.

"Besides you can't just fire off what is essentially a giant laser cutter into a cluster of Matrillion crystals and expect them to stop emitting power. I may not be much of an engineer but I do know that damaging those crystals won't stop them releasing energy. You can manipulate the electromagnetic field of chunks of Matrillion of any size or shape and they will release the energy stored within them. You could break every crystal in that reactor housing in half and all those halves would still emit power under the right conditions. Those things are pretty much bullet-proof. That's why we only have one, because they simply don't stop working."

"Until Keymaster."

"Until Keymaster," Hawkins repeated in agreement. "Also, I've said Keymaster so many times now that you owe me a whole keg, kiddo."

Blaine grinned.

"Clarke to Hawkins, could you please say the word 'Reeva' into the communicator please, Captain?"

"What the hell for?"

"Humour me."

Hawkins sighed and raised the communicator on his forearm. "Reeva."

"Thanks, that'll do. Is Blaine there with you, Captain?"

"Yeah, I'm here."

"Do me a favour and say –"

"Reeva," interrupted Blaine.

"Thanks, Blaine, Clarke out."

Hawkins and Blaine looked at each other. "Wonder what that's about."

"Who cares? How do we get out?"

"Sorry, Blaine?" Hawkins questioned.

"After we set off Keymaster and shut down the whole ship, its power should be off-line. It should go dark, right? Total shut down of any major system."

"If everything goes to plan, yes. Then we just need to make sure it stays down by locating Gatekeeper's system core and launching everything we can throw at it."

"Then how the hell are we going to get out of the bay?"

Hawkins stood in silence and looked at Blaine, as if trying to think of a reasonable answer. After a few seconds he reach into his pocket and took out a cigarette. After lighting it and taking a couple of hits, he took a thoughtful look around the bridge and returned his gaze to Blaine. "I think we both know the odds of getting out of that cargo bay once the outer door closes."

Blaine looked down at the monitor displaying the huge deck plan of the arrowhead vessel. After a thoughtful pause he nodded and looked back up at Hawkins. "The needs of the many outweigh the needs of the few."

"Yes, they do Blaine. Send a copy of Gatekeeper's vessel data to the mess hall wall monitor. I'm hungry. I'll look at it while I'm eating." Hawkins turned away from Blaine and headed out of the bridge. "Oh and, Blaine."

"Yes, Captain?"

"Stop quoting corny movie lines, or my foot will be boldly going where no one has gone before."

"Oh, now that was cheap."

Hawkins smiled to himself as the pair walked out through the bridge's main access door and off towards the mess hall. Hawkins could hear the metallic rattling sound of someone running along the grid metal floor of the corridor on the deck below them.

"Hawkins to Kane. Everything ok down there?"

"Yes, sir, everything's fine. Why do you ask?"

"I just heard someone running through the corridors. Guess I'm just a little on edge with that damn machine on board."

"It's just Clarke, sir, I sent him to fetch some spare computer components from one of the maintenance lockers."

"No problem, Kane. Me and Blaine are heading down to the mess if either of you fancy a break?"

"We're fine, sir. I'd like to finish up down here anyway, we're learning quite a lot from this thing."

"Such as?"

"Well for a start, I can confirm that Gatekeeper is in-fact after our navigational logs."

"How do you know that?"

"Clarke's managed to break this things programming, and it's amazingly complex, Captain. It's not controlled by a computer system like the repair drones, instead it actually seems to have the capacity to make its own decisions."

"What the hell are you telling me, Kane, that this thing can do whatever the hell it likes?"

"Not exactly, Captain, the best way to explain it would be to think of it as a soldier. For example, human soldiers have their own individual consciousness, free will, whatever you want to call it. However, they still follow the orders they are given without question. When the Auto-Repair system stops sending the repair drones orders, they simply stop moving. When the ship in orbit stops sending these things orders, they're free to do whatever they feel like doing."

"So, you're saying that even if we succeed in destroying Gatekeeper, we're still gonna have to take out every individual machine that's currently scurrying around this continent? Around that ship up there?"

"Basically, yes."

"Kane, tell me that thing's power source has a very short operational lifespan."

"Well, if you're thinking about giving these things a wide berth until they run out of juice, we'll be waiting for quite a while."

Hawkins sighed.

"It's powered by what looks like some sort of fusion generator, Captain. These things will probably still be ticking when we're all long dead."

Hawkins closed his eyes and took a deep calming breath. "This shit is getting better by the fucking minute."

"At least we know for certain that Gatekeeper wants the navigational logs. So at least the first part of the plan's going to work," comforted Blaine.

"Oh great, so Gatekeeper is definitely going to try to take us prisoner." Hawkins continued on down the corridor. "Now I feel much better!" he shouted as he disappeared through the mess hall door.

Blaine sighed and followed the captain through.

"What are you having, Blaine?" asked Hawkins as he punched buttons on the food dispenser.

"Whatever, it's all just as bad."

The food dispenser hatch opened revealing two steaming bowls of what looked like dark grey porridge. Hawkins carried them over to the table where Blaine had seated himself. After placing one down in front of Blaine he took a seat.

Blaine stared at the bowl of slop with a look of contempt as he stirred it around with his spoon. "Oh, that's it. I can handle hostile starships and killer robots but if I have to eat any more of these nutritional supplements, I'm going to have to surrender. Can't we go out and bag a few of those small squirrels or something?"

Hawkins grinned. "It's too quiet out there now. The weapons discharge from a plasma pistol is detectable on scanners. The only reason we got away with firing on that machine without being detected was that the power signatures from all those drop-pods masked our weapons fire."

Blaine picked up a spoonful of his meal. He turned his spoon and watched as it dribbled back into his bowl. "Great. I'm surrounded by hundreds of edible life forms and I'm still doomed to eat this snot."

The sound of approaching feet on the metal grid floor let Blaine know that someone had just entered the mess hall. From the seat he had chosen, Blaine's back was to the door and he was unable to see who had entered. Though it sounded like more than one set of boots.

"Changed your minds, guys? I suggest you try the slime, it's particularly good today," Blaine stopped his conversation as he looked across the table at Hawkins. The captain was staring straight past him wearing a look of dread. Blaine's attention turned back to the sound of the footsteps, which were much closer now and had slowed to a crawling pace. As he noticed Hawkins slowly reaching for his sidearm, Blaine glanced at the plasma rifles that they had propped against the food dispenser all the way across the room. He didn't know what was approaching behind him but from the look on the captain's face he could tell it wasn't anything pleasant. It hadn't attacked yet but that could all change if it saw him reach for his sidearm. He looked at Hawkins and tipped his head to the right, trying to indicate which way he was going to move. Hawkins seemed to understand what he meant and nodded.

"On three, Blaine," Hawkins whispered at a barely audible level. "One, two, three."

Blaine dove out of the way as Hawkins sprung to his feet and quickly aimed his pistol.

"Wait, don't shoot!"

Hawkins stopped as Clarke came running into the mess hall. "Don't shoot, sir, it's not going to attack," Clarke panted reassuringly. "Reeva, halt."

The metal beast turned to face Clarke and stopped. Hawkins lowered his pistol as Blaine picked himself up off the floor.

"What the fuck is going on here, Clarke?"

"We fixed it, Captain."

"What the hell do you mean you fixed it?" Hawkins started to sound angry as his shock subsided.

"Me and Kane managed to reprogram it."

"Go on."

"Like I said earlier, sir, it's like a soldier. It has its own unique consciousness but it takes order from the mothership via a communications link. After Kane repaired the pistol damage, I removed its up-link node and replaced it with one of our own communications nodes from the wrist-com's," Clarke paused and cleared his throat anxiously awaiting a response.

Hawkins looked at Blaine who was now stood behind one of the tables pointing a rifle at the machine. "Blaine, keep that rifle ready."

"Aye, sir."

Hawkins holstered his sidearm as he cautiously walked out from behind the table and headed towards Clarke. "So, it takes orders from us now?" Hawkins walked up to the creature that was still standing motionless looking at Clarke.

"Yes, sir, we've named it Reeva. That's also the password required to make it obey commands."

"Reeva." Hawkins jumped back in surprise as the metal cat swiftly turned to face him.

"Don't worry, Captain. It always does that when you say its name."

Hawkins quickly composed himself. "So, this thing is waiting for me to give it an order?"

"Yes, Captain."

"And it will take orders from anyone with a wrist-com?"

"No sir, as a safety precaution we programmed it to respond to our four voices only."

"Ah, that's why you needed us to say its name into the communicators."

"Exactly, Captain." Clarke looked down at Reeva. "You know it's just going to stand there until you give it a command."

Hawkins looked at the bright green light of Reeva's eyes as she looked up at him. He frowned and pointed to the other side of the room. "Go and stand over there."

Reacting instantly Reeva walked over to the far side of the room and turned to face the captain.

"Hmm, it works. Any idea what this thing's capable of?"

"Well, it has extremely high-tech visual and olfactory senses and from here it could hear a pin drop on the bridge. The statistical data we collected from its databanks says that it's capable of achieving speeds of up to forty miles an hour."

"So, out-running these things isn't going to be easy?" mocked Blaine.

"That's nothing, Blaine. This thing's also capable of jumping as high as fifteen feet. So, what it can't climb up, it can sure as hell jump over."

"You know, I'm starting to worry about these things more than the mothership."

"I thought these things did pretty much what they wanted in-between orders."

Clarke looked over at Reeva who was still standing motionless at the other end of the room. "That's because it's still carrying out your orders, Captain."

"How is it still carrying out my orders? I just told it to go and stand over there."

"And that's what she will do until you tell her otherwise. You see that's the kind of task that can't be completed. If you'd told her to kill Blaine for instance, the task would have been completed when he stopped breathing and her free will would be allowed to take over. Now, as there is no definable end-point to the task you set her, she will simply continue to obey the command until someone tells her otherwise."

Hawkins nodded.

"Could it actually be told to do that?"

"Told to do what, Blaine?"

"Told to kill someone."

"She'll obey almost any order that doesn't conflict with the directives Kane and I programmed into her."

"Which are?" questioned Hawkins.

"Well for a start you can stop worrying, Blaine, her primary directive is to protect us. You can order her to attack anything in the universe, except for the crew of this ship. Her second directive is to only take commands from people that she has a stored voiceprint of, which as I've already explained, is us. Directive three allows her to use whatever means are necessary to defend herself if she's attacked."

"Obviously that doesn't include us, right?"

"Of course."

"Hey, Captain, what about sending this thing out to fetch something edible? It'd be a chance to test these super-senses that Clarke's talking about."

"This thing would stand out like a priest in a brothel, Blaine. Gatekeeper is bound to know something's wrong if a missing and presumed destroyed drone suddenly reappears and starts dragging wildlife into the loch."

Blaine nodded.

"Clarke, do you think you can tap into this thing's optical systems?"

Clarke stood looking thoughtful for a moment. "I suppose I could get a picture of what she's seeing if I tie a transmitter into her optical wiring."

"Good, get it done as soon as possible. Maybe we can use it as a scout or something."

"I'll get right on it, Captain. Reeva, come with me."

Hawkins and Blaine backed off slightly as the machine followed Clarke out of the mess hall.

"This is fucked up," remarked Blaine after Clarke and Reeva's footsteps had grown sufficiently distant.

"Oh yeah." Hawkins walked back over to his table and sat down. "Are you going to eat this?" he questioned pointing at Blaine's unfinished bowl of food.

"Be my guest. I'm not really that hungry now anyway."

Hawkins picked up Blaine's bowl and began to spoon its contents into his own bowl. "As long as you're not doing anything, you might as well see if Kane needs any help. The faster we get this cannon online, the faster we can get out of here."

"Aye, sir." Blaine walked out of the mess hall and made his way back to the bridge.

"Blaine to Kane, where are you?"

"Down in the reactor room. I'm trying to hook up this damn power cable for the laser cannon."

"Need any help?"

"If I had someone to help me lift the deck plating, I could set this thing up permanently.

Otherwise, I'm going to have to trail this power cable down the corridors."

"No problem, Kane, I'm on my way."

"Thanks, Blaine. Kane out."

Blaine walked into the bridge' transport lift. "Engine rooms." The lift began its descent towards engine rooms.

As well as travelling vertically, the transport lifts could also travel horizontally throughout the length of the ship. This feature could save the crew vast amounts of time when having to cover the distances between the bow and stern of the half-mile long vessel. By the time Blaine arrived, Kane had already removed a couple of the large sections of deck plating and was struggling to lift another.

"Nice timing, Blaine."

"On three. One, two, three." Blaine and Kane pulled the floor plate up and rested it against the wall of the corridor.

"Jesus, how the hell did you move those two sections by yourself? These things must weigh over a hundred pounds."

"You know when you, Clarke and the captain are up on the bridge pushing buttons and pulling levers?"

"Yeah."

"Well, I'm down here lifting and carrying like a real man," Kane grinned.

"All hail the grease monkey."

"Very witty. Just help me get this power cable hooked up before any more of those machines decide to pay us a visit."

"Clarke to Kane, can you come up to machine shop two, I need a hand with something."

"Sorry, Clarke, I need to get this power cable hooked up. What's the problem?"

"Captain Hawkins has asked me to hook Reeva's optics up to a transmitter, so we can see what she's seeing. I'm just wondering if you know of a way of doing that without the mothership being able to pick up the signal."

"Hooking the transmitter up to a frequency modulator should make the signal harder to lock onto. If possible, try to give Reeva direct access to the transmitter, so that we can order her to cut the transmission when we don't require it."

"Ok thanks, Kane, Clarke out."

"Sounds like Reeva's gonna make a good addition to the crew."

"As long as she's on point instead of one of us, I'm happy." Kane looked down at the small screen on his wrist communicator as it started to beep.

"Kane to Hawkins, come in, Captain."

"Hawkins here, what is it, Kane?"

"The Auto-Repair drones have finished putting the cannon together, Captain. It'll be ready as soon as Blaine and I finish attaching the power cable."

"How long do you think that should take?"

"About forty minutes, Captain."

"Very well, I'll be on the bridge prepping the ship. Tell Blaine and Clarke that we leave at eighteen hundred hours."

"Aye, sir."

"Hawkins out."

The next hour passed relatively quickly due to the busyness of the crew. Kane and Blaine managed to run the power cable under the corridor deck plates, before hooking it up to the ship's new cannon. Clarke eventually got Reeva's optical transmission system online and after prepping the ship for take-off, Hawkins gave the crew a final rundown of the plans for the mission ahead. Sketchy as they were. With a great rumble of dissipating water, the Dark Star emerged from the loch. Animals and birds in the surrounding woodland panicked and scattered as the engines burst into action.

"Activating atmospheric thrusters, setting course for upper atmosphere."

"Clarke, give me a sensor reading."

"Bear with me, sir, I'm still waiting for all this damn water to drain off the sensor nodes."

"Blaine, the water in the port cargo bay isn't draining properly, can you give me a three-degree roll to port."

"No problem, Kane."

"Sensors are drying out and coming back online, Captain. They're still too wet for an atmospheric scan, however I am picking up several dozen small power signatures, heading at various speeds towards Loch Ness."

"I guess they found us."

"Breaking through the upper atmosphere in five, four, three, two, one. Bringing main engines online, Captain."

"Captain, I'm picking up a small ship in orbit, about two miles off our stern."

"Identify."

"It appears to be of the same configuration as the mothership, Captain, just a lot smaller. The sensors are having the same amount of trouble trying to scan it."

"Status?"

"The ship is heading this way, Captain. I'm picking up at least two separate power surges emanating from it."

"Shields up and weapons charging! Blaine, evasive manoeuvres now!"

Blaine threw the Dark Star into a hard turn seconds before the advancing vessel's main weapon discharged. The bridge rumbled as the energy-beam narrowly missed the ship.

"Wow, that was too close."

"I think it's safe to say that its weaponry is the same as the mothership's."

"Picking up another power build-up."

Once again Blaine changed direction as rapidly as the huge bulk of the ship allowed and once again narrowly dodged the energy weapons discharge.

"Captain, that energy-beam is significantly less powerful than the mothership's. If that's due to the scale difference of the crystalline reactors, then the shields should be less effective also."

"Well done, Clarke. Blaine, bring us about, we're through running."

"Aye, sir, coming about." Blaine turned the ship through a hundred-and-eighty-degree loop and levelled off. "It's no good, sir, this one's more manoeuvrable than us. It's followed us straight through the loop, I can't shake it."

"Clarke, load torpedo tubes one through ten. Prepare to fire a spread on my mark."

"Aye, sir, tubes one through ten are locked, loaded and ready to fly."

"Captain, the warheads on these torpedoes are still at full mining yield. I suggest we only fire one or two at this range."

"Noted. Blaine, try to keep her steady. Give Clarke a straight shot. Clarke, fire tubes one and two when you're lined up."

"Target locked, Torpedoes away." The tracking system on the tactical console began to beep as Clarke launched the torpedoes. "Impact in four, three, two, one. Negative impact, the vessel has moved to avoid torpedoes."

"Damn it, ready tubes three through ten. Launch in a random dispersal pattern on my mark."

"The vessel is powering for another shot. I'm going to set the launchers to fire manually and release them on differing trajectories. Ready to fire, Captain."

"Steady, Blaine. Get ready to increase speed as soon as Clarke launches the………." Hawkins stopped talking as Blaine barrel rolled in an attempt to avoid another incoming shot from his pursuer.

"Shit that was close." Blaine held the ship on course. "Holding course. Clarke, get that thing off me."

Clarke picked his moment and fired. "Torpedoes away."

Watching through the screen of the targeting scanner, Clarke manually fired off the torpedoes one after the other toward the vessel, knowing full well that the inaccuracy of his human targeting would create a much more spread-out hail of shots than the highly accurate computer would have fired. The pursuing vessel did its best to bank and correct its line of flight in order to pick a path through the haphazard onslaught of projectiles but didn't quite succeed.

"Pedal to the metal." Blaine threw the power lever into the red. Clarke and Kane slammed into their consoles as one of the torpedoes exploded, tossing the Dark Star around in the blast.

"Hit!" shouted Clarke triumphantly.

"Damage report!" shouted Hawkins through the din.

"Minor damage to the aft ventral hull plating and shield emitters. Repair drones have been dispatched."

"Clarke, status of the pursuing vessel."

"Pursuing vessel is adrift. My new ability to scan small sections of its interior would suggest that its hull plating is very badly damaged."

"Score one for the good guys."

"Any sign of the mothership?"

"There's no sign of it, Captain."

"Are you sure?"

"It's pretty hard to miss."

"Ok, everyone, relax," offered Hawkins. "Clarke is there any reason we can't load a mixture of standard mining yield and modified low-yield torpedoes into the launcher-pods, so we can choose? Cos I'm pretty sure that last explosion just burned the hairs off my ass."

"Good idea, Captain," replied Clarke, still breathing heavily. "In my defence, I was expecting an eight-mile-long mothership when I loaded the full yield warheads."

Hawkins nodded. "Let's just try to keep our options open shall we." Hawkins let out a long calming breath.

"Noted, sir."

"Blaine, bring us alongside that ship. Kane, go get your new toy ready for a little scouting mission."

Kane hurried into the transport lift as Blaine brought the ship about and headed for the battered vessel.

"Can we get a lock with the docking clamps?"

"We can probably lock onto one of the breaches in the hull, but it's not going to be very stable. One wrong move and whoever goes out there could end up spinning through space"

"Are you picking up any power reading?"

"Nothing big enough to be an active power source for the ship, it appears to be dead in space. However, I am reading several small moving energy signatures."

"Repair drones?"

"Couldn't say, Captain, but something's moving around in there."

"Coming alongside the vessel now, Captain."

"Ok, Blaine, all stop."

"Aye, sir, all stop."

"Lock us on, Clarke."

"Extending portside docking gantry now, sir. Contact in three seconds." The bridge jolted as the docking clamps came into contact with the other ship. "Docking clamps are locked and holding, Captain."

"Good job, guys. Hawkins to Kane, bring Reeva and meet us in the portside airlock."

"Aye, sir."

"Oh, and Kane, you'd better bring a rifle."

"Way ahead of you, Captain."

"Clarke, I need you to stay here and monitor Reeva's new optical up-link system. Blaine, you're with me."

Blaine left his position at the helm and after stopping to pick up his rifle, he followed Hawkins into the transport lift.

"Clarke?"

"Yes, Captain?"

"Keep an eye on the sensors. That mothership's out there somewhere."

"No problem."

"Deck five, section one." Hawkins and Blaine were lost behind the hissing doors of the lift and Clarke was left alone. He brought up an internal map of deck five on one of the four overhead monitors that curved around the roof above his console. If anything decided to wander off that ship through the airlock, he wanted to know about it before it got anywhere near the bridge. After setting the external sensors to scan for any incoming vessels or anomalies, he walked over to the main view port to take a look at the conquered ship. He couldn't see much of the ship from his position, but he could see enough to be impressed by its design. Even from this distance the hull looked silky smooth and seamless, with the obvious exception of the twisted and torn sections damaged by the torpedoes. Staring at this tool of destruction set against the backdrop of the planet, the clouds below reflected in its shiny black surface. He couldn't help but think that it actually looked quite beautiful.

"Kane to Clarke, are you receiving the signal from Reeva's optical transmitter?"

Clarke ran back to his console and started typing on his keyboard. "Hold on, Kane." Another one of the overhead monitors came online, displaying a strange and hazy bright coloured picture of what appeared to be a hand waving back and forth. "Confirmed, Kane. She appears to be using her infrared sensors at the moment."

"Yeah, that makes sense. The airlock is quite cold, life forms and anything else with a heat signature would show up quite well in here."

"Well, it works, you guys are shining like beacons. Even through the pressure suits." Clarke watched Reeva begin to walk forward as the outer airlock door opened.

"Clarke, we're sending Reeva in a few metres in front of us. Let us know the second you see anything. I don't want any surprises."

"Aye, sir."

Hawkins, Blaine and Kane activated their rifle torches and the backup lights on their E.V.A. suits and slowly crossed the docking gantry into the other ship.

"Ok, boys, this is a salvage mission. If you find anything that could be useful to us, data storage banks, technology etc, bag it and bring it with you. Watch your backs in here, guys."

The team walked on through the dark, still corridors of the ship. The sound of their magnetic boots grasping the metal floor was all that broke the deafening silence. Hawkins glanced up and out into space as they passed under one of the many breaches in the outer hull. "Be careful not to tear your suits on all this twisted metal."

"Hold on a minute." Kane stopped and removed a cutting torch from the satchel he was carrying. After deactivating his magnetic boots, he gently pushed away from the floor and grabbed onto a small piece of battered hull plating at the edge of the breach.

"What are you doing, Kane?"

"I'm trying to get a sample of this hull plating. If I analyse it, I might be able to explain why it screws up the sensors"

"Clarke to Hawkins, come in."

"What is it, Clarke?"

"The corridor ahead of you opens up into a large circular room. It's about twice the size of cargo bay four, Captain, and if I'm making it out properly through this damn heat vision, it's some sort of launch bay."

"Launch bay?"

"Yes, sir, there's dozens of launch tubes in here, all empty. I'm thinking it was this ship that launched the drop-pods, not the mothership."

"Then the mothership could have left days ago."

"Yes, sir. It could be anywhere by now."

Kane reactivated his magnetic boots and quickly drifted back down to the floor. "Damn this stuff's tough. I've never seen a laser torch take that long to cut through anything." Kane put the cutting torch and the sample of hull plating in his satchel and the crew walked on towards the launch bay.

"Jesus, this room must span all the way across the ship."

"There doesn't appear to be any way out except the way we came in."

"Hawkins to Clarke, can you get me a deck plan of this section?"

"Sorry, Captain, I can't scan enough of the interior to create a deck plan."

"Don't worry about it, Clarke, we'll just have to –" Hawkins was cut short by a loud thud. "What was that?"

"Sorry, Captain, I didn't catch that."

"Standby, Clarke."

Kane jumped as another larger thud echoed through the room.

"Over there, Captain." Blaine pointed towards a large indentation in the wall. As the crew watched, another large thud filled the room and the indentation grew larger. They watched as thud after thud the indentation grew until the bulkhead started to breach under the strain.

"Clarke to Hawkins, I'm picking up a moving power source in one of the chambers adjacent to your position."

"No shit, Clarke."

Hawkins and the crew stepped back in horror as the bulkhead gave way. Stood before them was a towering multi-limbed mass of pistons and shiny metal, standing at least five feet tall. Several small red lights spread across the front of the machine's main body, reflecting on the blade-like mandibles that twitched beneath them. Hawkins and Blaine slowly turned their heads and looked at each other in disbelief before quickly raising their rifles and opening fire. Kane followed suit and proceeded to discharge his rifle at the machine, which started to move quickly across the huge room towards them.

"Aim for the legs!" shouted Kane through the din of the weapons fire.

Hawkins and Blaine followed the suggestion but the monstrous mass of metal kept coming. Shrugging off the green plasma bolts thrown out by the three rifles.

"Everybody, aim for the top joint on the left claw."

"Which left?"

"Damn it, Blaine, our left." Hawkins' plan worked. The machine's left mandible was sent spinning through the air as the team hit it with the concentrated power of all three rifles.

"Yes, that's it. Quickly aim for the centre of the main body."

The crew fired at the machine, which was now only a few feet away. Kane closed his eyes as it closed in and Hawkins braced himself for the impact. The huge machine was ripped from the floor as Reeva smashed into its side at a sprint. The crew fired off shot after shot as it drifted helplessly through the zero-gravity environment and by the time it came into contact with a suitable surface, it had sustained too much damage to re-establish its grip.

"Hawkins to Clarke, nice timing."

"That wasn't me, Captain. Reeva did that by herself."

Hawkins looked at Reeva, who was stood watching the machine as it drifted around the room. "Hmm, maybe that thing's gonna come in handy after all."

"That was far too close."

"Yeah, but at least that thing was nice enough to leave the door open," returned Blaine jokingly as he pointed at the gaping hole in the wall.

"Come on, we'd better keep moving."

The crew followed Reeva through the new breach. The chamber beyond was little more than a shaft that led down past the range of the torchlight.

"Captain, we are going to have to leave Reeva here, the walls of this shaft are too smooth for her to grip."

Hawkins nodded. "Ok, Blaine, you're on point."

"Aye, sir." Blaine stepped up to the edge of the shaft and looked down. After shaking his head in protest, he allowed himself to slowly fall forward by ninety degrees before locking his boots onto the side of the shaft. "Ok, Captain, it's safe."

Hawkins and Kane followed Blaine's lead and the team proceeded to descend down the vertical wall of the shaft. Hawkins jumped and reached for his rifle as Reeva brushed passed him and headed towards Blaine at the front of the group. Hawkins steadied himself with a long sigh.

"That's amazing, she must be able to magnetise her paws," remarked Kane as Reeva passed by him.

"I thought her primary function was to protect us?"

"Yes, sir."

"Then why does she insist on trying to give me a fucking heart attack."

"Captain, there's a hatch down here."

"Don't open it till we get there."

"Aye, sir."

Hawkins and Kane caught up with Blaine who was standing next to the hatch on the adjacent wall of the shaft

"You're gonna have to blow the locking mechanism before I can open it, Captain."

"Ok, Blaine, stand back." Hawkins trained his rifle on the hatch and fired. Under a shower of sparks the hatch opened and Blaine ordered Reeva inside.

"Blaine to Clarke, is the room secured?"

"Hold on, Blaine, this room is full of equipment, it's gonna take a few minutes to check out."

"Copy that, Clarke."

Hawkins and Kane carefully walked round to the adjacent shaft wall where Blaine was now peering through the hatch.

"Clarke to Hawkins, Reeva's picking up multiple heat signatures, Captain, but no movement. It's as secure as it's ever going to be, sir."

Hawkins nodded at Blaine and he climbed in through the hatch.

"It looks clear to me, Captain."

Hawkins and Kane followed Blaine through the hatch and into the cluttered room.

"Bingo."

"Where are we, Kane?"

"The engine rooms, Captain." Kane took another look around. "Or at least some sort of engineering section."

Reeva walked out in front and led the team through the darkened chambers. Being certain that they were alone was almost impossible amidst the clustered silhouettes of a variety of large pieces of machinery and equipment but the team pressed on. After a few minutes of their torch-lit exploration, Kane came across something that interested him immensely. "Captain, hold up a minute."

The team stopped and while Blaine and Reeva kept watch, Hawkins walked back to where Kane was standing. "What is it?"

"This looks like some kind of databank."

"How much data could something this size hold?"

"Let's find out." Kane took a small piece of diagnostic equipment out of his satchel. Except for a larger screen and a number of small wires and clamps attached to it, the tool resembled a large calculator. Kane carefully removed a small panel from the databank and started to attach the diagnostic tool to its now bared wiring, within a few seconds the screen on the tool lit up and started scrolling through line after line of information.

"Now this is interesting."

"Let me take a look."

"See, this is the equation for calculating weight and this equation here seems to be something to do with mass and velocity. As for the rest of it, sir, I don't have a clue."

"Can you download information to the Star from that thing?"

"Yes, Captain."

"Hawkins to Clarke, we're sending some equations from a data storage unit that we've found, it should be coming up on Kane's console. See if the computer can work out what it does."

"No problem, sir."

Kane transmitted the equations to his console on the Dark Star and disconnected the diagnostic tool from the databank.

"Receiving information, Captain. Transferring it to the main computer now, standby." Clarke watched his monitors as the main computer started to create pictures of the small arrowhead vessel and strange funnel-like shapes. Other screens began to scroll lines of descriptive text and more algebraic calculations. "Jesus, Captain, there's a lot of information here, it's going to be a while before I can tell you what it means."

"Ok, Clarke, keep working on it. We're gonna keep exploring."

"Aye, sir." Clarke quickly turned and hurried towards his console as the long-range sensors started to beep out a warning. "Captain, I'm picking up a distress beacon from what appears to be an escape-pod."

"Can you identify it?"

"Reading now, sir. The pod is identifying itself as. . ." Clarke stopped as the information scrolled down his screen.

"What is it, Clarke?"

"The pod is identifying itself as life-pod three, of the Earth Fleet science vessel Phoenix."

After rushing back to the Dark Star, the crew set course for the source of the distress beacon. The Phoenix should have been on its way back to the colony by now, Hawkins thought. If this really was an escape-pod from the Phoenix then it must have been launched nearly a week ago.

"Coming up on the source of the signal now, Captain."

"Put it on the view screen."

The holographic view screen flashed up once again covering the main view port. A picture of the small spherical pod, emerged. The small craft had clearly been battered and buckled by its time in open space.

"Kane, bring it into cargo bay two."

"Aye, sir, depressurising bay two and arming grappling tether."

"Pod is coming into firing range of the tether now, Kane."

"Thanks, Blaine, opening outer door. Firing grappling tether now, Captain."

Hawkins watched the pod through the view screen as the claw like grappling tether hit and grasped tightly.

"Lock confirmed, retracting tether."

Hawkins stood up and walked towards the back of the bridge.

"Outer door is locked, Captain. Pod is secure."

"Ok. Kane, you're with me. Clarke, keep a look out."

Kane followed Hawkins into the transport lift. "Cargo bays."

The bridge was now quiet and Clarke took the opportunity to see how much of the databank information the computer had managed to decipher. Bringing the information up on a couple of his station's overhead monitors, he began the complicated task of working out what it all meant. Upon noticing the look of confusion on Clarke's face, Blaine's curiosity got the better of him and he walked over to take a look. "So, what is it, Clarke?"

"I'm not entirely sure. There appears to be information on most if not all of the ship's systems. This reading here shows us the frequencies that the ships shields are capable of working on."

"So, in theory we should be able to modulate the laser cannon to fire straight through this type of shielding."

"Well, it's actually a lot more complicated than that but I suppose it's possible, in theory."

"What's this?" Blaine pointed to a monitor displaying a picture of the small arrowhead vessel and another picture of what looked like a funnel positioned underneath it.

"I'm not sure, a lot of this stuff doesn't make any sense to me. I'm hoping Kane will have more luck when he gets a chance to take a look at it."

"Do you think we'll be able to use this data to fight Gatekeeper?"

"I hope so, Blaine. I hope so."

Meanwhile down in the cargo bays, Hawkins and Kane were attempting to open the battered escape-pod.

"Ok, Captain, after three. One, two, three." With a tug on the pry-bar the pod's hatch opened and Kane ducked as a plasma bolt narrowly missed his head. "Wow, we're the good guys remember, put the pistol down."

"Thank god, we thought we'd been picked up by the arrowhead vessel."

"Redmond?" Hawkins reached a hand inside the hatch and helped the commander out.

Commander Redmond introduced the other occupant as he emerged from the pod. "This is my chief engineer, Jonathan Drake."

Hawkins shook Drake's hand. "This is my only engineer, Adam Kane. My helmsman, Tyler Blaine and my first officer, Eugene Clarke are on the bridge. You can meet them later, but first, tell me what happened."

"We returned to the Jupiter gas refinery as ordered. Then we were attacked as we left orbit by the arrowhead vessel. We didn't stand a chance. It pulled the Phoenix into a large cargo bay beneath the ship. I ordered everyone to abandon ship but..." Redmond paused to compose herself. "I don't think any of the other pods made it."

"What about the mothership?"

"It disappeared off the escape-pod's sensors a few seconds after we launched."

"The ship's data?"

Redmond shook her head. "No data regarding Keymaster was ever stored in the ship's computer. O'Connor was pretty adamant of that. But the star charts, the travel logs...... It all happened so fast."

"Kane, take them down to the mess hall and get some fluids into them. I'll meet you back on the bridge."

"Aye, sir."

Hawkins watched the crew leave the cargo bay before activating his wrist-com. "Hawkins to Clarke, be advised, Gatekeeper has the navigational charts from the Phoenix."

"Then it knows the flight plans of every ship we have and…" Clarke paused.

"Yes, Clarke, and the location of the colony."

CHAPTER 6
Do not go gentle

"This is Captain Bridger of the Liberty, calling Colony command. Command, come in please?"

"This is Bastion, go ahead Liberty."

"We're picking up some sort of spacial anomaly in sector six. It appears to be some kind of gravity well."

"Sector six has no recorded anomalies, Liberty, are you sure it's not a sensor malfunction?"

"Negative, command, I can see the distortion from this thing through the view port. It just appeared on the scanners a few minutes ago. Be advised we are going in for a closer look."

"Acknowledged, Liberty, keep us posted."

"Standby, command, there appears to be something emerging from the anomaly."

"Say again, Liberty."

"There is what appears to be a ship emerging from the anomaly. Jesus it's huge!"

"Can you identify the ship, Liberty?"

"Negative, command, the sensors aren't even picking it up. However. we are reading a massive power build-up and..."

"Say again, Liberty… Liberty acknowledge… Command to Captain Bridger come in?" Commander O'Connor stopped the tape and the meeting room was filled with a deafening silence. He slowly walked towards the front of the meeting room, the sound of his walking cane against the floor the only audible sound. He turned to face the anxious members of Colony command.

"That transmission was sent by Captain Bridger twenty-six hours ago. Further attempts to contact the Liberty have failed. We have also lost contact with the Tomahawk, the Tempest and the Lexington. This hostile ship appears to be systematically destroying vessels along the patrol zone."

"What are you saying, O'Connor? Are we under attack?"

"I don't know." The sound of panic-stricken mumbles filled the air. "Be quiet all of you!" O'Connor shouted. "If it continues on the path it appears to be currently following, the ship will reach this solar system in under eight hours. We don't have time to fall to pieces."

"Then what do you suggest we do?"

O'Connor rested on his cane and contemplated his best course of action. "Captain Reed, start loading the women and children into ships. You will be responsible for their protection."

"Evacuation?"

"Preparation. You will lead the defenceless ships out of danger whilst I lead the rest to intercept the incoming vessel."

"This is madness, we're in no shape to mount an offensive. We'll be slaughtered."

O'Connor shook his head. "All these years of peace on this planet without so much as a passing comet. Do you think it is coincidence that this ship has turned up now, less than two weeks after the Dark Star was due to arrive in the Sol system? In Earth orbit?"

"Are you proposing that this ship was sent by the Gatekeeper system?"

"In all the worlds ever surveyed, we've never come across a life form bigger than a bug. The odds of one turning up here, now, are astronomical." O'Connor paused to catch his breath. "Of course it's Gatekeeper."

"Then the Dark Star failed. My god we need to get out of here."

"And where would you go, there's nowhere left to run."

"What about site B?"

O'Connor shook his head at the question. "The Dark Star crew did us a massive favour finding that planet, I wish all crashes ended so fortuitously. However, we are all aware that the colonist team there is struggling to get anything to grow reliably. The process takes time. Are we to just descend upon them on mass?" O'Connor sighed audibly. "I don't know about you but I'm too old to watch people starve again."

The room fell silent as the ship commanders realised that O'Connor was right. They stared at each other awaiting a new option, any option, but nothing came. One of the captains pushed back his chair and stood up from the table.

"I will fight."

Another captain rose to his feet. "I will fight."

The sound of scraping chairs filled the room as the rest of the table rose.

"What's the plan, Commander?"

"All mining torpedoes in the colony need to be gathered together and their guidance system removed. Share them equally between your ships and leave the warheads at full-yield. You'll have to launch them from a greater distance but low-yield warheads obviously didn't do the Dark Star any good or that thing wouldn't be here. You have less than eight hours, gentlemen, dismissed."

The ship commanders hurried out of the meeting room, leaving O'Connor with his thoughts. The Dark Star, the Phoenix and the Ulysses. Such a waste of life he thought. After all, if they had succeeded in their mission then this ship would not be here and Hawkins would have fought to his last to protect

Bastion. He walked over to one of the meeting room's windows and stared at the reflection of the old man looking back at him. So many years of waiting for word of the mission's outcome, waiting to know if he could return home. Well, he had his answer and if it wasn't for his responsibilities to this colony and his race he would give in right now and surrender to his fate. Then again no, death would not take him so easily. Too much running, too much pain and anguish, too many years of longing for the calm blue skies of home. All that was left now was revenge. That was his mission now. That was his purpose and if it cost him his life, he would make that bastard of a computer pay for what it had done.

"O'Connor to all hands, ready the Lynx for take-off. You have thirty minutes."

"Commander, this is Troy, the ship is in no condition for a take-off, sir."

"Then you have thirty minutes to make her ready."

"Aye, sir."

Panic gripped the colony as word of the impending danger spread. Many people were injured in the mad dash to secure a place on board one of the rickety vessels bound for orbit. Everyone not leaving with the evacuating ships were prepping the rest of the fleet to intercept the approaching vessel.

The hours passed quickly and in what seemed like no time at all, O'Connor was taking his position on the bridge. "Troy, report."

"Status reports have been received from all vessels in the fleet, Commander. The evacuating ships have started to take off and are setting course to rendezvous behind Vega as ordered."

"What about the intercepting ships?"

"Every ship that is still capable of breaking orbit has been prepped and armed to the best of its crew's abilities. They're awaiting your orders, sir."

"What's the status of the Lynx?"

"A couple of the atmospheric thrusters are damaged beyond repair and we have had to close off sections one and two of deck seven due to an un-repairable hull breach. We'll be ok as long as we stay away from atmospheric flight. If she needs to go down to the surface she won't be coming back up."

"Then we'd better make sure we keep the fight away from the orbital anchorages," O'Connor sighed and eased himself into his seat. "How long before the last of Captain Reed's evacuation fleet has cleared the atmosphere?"

"The last three ships are launching as we speak. Commander, what about the colonists that refused to leave? Surely there's some way to change their minds."

"Like what, hold them at gun point? If they want to stay let them, their fates are no more or less certain than ours." O'Connor fastened his safety harness and wedged his cane down the side of his seat. "Open a channel to the interception fleet."

"Channel open, Commander."

"This is O'Connor, the evacuation fleet is almost clear of the planet. All ships launch when ready." The bridge rumbled and shook as the Lynx pulled free of the orbital platform and began to pick up speed. "Troy, status of the fleet?"

"All but three of our ships have managed to disembark successfully, Commander. The first few ships in Captain Reed's fleet should be reaching the star in a couple of minutes."

"Excellent."

"Clearing orbit now, Commander."

"All sections report as stable and ready to fly."

"Set course heading three-nine-two-point-seven-one."

"Aye, sir, course heading confirmed."

O'Connor's interception fleet headed for the inner patrol zones of sector six whilst

Captain Reed's evacuation fleet took up their undetectable position behind the star of Vega. After a few minutes of flight, Troy picked up an anomaly on the ship's long-range sensors. "Commander, there's something big heading this way."

"Identify."

"I'm having trouble getting a sensor lock, sir, but it appears to be well over seven miles in length."

"Put it on the view screen."

The huge menacing image of the arrowhead mothership flashed up onto the bridge's main view screen.

"Now there's something you don't see every day."

"What the hell is it?"

"It looks like some sort of blade, or arrowhead, or something."

"Open a channel. This is First Commander O'Connor of Earth Fleet, identify yourself," O'Connor paused, awaiting an answer. "Shut down your engines and identify yourself or we will be forced to open fire." O'Connor watched the view screen as an orange glow began to engulf the mammoth vessel.

"Picking up a huge power increase from the approaching vessel, sir."

"No shit."

"The vessel has changed direction and is now on a direct collision course with the fleet."

"O'Connor to fleet, load torpedo bays and prepare to fire on my mark."

"The vessel is increasing speed and will reach the front line in fifty-three seconds."

"O'Connor to fleet, all vessels arm one torpedo and fire."

"Arming torpedo bay one, Commander. Target locked, torpedo away."

"Reading multiple torpedo launches, sir. Counting thirty-five warheads on course for the approaching vessel."

O'Connor watched the view screen as the torpedoes sped towards their target.

"The ship is making no attempt to avoid or intercept the torpedoes, impact momentarily, Commander."

The bridge of the Lynx shook as the shock wave from the exploding torpedoes passed through the fleet. O'Connor couldn't believe his eyes as he watched the ship continue unscathed through the blast cloud. "What the hell! O'Connor to fleet, break up, get out of the way."

The fleet began to scatter as the arrowhead vessel began to smash its way through the forward line of ships.

"Helm, get us out of here."

"Aye, sir."

"Several ships have been rammed, sir. The Glory and the Tsunami are requesting assistance and the rest are not responding to my hails."

"'O'Connor to fleet, fire at will."

Chaos broke out as the fleet began to launch everything they had at the attacking vessel. Wave after wave of hastily fired torpedoes indiscriminately destroyed any ship that was unfortunate enough to be in their way. A huge piece of debris from one of the many battered or destroyed ships punched through the hull of the Lynx causing O'Connor to wince as the force of the collision whiplashed his body, sending waves of pain through his neck and back.

"Damage report."

"Propulsion's down, sir, we're adrift. Auto-Repair system is responding but we're losing atmosphere through the breach"

"Close off the pressure doors to that section."

"I've been trying, Commander, but the breach extends through three decks and the power is down on two of them. I can't seal the breach fully until the repair drones fix the power grid in those sections."

"Can the repair drones fix it before the drain on the atmosphere becomes life threatening?"

"Not a chance, sir."

O'Connor was almost thrown from his seat as the drifting Lynx collided with another ship. "Report."

"Main power is off-line, and we've lost the main starboard side engine."

"Can it be repaired?"

"No, we've lost the engine, sir. It's no longer attached to the ship."

"Commander, there appears to be three huge doors opening in the top side of the attacking vessel."

"What? On screen." O'Connor watched as three small ships emerged from within the open hatches of the arrowhead mothership.

"Three ships, sir, all identical in shape to the larger vessel but one-sixteenth the size. I'm detecting power build-ups in all three vessels."

"Shields?"

"I don't think so, sir."

Through the view screen the crew of the Lynx witnessed the destructive power of the ship's energy weapons as they opened fire on the fleet.

"Jesus Christ."

"The mothership is moving away, Commander."

"What's its heading?"

"It's heading straight for Tartarus sir."

"We are out of torpedoes, Commander."

"Sir, one of the smaller fighter ships is heading straight for us.

"Is propulsion back online yet?"

"No, sir."

"Detecting a power build-up, Commander."

"All emergency power to shields." O'Connor turned to the view port to see the approaching vessel strafing through the wreckage of many destroyed ships, its hull covered in dancing arcs of electricity. "Now damn it, now!"

From the bridge of the Intrepid, Captain Hemmingway witnessed the destruction of the Lynx. Not a single life-pod was fired before the ship exploded under the effect of the arrowhead fighter's energy weapon.

"Taylor, how many torpedoes do we have left?"

"Nine, sir."

"Shoot that fucking ship!"

The Intrepid launched two torpedoes at the still-occupied enemy vessel, which took a direct hit and was lost in the scattering debris from the damaged vessels caught in the blast.

"Did we get it?"

"Standby, Captain."

"Enemy fighter ship is no longer registering on my scanners, sir."

"That's for the Lynx, you bastard."

"Captain, we are receiving a distress call from the Raven. They have a ship on their tail and are unable to shake it."

"Helm, bring us about, set course to intercept."

"Aye, sir."

"Intrepid to Raven, hold on, we're on our way."

"Hurry, Intrepid, I don't know how long we can –"

"The Raven has taken a direct hit, Captain."

"What's her status?"

"She's gone, sir."

"God damn it. Taylor, target that ship and fire."

"Targeting, Captain." Taylor shook his head. "It barely registers on the sensors. I..."

"Best guess, damn it!"

"Aye, sir, torpedoes away." The arrowhead fighter rapidly changed direction and the torpedoes sped on into open space. "Torpedoes have missed, Captain, reloading tubes one and two."

"Helm, bring us into a parallel position above the ship. Load all remaining torpedoes and prepare to launch them in a spread dispersal pattern towards that ship."

"Torpedo bays three and four loaded, target locked, Captain."

"Fire."

Once again, the torpedo tracking monitor started to beep and the crew of the Intrepid awaited the outcome of the launch. The beeps got closer together as the torpedoes drew closer and closer to the enemy fighter. A power conduit overloaded as the shock wave from an exploding torpedo slammed into the Intrepid, sending a shower of sparks flying across the bridge.

"Impact, Captain, we have a hit."

"How many?"

"Only one torpedo managed to hit the ship but it did the trick. The arrowhead fighter ship is spinning out of control."

Captain Hemmingway watched the view screen as the enemy vessel collided with a large piece of debris and exploded.

"Captain, the third enemy fighter has changed course and is heading straight for us. We don't have anything left to hit it with, sir."

"Evasive manoeuvres, get us out of here."

The Intrepid sped through the wreckage of the battered fleet in an attempt to evade the approaching vessel.

"The fighter is closing to two thousand metres, Captain. It appears to be charging its energy weapon."

"Helm, this isn't good enough."

"Sorry, Captain, that ship is way more manoeuvrable than ours, I can't shake it."

"Intrepid to fleet, requesting assistance from anyone who still has torpedoes to fire."

"Intrepid this is the Glory, set your heading to seven-zero-one-point-three and prepare to bank hard to port on my order."

"Negative Glory, re-calculate that course heading. That vector would put you on a direct collision course with the enemy fighter."

"You heard me, Hemmingway, course heading seven-zero-one-point-three."

"Carter, don't do this, we'll find another way."

"Our environmental systems are damaged beyond repair and the bridge's rear bulkhead is too badly buckled to open the doors. I won't let my men suffocate, Captain. Now veer to port in ten seconds and allow me the satisfaction of taking this bastard with me."

Hemmingway stood silent for a second staring into nothingness. "Helm, in six seconds bank hard to port and get us out of here as fast as possible."

"Aye, sir, banking in four, three..."

Captain Carter's voice came over the com as the helmsman counted down the seconds to his untimely demise. "Hemmingway, get that mothership for me."

Under the rumbling of a large explosion, Captain Carter's transmission ended and the Intrepid shook as a hail of debris bounced off the hull. Captain Hemmingway slammed his fist into the small control panel on his chair's armrest, causing it to flicker and buzz wildly. "Taylor, what's the status of the fleet?" Hemmingway waited for a response. "Taylor."

"All but seventeen ships have been destroyed, Captain. Twelve of which are heavily damaged."

"Jesus. Are any of the damaged vessels capable of rescuing survivors?"

"Standby, sir." Taylor scanned the fleet's surviving vessels. "The Hastings and the Nova are probably in the best condition, sir."

"Send them a message. Tell them to stay behind and look for survivors."

"Aye, sir."

"This is Captain Hemmingway of the Intrepid. With the exception of the Hastings and the Nova, all ships that are still capable of flight will follow me to intercept the Mothership." Hemmingway gave the order to return to the planet Tartarus. They had to intercept the mothership before it had a chance to wipe out the colonists on the surface. Though battered and almost out of torpedoes the six strong fleet followed without question.

"I'm picking up gravitational distortions from sensors on the orbital anchorages, Captain. I believe the vessel has stopped and is holding position just outside the range of the planet's gravity."

"How long is it going to take us to get there?"

"Two minutes and thirty-three seconds, Captain"

"Damn it."

"Captain, I'm picking up one hell of a power build-up in that ship."

"Helm, we have to go faster."

"Sorry, sir, that's just not possible."

"The mothership's power build-up is discharging, Captain. It's fired on the planet."

"On screen."

Hemmingway and his bridge crew watched the planet as the discharge of the mothership's energy weapon cut through the atmosphere. The cloud layers over the colony parted as a huge shock wave extended around the planet like rippling water in the aftermath of a thrown stone. The ground below took on a glow like the embers of a dying fire that spread outwards in a circular pattern extending for thousands of miles.

"No!" screamed Hemmingway as he rose from his seat.

The mothership ceased fire and began to move away from the planet. The faces of the crew shared a look of horror as they watched the burning planet through the view screen.

"Taylor, how many people were down there?" Hemmingway asked quietly.

"Approximately three hundred families refused to leave the planet, Captain." Taylor stopped to compose himself. "The mothership is on a direct course with the system's star, Captain. It's heading for the second fleet."

"There's no way it can scan the ships on the opposite side of the star. It's not possible," offered one of the crew in a desperate tone.

"That remains to be seen," replied the captain. "But one thing's certain, the second fleet can't detect the mothership approaching," Hemmingway sat looking thoughtful for a moment. If he sent a message ahead to the second fleet the enemy ship might intercept it. Maybe it hadn't detected the fleet, maybe they could lead it away from the colonists. "Intrepid to fleet, as soon as we're in range fire at will."

The six ships closed on the slowly moving vessel and opened fire. Hails of torpedoes were launched at the gigantic craft before they moved off to a safe distance to await the explosions. Taylor steadied himself on his console as the first torpedoes impacted, rocking the Intrepid in the shock wave.

"Report."

"No effect, Captain, we can't penetrate those damn shields."

"Send a message to Captain Reed. Tell him to take the second fleet into deep space."

"Captain, with all due respect, if we send the second fleet a message, we'll give away their position."

"It's heading straight for them, Taylor. If we don't warn them, they're fucked anyway."

"Aye, sir. Sending encrypted message to the Alabama." Taylor frowned and shook his head. "I'm sorry, sir, but I don't believe they are receiving the message. I'm trying to connect with them on the opposing side of the star. Too much interference maybe, but I am not registering a connection."

"The enemy vessel is increasing speed, sir."

"Shit, increase speed to match. Hemmingway to fleet, we have to stop this thing now."

"I'm detecting a power surge from the mothership. It's preparing to fire."

"At what? The fleets on the other side of Vega." Hemmingway stopped as he suddenly realised Gatekeeper's plan. "My god."

"The mothership is firing, Captain."

"On screen."

The view screen flashed to a view of Vega as the arrowhead vessel's energy weapon fired. The blinding light from the star grew dimmer as the beam hit.

"The energy beam is destabilising the star, Captain. The added noise from the star is disrupting long range communications. Boosting signal strength to maintain short range coms."

"What's the status of the second fleet?"

"I'm not reading them, sir. If they've moved at all it's in a parallel line with the star."

"The destabilising effect is reaching critical, Captain. At this rate the star is going to supernova in approximately seven minutes."

"Captain, there's no way we can clear the blast radius of a supernova in that amount of time."

"Hemmingway to fleet, we need to take this ship out now."

"Taurus to Intrepid, it's useless, we can't get through the shields. We need to get out of here, now."

"Go where? If this star explodes it will take Tartarus and most of the system with it. We can't outrun it"

"The Taurus is breaking position, Captain, and is heading into open space."

"Fuck them. Hemmingway to all ships. I want everyone to aim for the centre of the ship's stern and prepare to fire on my mark. Maybe if we hit one spot hard enough, we can buckle the shields."
Hemmingway stood up and walked to the view port at the front of the bridge. He stared at the enemy vessel and frowned. "All ships, fire."

The torpedoes from the surrounding ships shot into view and spiralled towards the mothership as Hemmingway watched through the view port. He shielded his eyes from the flashes as they impacted with the shields and exploded.

"Not a scratch, Captain."

"God damn it, there's got to be some way to stop this thing!" Hemmingway shouted in a desperate rage.

"Captain, the star is gonna lose cohesion in less than four minutes and at this range the.....sir, I'm detecting some sort of anomaly forming about thirty miles from Tartarus at co-ordinates two-zero-three-point-four-two. It appears to be some sort of gravity well."

"Taylor, pull up the information transmitted by the Liberty before she stopped transmitting."

"Way ahead of you, Captain. It's the same type of anomaly."

Hemmingway stood silent with an overwhelmed look on his face.

"There's something emerging from it, Captain."

Hemmingway noticed the puzzled look on the face of his first officer. "How many, Taylor?"

"One, sir. Its transponder identifies it as an Earth Fleet mining vessel," Taylor looked up at the captain, still wearing a look of confusion. "Call sign Dark Star."

"What? On screen," the view screen flashed up a picture of the Dark Star as it exited the anomaly and blasted past the fleet. "What the hell?"

"Captain, we're being hailed. They want to know who is in control of this fleet."

"Patch them through, put it on the viewer." The view screen changed to a picture of the Dark Star's Bridge and Captain Hawkins with an angry look on his face. "Hawkins? What? How?" questioned a baffled Hemmingway.

"I'll explain later. Just get the fleet ready to fire on the arrowhead vessel."

"But we can't penetrate its shield, Hawkins. The torpedoes –"

"Let me worry about that," interrupted Hawkins. "Get these ships ready to fire on my order. Hawkins out." Clarke cut the transmission and the view screen switched back to an external view of the ship. "What the hell is it doing, Clarke?"

"It appears to be trying to de-stabilise the star, sir, and it's working. At this rate the star will supernova in about two minutes."

"Blaine, get us over there."

"Aye, Captain."

"This better work, Clarke."

"I hope so, sir."

"Hawkins to Kane, bring the cannon online."

"Aye, sir, activating laser cannon now."

"Increasing power input into the crystalline reactor to compensate. Reactor power output is now at two hundred percent of normal, Captain."

"Ok, Clarke, raise the platform."

"Platform activated, Captain, standby," Clarke paused as the platform moved into position raising the cannon out into open space above the ship. "Cannon platform is locked in firing position, sir. Activating beam modulation upgrade."

"Are you sure our computer can keep up with that ship if it starts modulating its shields?"

"No."

Hawkins shook his head. "I'm too old for this shit."

"Coming up on the mothership's starboard side."

"Hawkins to Kane, we're ready up here. You and Drake stay down there and make sure this cannon keeps working."

"Aye, sir."

"Clarke, are you sure the shield generator is where you say it is?"

"The deck plan we got from the smaller ship shows a generator in the location I specified, Captain."

"John, are you sure the laser will penetrate the shields?" questioned Commander Redmond nervously from the diagnostic console.

"Yes, Commander, as long as our computer can match that ship's shield frequencies then the laser should pass straight through."

"In theory," added Blaine as he manoeuvred the ship along the arrowhead vessel.

"Ok coming into position in twelve, eleven, ten. . ."

"Rotating ship one hundred-and-eighty-degrees, Captain. Aligning dorsal hull with mothership."

"Seven, six, five..."

"Positioning cannon."

"Three, two, one."

"Fire!" shouted Hawkins, clenching his fists and gritting his teeth in anticipation.

The laser cannon spun to face the mothership as the Dark Star finished rolling onto its back and with a great flash of green light it fired. From the Intrepid, Hemmingway and his crew watched in amazement as the cannon cut through the hull, creating a thin scar as the Dark Star dragged it along the length of the huge vessel.

"Kane to bridge, did the cannon penetrate the hull plating?"

"Like a hot knife through butter, Kane," answered Blaine as he brought the ship round for another pass.

"The shields are still up, Captain. We missed the generator. Suggest we try a stationary shot. It will help with the accuracy."

"You heard the man, Blaine. Take us out to one thousand metres and hold position."

"Aye, sir."

"Commander Redmond, how's the cannon holding up?"

The commander looked over the displays on the diagnostic console. "It's holding up fine, John."

"In position, Clarke. Holding at one thousand metres."

"Repositioning cannon now." Clarke brought up a copy of the arrowhead mothership's deck plan and superimposed it over the image of the vessel that he had on the Cannon's targeting screen. He aimed the cannon at the superimposed picture of the shield generator and fired. The orange tint of the mothership's shields faded and disappeared.

"Clarke, open a channel to the fleet."

"Channel open, sir."

"This is Hawkins, all ships fire at will."

The mothership ceased its assault on the star as its shields fell and began to turn towards the previously inconsequential band of ships. Blaine engaged the Dark Star's ion engines and backed away from the immense vessel, as fresh multitudes of torpedoes were launched in its direction.

"That got its attention."

"The fleet's forward-most torpedoes will reach the arrowhead vessel in approximately ten seconds, Captain."

"Blaine, are we at a safe distance?"

"Yes, Captain."

"Clarke, launch a full spread."

"Aye, sir. Locking target. Tubes one through ten launched. Our torpedoes should impact three or four seconds before the rest of the fleets."

Hawkins found himself sitting forward in his chair, edging towards the view screen in anticipation of the torpedo strike. His heart quickened with the beeping from the tracking system as the torpedoes drew closer and closer to their target.

"Positive impact on at least eighty percent of our torpedoes, Captain," presented Clarke. "I'm reading heavy damage to the vessel's hull plating. The fleet's torpedoes are approaching, hold on," the bridge trembled as the fleet's wave of torpedoes started to hit.

"Blaine, back us off another eight hundred metres."

"Aye, sir."

"Several sections of the mothership's starboard and aft hull plating have breached, Captain. However, relative to the size the ship the damage is negligible. The mothership is still turning." Clarke smiled as his screen offered him new information. "The missing hull plating is allowing for a solid target lock," he explained triumphantly.

"Arm another spread. Target those breaches."

"Aye, sir, tubes one through ten are locked and ready."

"Fire."

"Torpedoes away, sir, impact in three, two, one."

Blaine squinted as he watched the bright light of the blast through the view screen.

"Impact confirmed, Captain. I'm reading heavy damage." Clarke looked at Hawkins. "Should we use Keymaster, sir?"

Hawkins shook his head. "You'll fry the entire fleet. Just continue firing at the breached sections."

"Aye, sir." Clarke's attention was drawn to his console as it began to beep. "Captain, we have incoming."

"A small object has just been launched from the mothership and it's heading straight for us."

"All emergency power to shields, Blaine, get us out of –" the captain's order was cut short as the small object impacted with the ship. "Damage report."

"We have a hull breach on deck four section two, energy seals are holding. Whatever that thing was, it didn't explode on impact."

"Kane to bridge, what the hell just hit us?"

"We don't know, Kane, standby. What are we looking at here, an unexploded warhead or something?"

"I have no idea, Captain, it knocked out the sensors in that section when it hit."

"Hawkins to Kane, can you and Drake get up to deck four and find out what hit us."

"No problem, Captain, we're on our way."

"Kane, take Reeva, just in case."

"Aye, sir. Kane out."

"What's the status of the mothership?"

"The fleet is still bombarding her, Captain, the hull is starting to come apart."

Through the view screen, Hawkins watched the mothership as it started to break up under the unrelenting barrage of torpedoes. "Back us off, Blaine, before the debris gets too thick to manoeuvre through."

"Aye, sir."

The Dark Star ceased fire and began to move away as the mothership's structure finally gave way. The once immense vessel had been reduced to an indecipherable cloud of charred and twisted alloy, smouldering against the backdrop of space.

"Clarke, can you pick up any power sources in the debris field?"

"Other than our ships, Captain, no."

Hawkins sat back in his chair and sighed, "Then it's over."

"Kane to bridge, intruder alert." The sound of weapons fire could be heard through the communication link.

"Report, Kane."

"Deck four is crawling with little metal insects, Captain. Drake's down and I'm not sure how long I can keep these things off us."

"Where are you, Kane?"

"Section three, at the laundry, Captain. These things are eating through the deck plating and the wiring. I suggest you lock down the deck before they spread to any major areas."

"Hold on, Kane, we're on our way. Blaine, you're with me."

Clarke picked up his rifle and walked over to join the rescue.

"No, Clarke, I need you here."

"Aye, sir."

Blaine and Hawkins entered the transport lift and headed down to deck four. Clarke immediately returned to his console and patched into Reeva's optical system. As the picture on the monitor cleared up, he saw dozens of what looked like small metal scorpions, spreading across the walls, floor and ceiling of the corridor where Reeva was standing.

"What the hell?"

No larger than a foot in length but infesting Reeva's entire field of view, the insects were actually eating their way through the bulkheads and wiring of the corridor. The small machines were exploding into pieces under a hail of plasma blasts coming from somewhere behind Reeva, who appeared to be trying to hold the wave of machines back. Blaine appeared from an adjacent corridor in the distance, followed closely by Hawkins. The pair froze for a moment when they first saw the swarm of machines but quickly shook off the initial shock and commenced firing.

"Blaine, try to clear a path to Kane and Drake. I'll keep them off us."

"Bring it on," shouted Blaine as he opened fire on machines.

Kane was standing behind Reeva in the doorway of the laundry room, trying to protect Drake who was sat on the floor clutching his badly burned leg. "Watch out for the jaws on these things, they excrete some kind of acid," warned Kane, as Blaine blasted and kicked the little machines out of the way.

"Hi, did you miss me?" remarked Blaine cockily as he reached the engineers. "Get Drake, I'll cover you."

Kane swung his rifle over his shoulder and helped Drake to his feet, as Blaine and Hawkins continued their assault on the swarm of metal insects. "Ok, Drake, let's go."

With a groan and a look of intense pain on his face Drake leaned on Kane and hobbled down the corridor towards the ship's mid-section transport lift. Hawkins and Blaine stood their ground, as the metallic swarm continued towards them.

"Captain, above you."

Hawkins swung his rifle upwards and fired at one of the machines that had managed to climb undetected to a position above his head. Reeva continued to attack the machines with a vengeance, crushing them between her powerful piston-fed jaws.

"How big was that thing that hit us?" questioned Hawkins in reference to the sheer number of machines still scurrying towards them.

"I don't know, but it really packed them in there," replied Blaine, as they backed off down the corridor still firing.

"Oh yeah, I'm starting to think Gatekeeper doesn't love us anymore."

The pair and their metal protector continued their assault on the machines for over two minutes before their numbers started to thin out, stopping their slow retreat down the corridor as the tables began to turn.

"Clarke to Hawkins, I'm starting to pick up movement in the adjoining section around you and on deck five. There's only a few but we could do with dealing with them before they get into any major systems."

"We're starting to get the situation under control down here, Clarke, we can live without Reeva if you think she can handle it."

"She shouldn't have a problem, sir. I'll direct her from up here."

"Fair enough, Clarke, keep me posted."

"Aye, sir. Clarke out."

Reeva dropped the metallic invader that she was currently chewing and sprinted off down the corridor in response to Clarke's orders. Hawkins and Blaine continued their eradication of the remaining machines.

"Can you see any more, Blaine?"

"A few of them backed off down that corridor."

Hawkins slapped a fresh power cell into his rifle. "Let's go."

The pair carefully advanced down the corridors of deck four destroying any invader that they came across. The walls and equipment in the corridors were covered in smouldering holes from the robotic insects' acidic secretions. The wiring in some sections had been damaged causing the lighting to flicker or fail entirely, making hunting the little creatures very difficult.

"Looks like some sort of drop-pod," remarked Blaine, as he and Hawkins stumbled upon the object that had previously punched its way through the hull.

The lighting in the section was out entirely, but the blue glow from the emergency energy shield that was sealing the breach between the object and the ship's hull provided plenty of light. Should it fail, the entire deck would instantly begin to depressurise, as its atmosphere bled out into space through the holes it was sealing.

"No, the shape's all wrong and look at the reinforcements." Hawkins pointed at the extremely thick and serrated hull of the battered bullet-shaped object. "This thing has been designed to tear through a ship's hull."

"So, it's some sort of breaching-pod."

"Exactly, designed to infiltrate vessels."

"It's in extremely good shape for something that just crashed through two feet of hull plating."

"Hawkins to Clarke, the object that hit us is some kind of breaching-pod."

"Breaching-pod, Captain?" questioned Clarke.

"As far as I can figure it, this thing is designed to smash through a ship's hull allowing for rapid deployment of troops, or in this case weird little metal insects."

"Do you think it's worth getting the repair drones to reverse engineer it before they scrap it?"

"I doubt a human could survive this kind of incursion, but the technology might come in handy."

"Ok, sir, I'll get on it."

"While you're at it, Clarke, can you tell if any of the other ships were hit by one of these things?"

"Standby, Captain." Clarke scanned the other vessels in the fleet, which were busying themselves either searching the debris field or returning to the sight of the original engagement to search for any signs of survivors. "This is the Dark Star calling the Argon, come in please?"

"Argon here, I don't know how the hell you got back here so fast but you saved everyone's bacon. You're all heroes in my eyes."

"Captain, sorry to interrupt but I'm picking up a large hull breach in your lower bow and –"

"Nothing to worry about Dark Star, we must have been hit by a piece of debris or something, the repair drones have already been dispatched."

"Negative, Argon, be advised, we have been hit by some sort of breaching-pod full of small insect-like machines that are capable of eating through the wiring and pretty much everything else. I suggest you send an armed team to check it out immediately."

"Thanks for the heads-up, Dark Star, I'll get right on it, Argon out.

Clarke continued to scan the ships. "Dark Star to Intrepid, come in please?" Clarke awaited a response. "Intrepid this is the Dark Star, please respond?" Again, Clarke gave the Intrepid chance to reply. "Clarke to Hawkins, I'm detecting two ships that could have been infiltrated. The Argon is checking out a large breach in their bow and I've not been able to raise the Intrepid."

"Keep trying, Clarke, we're on our way back to the –" Hawkins stopped talking and his voice was replaced with what sounded like weapons fire, through the communications line.

"Clarke to Hawkins, come in. Captain, what's going on down there?"

"Blaine to bridge, we're under fire, the captain's hit."

"The bugs have weapons?"

"No, there's something else down here."

"I didn't get a good look at it. It was hiding in the shadows." Blaine's voice was drowned out by the sound of his rifle. "Clarke, we're pinned, we need back-up down here."

"Hold on, Blaine."

"Hurry up."

"Clarke to Kane, what's your position?"

"I'm in the medical bay with Drake."

"Blaine and the captain are under fire. I need you to meet me on deck four."

"On my way."

Commander Redmond threw Clarke a plasma rifle, as he rushed into the transport-lift. After a few seconds of travel the lift stopped and the doors opened as Kane rushed in.

"Continue." The lift doors closed and it began to move.

"What the hell do you mean under fire, under fire from what?" asked Kane as he checked the power cell on his rifle.

"I don't know but it was hiding in the dark, waiting to ambush them."

"Jesus."

"Ok, get ready."

Weapons fire could be heard as the transport-lift doors opened.

"It sounds like it's coming from corridor C, you circle around through corridor F and we'll catch this thing in a cross-fire."

Clarke nodded in agreement and the pair set off through the corridors. Clarke quietly followed the sound of weapons fire until he reached the junction of corridor C. He could make out the sound of a single plasma rifle and what must be another weapon. It didn't sound like any weapon that he was familiar with but from the noise level he could tell it was close, maybe even just around the corner. He backed up against the wall as a whispered voice spoke his name over his wrist communicator.

"Clarke, are you in position?"

"Mother-fucker, when I get my hands on you, I'm gonna fuck you up." Blaine's quaintly-voiced objections to the situation could be heard from Clarke's position at the far end of the corridor.

"Yes, Kane. Are you ready?"

"I'm in position, but I can't quite make out where it is."

"I think it's standing behind one of the roof struts at my end of the corridor. It sounds really close."

"Ok, let's do it."

Clarke leaned partially around the corner in the hope of using the bulkhead as a shield. He was surprised at what he saw as he trained-in his rifle. Not another blade covered insanity of a machine or a small-insect like abomination, but what looked like the shadowed figure of a man. Who was this shooting at his crew, why would anyone help Gatekeeper destroy his own race?

"Hey, asshole, drop the weapon." Clarke's face dropped as the dark figure turned, the glow of its green eyes, fixing on him. It was a machine! A machine built in the image of a man. The light shined off its cold metal body as it raised its arm and fired. Clarke dove back behind the safety of the adjacent corridor's corner, narrowly escaping the attack. "Clarke to Kane, it's some kind of android or something. It has an energy beam weapon attached to its left arm."

"A what?"

"An android. It's a machine but it's shaped like a man." Clarke leaned back round the corner of the adjacent corridor, still low to the ground where he had landed. Hastily he pointed his rifle and fired. The plasma bolt hit the roof strut and the android returned fire. "Shit that was close," Clarke whispered quietly to himself after he ducked quickly behind the corridor's corner wall.

Kane and Blaine took the opportunity to open fire whilst the machine was distracted and blasted wildly in its direction. Blaine and Hawkins were trapped in the doorway of a small maintenance room and were too far away from any adjoining corridors to attempt retreat.

"How's the Captain?"

"He's passed out, his arm is really messed up." Blaine ducked back into the doorway as the android opened fire. "This is starting to piss me off. Clarke, get its attention."

"That's easy for you to say." Clarke took a couple of deep breaths and stepped out into the corridor. "Hey, ugly!" he shouted as he raised his rifle. The android reacted quickly and raised its free arm at Clarke, which unknown to him was also armed with an energy weapon. At the same time, Blaine boldly stepped out into the corridor and took aim.

"Fire."

A dazzling light forced Hawkins to shield his eyes as he awoke. He could just make out the blurred shape of someone over him and for a second, in his disorientation, he found himself wondering if the wound he had sustained could have been fatal. After having a few seconds to come round and adjust to the light, he suddenly became aware of three things. He was laid down, he was alive, and the blurred figure standing over him was Blaine and not death himself. This amused him and he began to laugh.

"What's so funny?"

"For a second there, Blaine, I thought you were the Grim Reaper, here to save me from my life."

"Nah, I've seen pictures of the Grim Reaper and he isn't that ugly," Clarke mocked from the back of the room. "How are you, sir?"

"Confused. Our medical bay isn't this clean, where the hell am I?"

A young woman stopped Hawkins as he tried to sit up. "Try to stay still for a few minutes, Captain. You're onboard the medical ship Apollo."

"The Apollo. There weren't any medical ships left when we got back here. Will someone please explain what's happening?"

"Well, sir, it's like this. When Commander O'Connor heard that Gatekeeper was heading this way, he split the fleet into two groups. The first fleet, consisting of all the ships that could be armed, were sent to intercept the mothership. All other ships were loaded up with colonists and sent to hide behind the star in case the first fleet failed."

"Smart idea, go on."

"To cut a long story short, Captain, all but eight ships in the first fleet were destroyed in a matter of minutes. Two of those where heavily damaged and Captain Hemmingway of the Intrepid ordered them to stay behind and search for survivors."

"The mothership wasn't manoeuvrable enough to destroy an entire fleet of ships. Why the hell didn't they retreat?"

"Well apparently the mothership didn't attack the fleet at all. It released three small fighter ships as it broke through the lines. From the descriptions I've heard they sound like the same kind of ship we took out in Earth's orbit."

Hawkins slowly sat up and checked himself for holes. "O'Connor?"

Clarke shook his head. "The Lynx was destroyed with all hands still aboard, Captain. The crews of the Argon and the Intrepid have also been lost to the same kind of breaching-pod attack that we were subjected to."

"What's the status of the infestation on those ships?"

"The Intrepid has been cleansed but the invading machines on the Argon managed to tap into the propulsion systems before an armed team could get onboard. It was destroyed by the fleet under my request, sir."

Hawkins nodded. "May they all rest in peace." Hawkins sat looking thoughtful for a moment. "How many ships do we have left?"

"The fleet presently consists of twenty-one vessels, all jammed full of pissed off and hungry people."

Hawkins' attention turned to his bandaged arm. "What's the deal with this?"

The nurse pulled a smiley face that Hawkins immediately recognised as a well-practiced response to accompany bad news. "Your forearm and hand were very badly burned, Captain," the nurse explained. "We've done what we can with what we have available, but it may require more surgery in the immediate future I'm afraid. The meds we gave you will help with the pain while it begins to heal. Then we can see how the grafts respond."

Hawkins paused for a moment looking at his bandaged limb. "We don't have time to stand here talking," Clarke helped Hawkins to his feet.

"Captain, I really must insist you stay in bed. You are in no condition to leave at the moment," the nurse ordered in a stern voice.

"Thank you for your assistance, it is much appreciated. But there are things to do that can't wait." Hawkins stumbled as he took a step. "How long have I been laid here? My legs feel like I haven't stood up in months."

"You've been unconscious for over forty-eight hours, sir. Most of the repairs to the fleet are well under way."

"Two days. Damn, no wonder I'm so hungry." Hawkins thanked the nurse, dressed himself and walked towards the door. As he reached the archway that led to one of the ship's corridors he stopped and turned back to the crew. "Where is my ship?"

"Those little insect things did a lot of damage to the wiring on decks four and five. She's docked at the port airlock, Kane's over there supervising the repairs."

Hawkins turned back to the nurse who was now stood cleaning a small tray of medical equipment. "How do I get to the mess hall?"

"I'm sorry, Captain, we're out of food supplies."

Hawkins sighed and looked at Clarke. "Any idea how long it will be before we're ready to return to Tartarus?"

"Tartarus is no longer an option, Captain."

Hawkins looked puzzled.

"The mothership attacked the colony from orbit, destroying several thousand square miles of the planet's surface. The resulting shock wave has totally devastated the atmosphere, sir, the planet is no longer inhabitable."

The stress levels in Hawkins' face were clearly evident. "Hawkins to Kane, what's the status on the repairs?"

"Good to hear from you, sir. The wiring on deck four is shot to shit but the hull's back in one piece. I'm just in the middle of repairing the sensor grid."

"How long before we can get under way?"

"She's ready to fly now, sir. There's nothing down here that I can't fix on the move."

"Very good, Kane, Hawkins out." Hawkins and the crew left the medical bay and headed towards the port airlock. "Where's Commander Redmond and the engineer?"

"Commander Redmond has been given command of the Intrepid. Her and Drake have been onboard for about a day."

"The Intrepid is a good ship." Hawkins pressed the inner door activation button as they reached the port airlock. "Not very big but it's supposed to be one of the fastest in the fleet." The airlock door hissed shut behind them as they walked in.

The voice of the ship's computer sounded a warning as the crew waited for the button on the outer door of the airlock to change from red to green. "Running diagnostic check on interior pressure door seals, please standby."

"Our ship isn't much older than this one, is it?" questioned Blaine.

"No, they started building this class of medical ship about three years after the Dark Star was launched."

"So why doesn't our computer talk?"

"It did, I disconnected its vocal processors when I was promoted to captain. Damn thing used to get on my nerves."

Blaine pressed the button on the outer door as it turned green and it hissed open. They walked through the airtight passageway of the Dark Star's starboard docking gantry. After a few seconds of waiting in the Dark Stars airlock, the inner pressure door opened and they made their way to the bridge.

"Clarke, give me a systems check?" asked Hawkins as the crew sat down at their stations.

"Running diagnostic now, Captain, standby."

"Blaine, prep us for flight."

"Aye, sir. Initiating engine warm up sequence."

"With the exception of deck four's wiring and sensor grid, systems are working within flight tolerances, Captain."

"Very well, open me a channel to the Apollo." The view screen flashed up a picture of the Apollo's bridge. "How are you, Aiden?"

"Ah, John, I trust you're feeling better?"

"I've been worse. We're ready to get under way over here. I just wanted to thank you for the hospitality."

"No problem, my friend. Anything for the saviours of mankind."

Hawkins shook his head and grinned. "We did nothing more than the rest of the fleet."

"Ah, the famous Hawkins modesty. You and your crew saved all our necks and you know it. You got my vote for leader on your timing alone, that was one hell of an entrance."

"Leader? What are you talking about?"

"The fleet captains had a conference whilst you were healing and unanimously voted for you to replace O'Connor. Has no one told you?"

Hawkins turned and looked at Clarke with a frown.

"Oh yeah, I knew I'd forgotten something," Clarke responded uneasily.

Hawkins returned his gaze to the view screen. "Give me a fucking break, Aiden. I run a mining boat."

"From what I've seen, you're running our best gunship. With one arm tied no less." Captain Aiden grinned.

Hawkins took a look at his bandaged arm and grinned.

"Let me ask you this, John. With O'Connor gone, if not you, who else?"

Hawkins looked at Clarke, who smiled and saluted. Blaine followed suit, even if it was just for his own amusement.

"Do I get a vote?" Hawkins asked.

"Everyone in the fleet has been notified," Captain Aiden continued, "Congratulations."

Hawkins stood silently for a moment still wearing a troubled frown. "Clarke, detach the docking clamps and retract the gantry."

"Aye, sir."

The bridge shook slightly as the two ships parted.

"Well, Aiden, it would appear I have an exodus to co-ordinate."

Captain Aiden smiled. "Good luck, John, you're going to need it." Aiden saluted wearing a grin.

"Thanks. I think. Hawkins out." The view screen deactivated allowing Hawkins a view of space through the main viewport. "Blaine, take us to a position just outside the fleet's main cluster."

"Aye, sir." Blaine carefully navigated the Dark Star through the stationary fleet and brought her to a full stop outside the cluster.

"Clarke, I need a channel opening to every ship here."

Clarke played around for a few seconds on his keyboard before activating the view screen. "All ships have been hailed, Captain, and are awaiting your message."

The view screen brought up a slightly disorientating split-screen of all the bridges of every ship left in the fleet. Hawkins stood up and calmly took a moment to scan the faces on the screen. He nodded at the image of Commander Redmond, who smiled back at him.

"Thank you all for responding so quickly. I have called this little meeting to assess the fleet's status. I need to know if anyone is incapable of short-range flight." Hawkins waited for a response.

"If you're planning on taking us back to Tartarus, you should remember that it is no longer habitable."

Hawkins fixed his view on the face of a rather scrawny looking young man on the screen. "Who are you, boy?"

"I am First Officer of the Aurora. My captain was injured in the battle and I have assumed command of this ship until his return," answered the first officer in an extremely snide and pompous tone.

"Tell me, what is the full classification of my ship?"

The first officer looked suddenly puzzled. "Err, your ship is an Earth Fleet mining vessel. Classification Mark five Dreadnought, call sign Dark Star."

"Very good. I want you to remember that, because if you ever use that tone with me again, you're gonna need to let the nurses know where to send my boot back to, after they remove it from your ass, do I make myself clear?"

The officer nodded nervously. "Yes, yes, Captain. Sorry, sir."

"As I was saying," Hawkins continued, "Does anyone have a problem with a relatively short-range flight?" Hawkins waited for a response. "I'll take that as a no." Hawkins took a deep cleansing breath. "Gatekeeper followed its programming to the letter. It even went as far as to remove itself from Earth after its task was completed. That mothership was Gatekeeper's final solution to returning the earth to its pristine former glory. Gatekeeper is gone." Hawkins paused to let his words sink in. "We have somewhere to go. I want all ships to prepare to return to Earth space." A silence descended.

"With all due respect, Hawkins, I'd hardly call returning to the Sol system a relatively short flight," replied one of the captains.

"Yes, and most of our ships are packed full with people. We don't have anywhere near enough stasis pods for everyone," stressed another captain with a panicked look on his face.

Hawkins halted the conversation by holding up his hand. "Clarke."

Clarke nodded and returned to his keyboard

"Gentlemen, and lady."

Redmond smiled.

"If you calm down for a second, my first officer will put your minds at rest."

The heads on the view screen all turned to look at Clarke who looked briefly before smirking and returning his attention to his console. "With all due respect, Captains', you need to keep up with up times." Clarke hit the enter key and smiled.

The Dark Star's bridge crew watched the view screen, as officers aboard the fleets' other ships scurried around frantically in response to new warnings coming from their sensor displays. Entire bridge crews could be seen looking out of view ports to catch a glimpse of the enormous anomaly that was forming just off the Dark Star's bow. Like a miniature blackhole the anomaly concaved into itself. Sucking in the space around it like whirlpools swallow water. A few of the captains returned their gaze to Hawkins, most of them with gaping mouths and all of them wearing questioning looks. Clarke licked his lips and leant over his console towards the view screen. A huge smile spread across his face. "Stasis pods are a thing of the past."

CHAPTER 7

Sol

Within a matter of hours, the last of the fleet's ships had touched down on the welcoming soils of Earth. After weeks of extensive and time-consuming repairs had been made to the battered and rickety vessels, Hawkins returned the ore miners to space to continue the task for which they were built. Only this time they were collecting ore for a greater purpose, not to increase the already overflowing purses of greedy corporations, not for minerals and precious metals to make trinkets and expensive jewellery for the fat upper-classes, but to collect any and all materials necessary to create a city for the new colony, the new brotherhood of man. Before one flower had been picked, before more than a few breaths of air were taken, Hawkins called a meeting of the whole colony to dictate the rules of the second age of man.

"Well, we made it, we're home."

A great cheer rose from the crowd that stood at the base of the Dark Star's main access ramp, in anticipation of their leader's speech from above.

"Look around you. Out of the misery of our exile this planet has flourished, and that shows me what must be done. We must live in harmony with this place, we must find a natural equilibrium that benefits the Earth as much as it benefits us. With our crystalline reactor and recycling technologies in place from the very start, there is no reason why this planet should have to suffer the damage that we subjected it to in our past.

"Never forget that the price for this paradise on which you stand was the slaughter of over ninety-nine percent of our race. Remember this when you breathe the air, when you walk through the hills and drink from the pure water of the streams. Remember the mistakes of the past and remember that what once was, can never be again.

"Your captains and I didn't choose to land in Peru at random. This is to be the site of the greatest and only stronghold of man. Once we have completed construction of our city, the Earth will be yours to roam but only here will there be evidence of human settlement on this world.

"But what if we wish to settle on our own, away from the colony? One building won't make a difference. No, one building won't make a difference and in times to come neither will ten buildings or a hundred. Have you realised that this day, this moment, is the first and only time that the entire human race has stood together as a family instead of standing apart as factions, as continents? We can't afford to walk the same path as our ancestors. It only leads to destruction."

The group broke into applause as Hawkins stopped talking.

The city was designed using the latest of technologies taken from Gatekeeper's fighter-ship databank. New alloys previously unimagined and state-of-the-art equipment to go with it. Over the next few weeks all ships that had been deemed unnecessary since the landing on Earth were stripped of their equipment and materials. The propulsion and navigation systems on the Jupiter gas refinery were painstakingly repaired and the entire station and all of its sister stations were brought back to Earth to be dismantled. Their repair systems and hundreds of repair drones were upgraded and used in the city's construction.

Carved deeply into the mountainside, the great saucer-like domes of the city began to take shape. Sitting against the rock faces, their forms resembled the mushroom or fungal clusters that grow on the trunks of large trees. Form following nature, another concept borrowed from Gatekeeper's logic. From their lofty positions over the lands below the domes of the city, when finished, would offer a truly remarkable view over miles of open plains and rainforest. The abundance and diversity of the plant and animal life in this region would easily support a colony of this size. As a community they could easily live and grow here without endangering the complex and precious equilibrium of the surrounding biome. Eventually the city's machine shops were completed and brought online and from them sprung a whole new range of vehicles and equipment such as the world had never seen. Compared to the complexities of maintaining a starship, the construction of the dozens of small open-top vehicles was relatively easy. The first of the sturdy six-wheeled vehicles were built with battle in mind, and were therefore equipped with the first of the prototype pulse cannons. These original vehicles were directly responsible for removing traces of the leftover Reeva units and drop-pods from the former British Isles. After being airlifted in, the small group spent three weeks in the Scottish Highlands, tracking down and eradicating the mechanical abominations before returning to the drop-off site for extraction.

"Morning, Captain," greeted Kane as he entered the city's partially completed operations chamber.

"Kane, I haven't seen you for days man, where the hell have you been?" returned Hawkins happily as he slapped Kane on the back.

"I've been trying to get the power grid in the third dome working. I'm starting to think that re-using the reactors from the dismantled ships was a bad idea."

"How so?"

"Some of these things look like they've been maintained by chimps, Captain. Frankly, I'm amazed that some of them are still working."

Hawkins shook his head.

"Still, we're making progress," Kane offered. "Anyway, Captain, how are you doing?" Kane glanced around the cluttered half-built room and out over the rainforest through one of the gaping holes in the wall.

Hawkins removed himself from the path of one of the room's four repair drones and shook his head. "I'm bored out of my fucking mind. If I don't find something to do soon, I'm gonna have to shoot myself." Hawkins continued to whine as he strolled across the room and kicked another repair drone that was in the way of his chair. The drone hovered off to the other side of the room and continued the construction work. "All I've done since we got here is look over progress reports." Hawkins sat down at his desk facing Kane. "What brings you here anyway?"

Kane held up three small progress reports and shrugged. Hawkins lit a cigarette and sat back in his chair. "You see what I mean. Nothing but progress reports."

"Brent to Kane, come in please."

"Sorry, sir, hold on a second. What is it, Brent?"

"We've solved the problem with the city's communications array. We're ready to bring it online."

"Ok, Brent, fire it up whenever you're ready."

"No problem, Kane, it'll take a few minutes to warm up. I'll keep you posted."

"Thanks, Brent, Kane out." Kane turned back to Hawkins. "You think you're having a hard time. Since you put me charge of the construction, all I've done is wipe everyone's asses for them. These guys can't take a piss without asking me my opinion."

Hawkins chuckled. "What about the Dark Star, Kane, are the repairs finished yet?"

"I haven't had time to patch into the repair system today, Captain. Still, last time I checked the drones had finished replacing the long-range communications array, that we removed to install the cannon," Kane huffed. "I'm so tired of hearing 'communications array' this week." He shook his head. "Anyway, they should have started the weapon upgrades by now."

"Weapons upgrades?" questioned Hawkins.

A look of anxiety suddenly crossed Kane's face. "The new weaponry upgrades. I mentioned it in one of last weeks' reports didn't I, Captain?"

Hawkins shook his head.

"Oh, damn. Well, the repair drones were already building the new long-range communications system and Blaine and I thought it would be a shame to just scrap the laser cannon. So, we sort of found a way to keep it."

"Go on."

"We had it re-installed a little closer to the bow." Kane licked his lips nervously and took a deep breath. "Well, actually, Captain, we had the design copied and installed a few."

An ambivalent look spread across the captain's face.

"All in the interest of being prepared, sir," Kane continued as if rambling would somehow soften the news.

"Really?" replied Hawkins questionably. "And how many cannons does a Dreadnought require before it is sufficiently prepared?"

"Err, well, four, sir."

"Four!" shouted Hawkins.

"Yes, sir, but in our defence, with the new anomaly jump-drive at our disposal we're gonna be heading deeper into space than ever before. There's no telling what we could run into."

Hawkins shook his head and sighed, "Cut the shit, Kane."

"Aye, sir."

"How the hell did you manage to get the materials to build three new cannons without anyone noticing?"

"One of the perks of being the city's chief engineer. All the stock lists have to go through me."

"Where did you get the man power?"

"I sort of, borrowed a few repair drones to do the bulk of the work."

"Damn it, Kane, those drones are supposed to be working on this complex."

"Yes, I know, sir, but I made sure all the teams still met their weekly quotas."

Hawkins frowned. "Well, I suppose there's no harm done."

"Thanks, Captain. If it helps my case, I'm pretty sure we can use these cannons to mine as well as fight."

"Don't thank me, Kane, the only reason you're getting away with it is because I happen to agree with you."

Kane looked surprised. "Sir?"

"Let's just say I like the idea of having a little muscle in case we need it."

"My thoughts exactly, sir."

"Where are the new cannons?"

"Here, I'll show you. I should be able to patch into the Dark Star's repair system from here." Kane leant over the desk and started punching keys on the keyboard. Hawkins watched as a blueprint of his ship loaded up on the screen.

"We installed one on the belly of the ship." Kane pointed to the spot on the screen. "Then we installed the other two on the port and starboard flanks. And the original cannon we moved to here, still on the dorsal hull."

Hawkins raised an eyebrow and nodded approvingly.

"If I ever manage to get the targeting scanners aligned, we should be able to hit four targets at once. Blaine named it the Laser Sword System."

"Colourful. What's this in the spare mid-section crew quarters?" Hawkins made reference to a new blue marker on the blueprints.

"Well technically, sir, the spare crew quarters are now known as the Laser Sword Reactor room. I had to install a separate reactor to be able to run four cannons at once; they simply draw too much power. Otherwise, we'd have been standing in the dark every time we opened fire."

"A separate reactor? When the mob turns up asking why we're using all the colonies resources on the Star, I'm sending them your way."

"Brent to Kane, the long-range coms should be online in a few seconds."

"Thanks, Brent. How are the sensor arrays coming along?"

"Well, we've managed to integrate them into the computer system but we're having trouble with this Gatekeeper technology. If I'm honest it doesn't make a whole lot of sense."

"Tell me about it, Brent. Keep at it. Co-ordinating landing times for the ore miners will be a lot easier once we can track them at a distance."

"Ok, Kane, I'll get on it as soon as possible. Brent out."

Hawkins covered his ears as a high-pitch squeal suddenly filled the room.

"It's just the city's communications array coming online, Captain. They haven't calibrated the sensors properly," Kane accessed the new arrays system through the computer console on the captain's desk. After a few seconds of typing, the ear-splitting sound cleared up into a voice.

"Alabama to anyone who's listening. Is anyone there?"

Hawkins pushed the answer button on his keyboard.

"There you go," Kane offered triumphantly.

"This is Hawkins, go ahead, Alabama."

"Finally, I was starting to think something was wrong down there."

"Yeah, the new communications system still has a few bugs in it. It's a pain in the ass but it should be working fine from now on."

"Fair enough, sir. We're gonna be hitting the atmosphere in about thirty minutes, I'm gonna need a landing plan."

"The landing preparations are being co-ordinated from the Rochdale until we get the operations chamber up and running. You need to contact Captain Newton."

"Thanks, sir, oh and it's nice to see those engineers finally figured out how to reproduce that anomaly drive of yours. It will save me weeks of travel time and –"

"Wait a minute," interrupted Kane. "I don't know who you're getting your information from, but the original anomaly drive we took from the fighter we destroyed is still the only one we have."

"Whom am I speaking to?"

"This is Kane, the fleet's head engineer."

"Well, I'm sorry, Kane, but it looks like you're overdue for a progress report or two. There are gravity wells forming all over the place up here."

"What? Are you sure?"

"Yeah. In fact, I'm picking up a ship emerging from one off my port bow."

"Alabama can you identify it?...Alabama!... Alabama!…"

CHAPTER 8
Dogs of War

The year is 2336 and the Earth is in peril. For the last hundred year's this small orb has been subjected to a constant and relentless attack by an apathetic and relatively unstoppable force, utilising many hundreds of different methods of attack to poison the planet. Rendering the ecosystem almost incapable of supporting life.

By the early twenty-fourth century, the planet had all but lost the war. Animals of all descriptions were forced to take shelter on a daily basis from the very thing that once brought life. The dark black clouds that once heralded the life bringing and replenishing rain, now warned of a burning bombardment of acid from the skies. The great oceans of the planet that once teemed with life existed now as little more than a lifeless cocktail of chemicals that supplied the deadly rains with their power. Plant and animal life grew less abundant by the day and the only hope for salvation lay in the hands of the force responsible for the cataclysm… man.

In January of 2336 the leaders of the world held a summit to find a solution to the decay. After a long and heated discussion, they came to the conclusion that the technologies required to reverse or neutralise all the pollution and poisons simply did not exist. Furthermore, the creation and development of such technologies would take years and the Earth simply did not have that long left before the ecosystem collapsed entirely. The only viable solution came in the form of two unwelcome guests that suddenly burst through the huge doors of the hall and collapsed under the weight of several security officers.

"What the hell is this, how did those men get in here?"

"I'm sorry Mr President," apologised one of the security staff as the two men were dragged towards the door.

"Wait, we can help!" shouted one of the intruders before being quickly muffled.

"Wait." The security staff halted as the Japanese delegate began to speak, "Are they unarmed?"

"Yes, sir.

"Then let them speak."

The security staff released the two men who proceeded to brush themselves off as they walked back into the room.

"Who are you?"

"Their names are Jake Evans and Thomas Bradley," announced one of the British delegates. "They've been pestering me for weeks regarding funding for a new computer they've designed."

"Is that why you're here?"

"Yes, Mr President."

"And how can your computer design solve this problem?"

"It's not a computer system, Mr President, it's a design for an artificial intelligence." The sound of chattering filled the room.

"Ladies and gentlemen, please." The noise dimmed. "Go on."

"As you're all aware, the ecological degradation of the planet is developing faster than the technologies that are required to counteract it. What I'm basically saying is that we, the human race, cannot develop our technologies at a sufficient rate to be able to reverse the decay in time."

"But your computer can?"

"Yes, sir."

"How is that possible?" questioned the Japanese delegate.

"It's possible because this system is more than just a computer, it is a sentient, free-thinking entity."

"Are you saying it would be alive? That's preposterous."

"It is not preposterous, it is fact." Evans stopped to compose himself. "Our system may not have a beating heart or require oxygen to sustain its muscles, but its mental capacity will be like nothing the world has ever seen. Capable of remembering everything it has ever learned with perfect clarity and total recall. With the ability to process that information at the speed of a super-computer."

"And you're sure you can build this thing?"

"I have the blueprints right here." Bradley held up a small memory core.

"And you're sure this thing will be capable or understanding any ideas we give it?"

"Why even bother?"

"Excuse me?"

"No offence ladies and gentlemen, but this system will be perfectly capable of finding its own solution to the problem. Which coming from a memory that contains all the knowledge in the world, will probably be more effective than anything your scientists can give it to work on."

Once again, the room filled with the droning sound of a hundred different conversations. After a few seconds, the president of the United States of America stood up and leaned over to his microphone. "And what would you need to make it work, son?"

3:01AM 15/12/2336

Evans knocked over the lamp on his bedside table as he fumbled around in the darkness for his communicator. "Hello."

"Jake, it's me."

"Thomas man, it's three in the morning."

"I've done it, Jake."

"I've solved the processing problem. It's finished."

"My god. Call the partners, I'll be there in a couple of hours."

"What is it, Jake?" questioned a voice from the bed as Evans hurriedly got dressed.

"Bradley cracked the processing problem on the system. I have to go down to the lab to meet the partners.

Evans' wife sighed and sat up. "I suppose this means the bed's mine for a few days."

Evans sat down on the bed beside her. "If I'm not back in a week you have my permission to re-marry." He smiled. Evans kissed his wife goodbye and quickly exited the apartment. After taking one of the complex's many lifts down to the transport storage area he climbed into his vehicle and headed out of the building.

The complex's main door slowly opened and Evans drove out into the darkness of the city. He hovered down the vast network of roads that weaved through the looming forest of dull metal and concrete that stretched out before him. Enormous cylindrical skyscrapers and towering apartment complexes that rose high into the sky, covering the whole area as far as the eye could see in an attempt to house the ever-growing population.

5:59AM 15/12/2336

"Ah, here he is now," introduced Bradley as Jake entered the room.

"Mr Evans, nice of you to join us," remarked one of the many people who had gathered in the room.

"Sorry to keep you all waiting, the hyper-link was packed solid, I couldn't get above one-fifty all the way here. If you'll follow me."

Bradley and Evans led the group into a large lift at the far end of the room. Upon entering they each placed their left hand on a small pad on the wall. A sweeping beam of light moved back and forth from their palms to their fingertips several times and as it stopped the lift doors closed and it began to move.

"Now I see where my money's been going," remarked a member of the group as he watched the numbers on the floor indicator ticking over. "How deep are we going, Evans?"

"The system chamber is exactly one mile down."

"One mile?" replied another member of the party. "Judging from that counter we should have stopped, shouldn't we?"

"The chamber is exactly one-mile underground, Miss Walker, but this lift shaft is over two miles long. You see we built the chamber as far under the mountain as possible for extra security."

"Oh, I see."

"Don't you think you're being a little paranoid, Evans?"

"You said to spare no expense on this system's security. This complex can withstand a nuclear strike, and I assure you that no sensor system in the world can penetrate this much rock. Your system couldn't be any safer if God himself was protecting it."

The lift stopped and the doors opened to reveal a long, well-lit corridor. The group followed Evans and Bradley along it until they reached an extremely large door.

"Cry havoc and let slip the dogs of war."

"Voice-print identification verified," indicated a light feminine voice from nowhere as the great doors opened. "Welcome, Bradley."

"Is that it?"

"No, Miss Walker, that's just a standard series seven security system. What you're interested in is through that door."

The group was startled as they walked towards the door, by two large chain cannons that suddenly dropped out from the ceiling in front of them. Positioned at either side of the unopened door, the cannons sprung to life and trained on the group.

"Warning, retinal scans required to access this section. You have thirty seconds to comply."

Evans and Bradley quickly walked over to two small panels on the wall at either side of the door. They both looked into a small round opening that pulsed with a green light. After a few seconds the pulsing stopped and as the immense solenoid locks retracted, the doors began to open.

"Ladies and gentlemen, let me introduce you to the first and only true artificial intelligence ever created. The Gatekeeper."

The group looked in awe around the small room as they entered. In the centre of the room stood a large black cube of at least ten feet in height. Built into the walls of the chamber were dozens of large computer monitors and keyboards, presently powered down and inactive. Below the raised metal grid floor, hundreds of wires and cables stretched out from the cube and disappeared into the walls.

"So that's it?"

"Don't let the looks fool you. The cube is only to shield the system from electromagnetic pulses. Inside that shell is the most complex computer processing system that's ever graced the planet. It is capable of accessing any and all satellite and terrestrial information systems with up-link capabilities.

"This complex has been fitted with fifteen state-of-the-art automated machine shops and with the number of raw materials stored down here, the system should be able to create just about anything it can dream up to aid it in its task." Whilst Evans gave the group a rundown of the system's capabilities, Bradley attached the final component to the system.

"That's all very impressive, Evans, but is this thing actually capable of reversing the damage to the ecosystem?"

"Jake, it's ready."

Evans nodded at Bradley.

"Well, General, if you'll be good enough to wait a few moments. You can ask it yourself." Evans turned to Bradley. "Ok, Thomas, fire it up."

With the flick of a master circuit-breaker positioned in a deep crevice in the wall, the dozens of monitors and lights exploded into action.

"Thomas, you did it man, it's working," congratulated Evans as Bradley started to laugh.

"We did it, Jake."

The pair excitedly shook hands, taking their eyes off the flickering screens for barely a moment.

"What's it doing?"

"It's learning, Miss Walker."

"What do you mean it's learning?"

"Well, General, at this point it only has the mental capacity of a new born child. You see, it would have taken months to programme it with all the information it requires to function as a sentient being. But with its internet and other information links, it should be able to learn everything there is to know in a matter of minutes."

"What exactly do you mean, everything there is to know?"

"Imagine this thing as a life form with the processing power of a super-computer. It only has to be told something once and it will remember it indefinitely with perfect clarity. Our minds are childlike in comparison to this system."

Suddenly the racing monitor screens shut down and the sound from the busy processors stopped. Everyone in the room stood silent and looked at Evans and Bradley.

"Jake, look." Bradley drew Evans' attention to the monitors covering the walls. On every single screen, one word had appeared in small green writing.

"STATUS."

"What does it mean?" questioned one of the group members in a whisper.

Evans gestured for the group to be quiet with a raised hand. He walked over to one of the keyboards on the wall and began to type. "RE-PHRASE THE QUESTION."

Immediately a new line of text scrolled across the screen. "REQUIRE INPUT. WHAT IS PURPOSE?"

"It's not making any sense."

"It's making perfect sense. Gatekeeper has essentially just been born. It wants to know why it is here, what its purpose is." Evans turned to Bradley. "Are we ready to give it its orders?"

"Everything seems to be working just fine," answered Bradley who was looking over the complex's systems on one of the consoles. "It's as ready as it will ever be."

"Ok, General, time to answer your question." Evans began to type. "PRIMARY OBJECTIVES: CLEANSE THE EARTH BY ERADICATING ALL POLLUTIONS AND INFECTIONS. PROTECT THE EARTH FROM ALL POSSIBLE THREATS."

Gatekeeper immediately responded, "PRIMARY OBJECTIVES INPUTTED @ 6:27AM 15/12/2336. MISSION PARAMETERS ARE ACCEPTABLE."

Once again, the monitors in the room began to scroll through information faster than the group could read. Every so often a noticeable image would flash up on the screens, such as a picture of the Earth or the anatomy of a recognisable animal or plant.

"Well, that answers your question, General."

"Very well done, both of you. The president will be pleased."

"As will my government," added Miss Walker with a smile on her face. "This is the start of a new era and it's all thanks to you two gentlemen."

"Well, we can't take all the credit," replied Bradley. "It took hundreds of people to make this place a reality."

"You are too modest I think," added another member of the group in a broad Russian accent. "My superiors will be pleased by this news."

"Does anyone have any questions?"

"What powers the system?"

"We managed to acquire a crystalline reactor to run the facility. The entire complex is completely self-sufficient and has even been equipped with its own repair drones in case it runs into any problems."

"What about security? I didn't see any guards at the front entrance."

"The security system I installed is second to none. The entrance alone is equipped with two anti-tank guns, a set of chain cannons and three surface-to-air missile launching systems. Human guards are not required to defend this installation."

"Well, it seems like our government's funding has been put to good use."

"Any other questions?" Evans paused to allow for a response. "Very well, then if there's nothing else, I wonder if you would all like a tour of the complex. Bradley needs to concentrate on the online checks."

The Russian delegate chuckled. "Da, we will leave him in peace."

"This way please."

Several days later outside the White House in Washington D.C, Evans and Bradley joined the president and delegates of the other nations involved in the project to announce their exciting news. T.V. companies from all over the world were invited, allowing the conference to be sent out on a live feed to homes across the globe. A gathering such as this had not taken place since the discovery of the Matrillion crystals that revolutionised the power industry in the form of the ecologically-sound crystalline reactors.

"That's a good question, I'll let the system's designers answer that one. May I introduce, Jake Evans and Thomas Bradley."

A light, half-hearted applause came from the crowd as Evans and Bradley stepped up to the podium.

"Thank you, Mr President. Morning, my name is Jake Evans and this is my associate, Thomas Bradley. I've never been in front of an audience before but if you bear with us, we'll try to answer all your questions. Let's start with you, sir, would you mind repeating the question?"

"I was wondering how it works. Obviously, the term artificial intelligence states that this computer can think for itself, but are you actually saying that it can comprehend like we can?"

"Not exactly. You see it isn't really a computer technically, it is silicon-based life. The system is sentient in the respect that it has its own consciousness and thoughts. However, it doesn't process information the same way we do. You see, the information in our brains is stored and processed in a frankly very limited way, that allows us to add emotion, desires, preferences and bias to the recall of the information. This created the potential for us to become confused, lost in personal opinion, influenced in ways that inevitably corrupt the big picture as we see it. Gatekeeper's brain, or neural-net as we like to call it, stores all information in neat separate files that can be referenced at any time with perfect recall and clarity. This means that the system's train of thought works on pure logic and is not affected by the hindrance of emotion or confusion that hinder all of us. It also process's information thousands of times faster than us without becoming overwhelmed."

"Is it dangerous?"

"Excuse me?"

"If it thinks for itself, isn't it possible that it could decide to take over the world or something?"

Bradley laughed and stepped up to the microphone. "At the risk of sounding judgemental, the system isn't interested in power or profit as we are. It simply does what it's been asked to do."

"Then how do you explain the new sickness?"

"I assume you're referring to the mystery illness that's sweeping the globe. Let me clear this up once and for all, right now. Gatekeeper does not have the type of equipment necessary to create viruses or pathogens of any kind. Any information you have heard to the contrary is little more than rumour and speculation spread by conspiracy theory fools."

"So, you expect us to believe it's a coincidence that the world is being plagued by a deadly virus, only seven days after the Gatekeeper System was brought online?"

"That's exactly what I expect you to believe because that's the truth."

Evans and Bradley were removed from the stage as the crowd began to get unruly. They were surrounded by the president's men and ushered into the White House and up to the famed oval office where the president and his aides were already sat waiting.

"It is confirmed gentlemen, the virus that is sweeping the planet has been traced to contaminated crops and reservoirs in thousands of different locations across the globe. The report states that the virus works on a genetic level. Apparently, it is spread by touch and ingestion and I have it on the best authority that no one in the world is capable of creating a virus of this complexity."

Evans shook his head. "I'm sorry but this is ludicrous," he barked. "Gatekeeper is not designed for this. Those people out there have no idea what they are talking about."

"And for the moment that is exactly the standpoint you will continue to take," the president replied with conviction. "But let me make something clear, Mr Evans. You are looking at this through a father's eyes."

Evans screwed up his face.

"My top scientific advisers are not to be confused with those people out there, and they are all telling me to look toward Gatekeeper."

"With respect, Mr President, Gatekeeper is not capable of –"

"It is."

Evans stopped as Bradley interrupted. "What the hell are you doing?"

"I'm sorry, but they're right. You are too close to this." Bradley placed his hand on the shoulder of his friend. "Gatekeeper is absolutely capable. However far from its task it may appear to be… it's possible. You know it has the capacity." Bradley looked at Evans for a moment.

"That's exactly what you two are going to find out."

Both men looked at the president.

"Sorry sir?"

"The European Alliance are sending an armed response team to the Gatekeeper facility to find out what's going on. We are sending a squad of our own to accompany them and you two are going with them. We've had clearance from your government to take you along. All going well you can simply walk in and make some enquiries and put this idea to bed once and for all."

Evans and Bradley nodded.

"Sergeant Miller here will have tactical command but you two will be responsible for getting the team into the complex and working out what, if anything, is going on."

"Of course, Mr President."

"Time flies, gentlemen."

"Ok, boys, you're with me," demanded Sergeant Miller as he walked towards the door. "You can inform me of anything I need to know on the way to the base."

"We're leaving now?" questioned Bradley.

"That's right, the team is already prepped and waiting at the drop-ship."

Evans clung tightly to his safety harness as the military drop-ship lifted off and began to climb. From his window he watched the concrete covered ground of the military base grow smaller and smaller as they ascended towards the clouds.

"Entering low orbit now, sir. Igniting primary boosters."

Bradley's seat rocked as the engines of the drop-ship ignited, propelling them forwards.

"Flight path is stable guys, sub-orbital hop underway, E.T.A. for re-entry window is six minutes."

Bradley watched the soldiers for a few minutes as they talked amongst themselves. Wearing white, grey and black 'urban' camouflage and covered in many different pieces of equipment and weaponry the soldiers made him a little nervous. The soldier across from him undid his harness and leaned over. He was a large African-American man with muscles that seemed to strain the stitches on his uniform, and a long thin scar that ran down the left side of his face.

"Name's Zeus, what's yours little man?"

The soldiers laughed.

"Thomas. Thomas Bradley."

"So, what the hell are you two doing on this mission?"

"Maybe they're the backup," mocked another soldier and once again the squad broke into laughter.

"Actually, asshole we're the brains of the operation," Evans interrupted. "They brought us along in case your bootlaces come undone."

The soldier suddenly looked unimpressed as the rest of the troops pointed at him and laughed. Evans just gave a small victorious grin and turned his attention back to the view through the window.

"So why are you here?" questioned yet another member of the squad.

"We're the only ones who can get into the complex without kicking down the door."

"So, you're the geniuses that built this thing. All this is down to you two fruits," insulted yet another brick wall of a soldier.

"All this was built at the request of government agencies from around the world. Including your government before you get started."

"Look who's suddenly on the defensive. What's the matter, boy, is the 'saviour of the world' title starting to slip away?"

"What the hell is your problem, redneck?"

"Redneck? You're dead, boy."

Sergeant Miller stood up and grabbed the soldier as he started to head towards Evans, "Check that shit, Deacon."

The soldier didn't move.

"I gave you an order, soldier!" shouted Miller about two inches from the soldier's face. "Now sit down and put your fucking harness back on before I knock you down and hog tie you with it."

The soldier grunted at Evans before nodding at Sergeant Miller and returning to his seat.

"Now cut the shit all of you. This is a military operation not a fucking picnic."

"Aye, sir," shouted the squad.

"And you," shouted Miller as he pointed at Evans. "Stop fucking with my men before you get yourself hurt, you understand me?"

Evans nodded and sat back in his seat.

"Everyone better be strapped in back there, we're going in."

Bradley's stomach churned as the ship suddenly began to dive. It was descending at such an incredible rate that he had to push to keep his feet on the floor. He watched the soldiers as their looks hardened and they checked over the equipment that was already strapped to their bodies.

"Picking up a small contingent of troops about half a mile from the installation, Sergeant. Do you want me to set down near their co-ordinates?"

"Affirmative, stay frosty, this place is equipped with aerial defences."

The squad was on its feet within seconds of the drop-ship touching down.

"Frost, Stone, prep the APC."

"Aye, sir."

"Deacon, Zeus, check the equipment."

"Aye, sir."

"You two come with me."

Evans and Bradley followed the Sergeant to the hatch at the front of the chamber. Miller typed a code into a small keypad on the wall and under the groan of its pistons the hatch opened. The snow around the base of the hatch's ladder had been melted by the heat from the drop-ship's engines and Bradley almost lost a boot in the resulting muddy ground. A man from the European Alliance team was walking towards the ship. Sergeant Miller saluted the fellow soldier as he stopped.

"Good afternoon, gentlemen."

"Afternoon, Sergeant, I'm Sergeant Smith of the British Army. Nice to know we can still count on the Yanks to make an over-the-top entrance."

Miller grinned. "I'm Sergeant Miller and these two sorry looking specimens are the reason we're all out here freezing our asses off."

"Ah the system designers I take it." Smith hazarded a guess as he shook the pairs' hands. "So, we're relying on you two to get us in here."

"Yes, I suppose so."

"Well, you have the designers, Miller. How do you suggest we approach this situation?"

"I think these two are the best ones to answer that question."

"We'll need to get inside and down into the system chamber," Bradley offered.

"Fair enough, we'll take a nerd each," Smith replied.

"That won't work," replied Bradley, "Either of us can get into the complex but it takes both our retinal scans to activate the system chamber door."

"Why isn't there some kind of remote shut down for this system?"

"Gatekeeper was designed to save the planet, not to harm it," Evans replied aggressively. "It was built in this bunker to protect it not imprison it. An off switch outside the bunker would make all that defence a bit pointless don't you think. We didn't want some mindless conspiracy theory idiot to have access to the world's best hope for renewal if they hopped the fence. The only shut off switch is located inside the system chamber."

"Damn, relax, we're on the same side here."

Evans grimaced at Miller.

"Ok then both of you will have to go in." Miller turned back to Sergeant Smith. "I suggest we hold one team back in case there's any surprises."

Smith nodded. "Sounds reasonable, but who gets to go in first?"

Deacon ran in from somewhere behind the drop-ship as Miller was pondering the question. "The equipment's still in one piece, Sarge." Deacon handed Miller one of the two plasma rifles he was carrying.

"Thanks, Deacon, carry on."

"Aye, sir." Deacon quickly turned and ran back behind ship.

Miller pushed a button on a small black piece of equipment that was attached to his ear. "Miller to Frost, what's your status?"

"APC is prepped and ready to roll, sir."

"Fire it up."

"Aye, sir."

The roar of another engine became apparent through the din from the waiting drop-ship. From the rear of the ship emerged a heavily armoured six-wheeled vehicle that advanced out into the open and stopped. The wheels on the vehicle were mounted on six long struts that spread out from its raised rectangular body. The ground clearance of the machine was high enough for Evans to view its entire underside without even having to stoop.

"Impressive hardware, Miller," remarked Sergeant Smith. "With that kind of fire power your team would best serve the mission by covering us as we advance."

"Well, frankly, I'd have to disagree. The armour is the smart way to take point if you ask me."

"Now, now, Miller. We were on the ground first old boy."

Miller shrugged. "Hell, can't say I didn't offer. If you want to volunteer to test the defences, I'd be an asshole to argue. I'll set up position a few hundred metres from the main entrance, check the place out before your boys move in."

Smith nodded. "See you on the inside, Sergeant." After saluting Miller, Sergeant Smith took Bradley and Evans and returned to his troops.

A large section of the underside of the APC lowered to the floor as Miller walked over.

"Ok, marines, this ain't no social gathering, let's go."

The squad ran over and joined Sergeant Miller on the lift and it retracted back into the APC.

"Miller to Davidson, get that bird in the air. Back off to a safe distance and wait till I call you."

"Consider me gone, Sergeant." The APC. shook as the drop-ship's engines fired up.

"Ok, Frost, take up position a few hundred metres from the installations entrance."

"Hold onto something, guys, we're going in," the APC engines roared as it started to advance towards the complex.

"Deacon, how's it look?"

"Quiet, Sarge'. No sign of any activity from the installation."

"What about the Allied team?"

"Their two vehicles are right behind us, sir." A couple of the men fell over as the APC bounced over a large snowdrift at high speed.

"Damn it, Frost."

"Sorry."

The sound of pistons filled the compartment as Deacon activated two large chain cannons that emerged from the roof of the APC. "Coming up on co-ordinates, Sarge' E.T.A thirty seconds."

"Ok, Deacon, keep your eyes open."

The APC jerked to a halt in the deep snow surrounding the complex. Deacon trained the chain cannons on the large steel door as the Alliance vehicles raced past.

"Still no reaction from the installation's security systems, sir. Maybe the nerds were right about it being a none combatant."

"Maybe."

The Alliance vehicles slid to a halt by the outer doors of the complex. After the British and French soldiers rushed out and secured the area, Evans and Bradley exited the vehicle and walked over to the door. As they did so, the entrance's anti-tank guns rose from their compartments in the ground and a large set of chain cannons quickly followed.

"No wait!" shouted Evans as the soldiers raised their rifles. "It's just the security system. It's supposed to do that. They won't fire unless you give them a reason to fire." Evans nodded at Bradley who opened a small concealed panel on the wall and began to type a code into the keypad.

"Gentlemen, welcome to the Gatekeeper bunker." Bradley hit the enter key and stepped back. Nothing happened.

"Oh yeah, best built complex ever," mocked one of the soldiers after a few seconds with no change

Bradley gave a confused frown and re-typed the code. "Jake, it won't accept my code."

Upon Bradley stating this fact, Evans noticed one of the anti-tank guns very slowly turning towards the Alliance vehicles. "Oh god." A great swell of fear ran through Evans as he realised what was happening. "Get outta here, it's a trap!" he screamed to the squad. In instant response to his warning, the chain cannons perched above them began to fire. Bradley was splattered by blood as the bullets from the cannons tore mercilessly through the screaming soldiers.

"Stone?"

"On it, sir."

The chain cannons on the APC screeched into action. Evans shielded his face from the speeding chunks of concrete that were now flying chaotically through the air as the cover fire laid waste to the entrance frame above him. Three men were crushed under the weight of the complex's mangled twin cannons as they were sent crashing to the ground.

"The installation's anti-tank guns have opened fire on the Alliance vehicles."

"Take 'em out."

"I can't, sir, not without hitting the troops."

"Fuck. Frost, take us in."

Frost hit the throttle and the APC burst into action. "One of the Alliance vehicles is retreating, sir, the others under heavy fire."

"Get us to those scientists now."

"Brace for impact."

Miller took hold of a roof support as Frost smashed the APC through the battered Alliance vehicle. Zeus and Stone ran onto the lift followed by another two members of the squad. Miller pulled a rocket launcher from its rack on the wall.

"Hanson!" he shouted as he threw it to one of the soldiers. The lift quickly descended and before it had even reached the floor the troops opened fire on the antitank guns.

"Down!" shouted Hanson as he raised the rocket launcher. The gun was totally demolished as the rocket hit it and exploded.

"Get over here!" shouted Zeus to Evans and Bradley who were still cowering in the doorway. "Now damn it now!"

The other marines concentrated their fire on the remaining gun as Zeus dragged Evans and Bradley on to the lift. The lift quickly retracted into the belly of the APC.

"We have to go back down, sir, there's still men alive out there." The APC began to shake lightly as the soldiers pushed Evans and Bradley off the lift.

"Deacon, report."

"I don't know, Sarge, some sort of low-level seismic activity I guess."

"No," stated Bradley as he tried to wipe the blood from his face. "It's a machine shop door."

"A door?" questioned Miller in disbelief.

"Sergeant, with respect, I suggest you get us out of here."

Miller stood and looked at the expression on Bradley's face for a second. "Frost, fall back."

"But."

"Fall back!".

"Aye, sir."

"What about the Alliance troops, sir?"

"We'll come back for them. I want this area secured."

As the APC cleared the wreckage of the damaged Allied vehicle, Frost spotted the opening door of the underground machine shop. "Err, Sarge."

Miller looked out of the window in disbelief as he watched the snow parting. "Jesus that thing's bigger than a football pitch."

"Twice as big if you want to get technical," informed Evans. As they watched, a large tracked vehicle sped out of the gaping chasm that opened before them.

"Now there's something you don't see every day."

Standing as tall as the APC the shiny steel vehicle slightly resembled a battle tank. Even under the weight of its veritable arsenal of turrets and cannons, it moved with ease at incredible speed across the rugged terrain. The machine was lost behind the debris of a large explosion as the surviving Alliance vehicle opened fire. Emerging unscathed from the blast-cloud, it raised a single cannon and returned fire.

"Shot fired, sir, the Allied vehicle managed to get out of the way."

"Deacon, teach that thing why it shouldn't fire at our friends."

"With pleasure, sir." Once again, the sound of moving pistons filled the compartment as three large multiple missile launchers emerged through the outer armour of the APC. Deacon hit the fire button and two of the three launchers fired. "Hellfires launched, impact in three, two, one."

"Status?"

"Target remains."

"What the hell? Hit it again."

"Hellfires away, sir, standby. Target is still moving, Sarge, and it's turning towards us."

"Use the Firestorm missiles."

"Aye, sir, Firestorms away." The APC rocked as the missiles impacted against the attacking tank. "Target is down, sir."

"I should fucking hope so."

"Picking up four more vehicles emerging from the opening, sir. They appear to be of the same configuration as the first."

"Give 'em hell, Deacon."

"Aye, sir, priming Firestorm missiles."

The sound of an explosion rattled through the compartment as one of the tanks opened fire.

"Report."

"I don't know what those things are firing, Sarge, but the Allied vehicle is no longer on my scopes."

"Sarge." Frost drew Miller's attention to yet more tank-like vehicles as they burst into the open through the immense doorway.

"Get us outta here."

"Hold on." Frost pushed the steering assembly forward and the APC began to move.

"Deacon, do you think our armour will hold long enough to rescue the Allied troops."

"Armour or no armour, one direct hit from those weapons and we're toast, Sarge."

"Frost."

"I know, Sarge." Frost turned the APC away from the complex and the wounded Allied troops and began the retreat.

"Incoming."

The soldiers stumbled around the compartment as a number of explosions narrowly missed their vehicle. Frost strafed erratically as they sped away, desperately trying to avoid being hit.

"Pedal to the metal, Frost."

"I'm going as fast as I can, sir."

"Incoming," warned Deacon.

"Veer left now." The proximity of the latest explosion caused one side of the APC to momentarily leave the ground. The soldiers struggled into their seats and strapped themselves in.

"Miller to Davidson, we need evac' now."

"On my way, Sarge."

Another assault covered the windscreen in snow and dirt, temporarily obscuring Frost's view.

"God damn it, return fire."

"I can't get a missile lock while we're bouncing around like this."

"Then use the cluster missiles, do the whole area."

"Cluster missile locked and loaded, launching now."

The central missile launcher rose high into the air before launching the large cluster missile. After gaining altitude for a few seconds the missile's outer shell burst off to reveal several smaller, tightly packed missiles. Launching in slightly different directions these small projectiles effectively blanket-bombed the whole area behind the APC where the attacking tanks were positioned.

"Confirmed hit on two targets. Five more are still in pursuit."

"We're running out of road, Sarge," stated Frost as the valley before the APC began to rise into the base of a mountain.

"It's not that steep, Frost, we can make it."

"Not fast enough to dodge the weapons fire, sir."

"Enemy vehicles are closing, Sarge."

Through the noise of the APC engines, Miller picked up the sound of distant explosions.

"Booyah, here comes the cavalry." Deacon referred to the drop-ship that was approaching rapidly from behind, laying waste to the enemy tanks as it passed overhead.

"Davidson to APC, prepare for extraction."

"Copy that Davidson, nice timing, brother."

"Sarge, I'm picking up more activity. There's something rising out of several small hatchways in the ground in-front of the bunker."

"Surface to air missiles," Bradley barked.

"Shit," Miller exclaimed. "Take those things out now."

"Locking targets, Sarge. Hellfire missiles away."

The drop-ship blasted over the APC and slowed to a stationary hover. As it descended towards the ground the large entry ramp at its rear began to open. The APC slid from side to side as Frost braked heavily and with a final screech of the rubber tyres on the metal ramp, he brought the vehicle to a halt.

"S.A.M.s are down, sir."

"Good work."

"Frost to Davidson, we're in, get us outta here."

The sound of metal on metal filled the APC like hammer blows, as the drop-ship's clamps locked down the APC for transport. The vertical thrusters of the drop-ship burst into action and it began to ascend up the mountainside. Miller and the soldiers quickly placed their weapons back in the APC weapons locker and hurried towards the ship's seating area. Miller ran into the ship's cockpit as Evans, Bradley and the squad strapped themselves in.

"Open me a channel to command."

"Channel open, sir."

"Arch Angels to command, come in please. Command this is Sergeant Miller, please acknowledge."

"This is West, go ahead, Sergeant."

"Be advised, General, we are under heavy attack from an extremely well-equipped and hostile force. The United Nations team has been neutralised and the enemy has control of the area."

"Elaborate, Sergeant."

"Gatekeeper, sir. It has some sort of new battle tank, sir. Bigger and more heavily armed than anything we have."

"Report back to base for debriefing on the double, Sergeant."

"Yes, sir. Miller out. You heard the man, Davidson."

"Aye, sir, best speed for Washington."

CHAPTER 9
Semper Fi

5:00 PM 22/12/2336

Evans and Bradley followed Miller into the meeting room. Several men stood around the large oval table that all but filled the room. All easily over forty years old and wearing finely pressed uniforms, the men returned Miller's salute before calmly sitting down.

"Let's get to it, Sergeant," suggested the man furthest away from Miller at the far end of the table.

"Well, General, as you know, my team was ordered into the Alps to assess the Gatekeeper situation. After these two men and the European Alliance team reached the complex, they came under fire from its sentry guns. We managed to rescue the developers and take out the entrance's armaments but were engaged by hostile vehicles before we could rescue the Alliance troops."

"Yes, these hostile vehicles I've heard about. Didn't you say they were some sort of tank?"

"Yes, sir. The vehicles were heavily armed and had armour like nothing I've ever seen. We had to hit the first target with a high-yield Firestorm warhead in order to take it out."

"If I'm not mistaken, Sergeant, Special Forces drop-squads are equipped with the new Mark four armoured personnel carriers, aren't they?" questioned another member of the group.

"That's correct, Colonel."

"Are they not equipped with Hellfire missiles?"

"Yes, sir, they are, however they proved ineffective."

"How do you mean, ineffective? Be more specific, Sergeant."

"We hit one of the tanks with at least a dozen Hellfires, sir and they didn't even slow it down. I'm sure that enough Hellfires would stop one of these things but not fast enough to be effective in battle."

'Thank you, Sergeant. Please continue."

"Yes, sir. The tank emerged from a huge door in the ground that apparently leads to one of many subterranean machine shops."

"Yes, thank you, Sergeant, we are aware of the facilities design parameters," interrupted the colonel.

"Of course, Colonel. Anyway, we took out the first tank before several more emerged from the machine shop entrance. After witnessing the destruction of the Allied vehicle, I decided it would be a good idea to fall back."

"You mean run, Sergeant."

"I mean remove my team from a non-survivable situation, sir," snapped Miller who was obviously offended by the colonel's remark. "The Allied transport was totally destroyed with a single direct hit from one of those vehicles. My squad would have been dead in seconds if I hadn't ordered the retreat."

"You should have tried to secure the area, soldier."

"I blanketed the whole area with a cluster missile strike and those tanks still kept coming, sir. In my opinion, sir, the only way to secure that area is with a full contingent of hover tanks and preferably air support. Which if I may be so bold sir, is exactly what I suggest we do."

"The European Alliance has already dispatched three tank squadrons to mount an assault on the complex. We have the command carrier, Philadelphia, positioned over the site in orbit to offer assistance if it is required." The General slid a small folder across the table to Miller. "Your mission is to return these two to the site and make sure they survive long enough to fix this mess. You will rendezvous with the Philadelphia and wait aboard until the Allied forces are ready to engage Gatekeeper's defences. Do you have any questions, Sergeant?"

"Permission to speak freely and make a request, sir."

"Anytime, Sergeant."

"I'm gonna need my APC re-arming with Firestorm missiles. I can't guarantee the safety of these men if my arsenal is still eighty percent Hellfires."

The general nodded. "Agreed, I'll have the command carrier's armoury at your disposal by the time you get there."

"Wait a minute," interrupted Evans. "I'm not going anywhere near that place. It was pure luck that we got out the first time.

"I was under the impression that you two were the only people that could access the bunker."

"Well, yes but –"

"Then you're going."

"But –"

"Stop fucking me around, man!" shouted the colonel as he stood up and slammed his fist against the table. "I have fighter squadrons napalming crops all over the county to contain a deadly virus that your invention appears to have created. If we don't come up with an antidote soon, I'm going to have to order my troops to start forcibly locking down cities."

Evans and Bradley suddenly looked horrified at this news.

"Yes, that's right. New York, Seattle, even Washington are starting to show signs of infected people, on mass." The colonel leant over the table towards the scientists and continued in a calm, disturbing tone. "If you two don't find a way to fix this soon, American troops are going to have to start burning their own people to stop this spreading. The contingency plans are already on my desk."

6:30PM 22/12/2336

"Black Hawk to Philadelphia, come in please. This is the drop-ship Black Hawk to command carrier Philadelphia, please respond."

"This is Philadelphia, what can we do for you Black Hawk?"

"We have orders to report here and re-arm before joining the UN ground forces in the Alps."

"Standby, Black Hawk."

Davidson sat and waited.

"My god, that's a big ship," remarked Bradley as the carrier came into view of his porthole.

"Yeah, the command carriers are the biggest things up here. Bigger than the Dreadnought class ore miners even."

"Yeah, only three of them were ever built, and two of them are ours. This computer picked a fight with the wrong assholes."

Back in the cockpit Davidson received his confirmation.

"No problem, Black Hawk, you're cleared for bay two."

"Thanks, Black Hawk out." With a short burst of its thrusters the drop-ship began to move slowly forward. A bead of sweat ran down Davidson's brow as he concentrated on avoiding the sides of the docking bay entrance. The ship rose slowly through the entranceway and into the stillness of the deserted bay area. As the bottom of the ship cleared the floor level, the huge pressure doors closed beneath it and Davidson lowered the landing struts.

"Standby for re-pressurisation." Through the view port of the drop-ship's cockpit, Davidson could make out a young man standing behind a small window in the landing bay's wall. The man nodded at Davidson before pushing a button on the control panel in-front of him. As he did so a great flood of air began to rush into the chamber and the drop-ship fell a few inches and hit the ground as the gravity-field in the room was restored.

"Bay re-pressurised, Black Hawk, exit at your leisure and report to the bay's control room."

"Acknowledged, Control." Davidson locked down the drop-ship and removed his flight harness and helmet. After double-checking that the flight systems were on shutdown, he exited the ship through the seating chamber door and joined his squad.

"I've been told to report to the landing bay control room, Sarge. I'll sort out the extra missiles we were promised while I'm there."

"Thanks, but I've got it. The Allied squadrons are moving in over ground, they won't be in position to start the offensive for at least three hours. Why don't you guys see if this place has a mess hall or something?"

The rest of the squad thanked the sergeant and quickly exited the area before he changed his mind. Zeus dragged Evans and Bradley along under the chant of, "Come on you two, let's get some red meat into those skinny little bodies of yours. God knows you could use the protein."

"You sure, sir?"

"Yeah, Davidson, I have to go up and see the captain anyway."

"Ok, sir, see you in the mess." Davidson turned and ran after the squad.

Miller walked into the landing bay's control room and returned the salute of the controller. "Sergeant Miller of the twenty-fifth. I'm going to need access to your armoury." Miller handed the officer a copy of his orders.

"Hmm, clearance from General West himself." The officer closed the folder and handed it back to Miller. "Apparently, our armoury is at your disposal, Sergeant."

Having found the mess hall, the squad got down to what seemed to be the very serious business of eating. Bradley was quite shocked by the way the soldiers piled food onto their trays. Huge mounds of cold mashed potato and as many fatty, bloody pieces of steak as the food re-hydrators could handle.

"Here you go, ladies." Deacon smirked as he dropped a couple of trays in front of the developers. "Enjoy it, probably gonna be the last meal you fags ever eat."

Zeus walked over and sat down across from Evans. The metal bench creaked under the weight of his enormous frame. "Don't pay any attention to Deac'," he said loudly. "He's just pissed because I fell asleep on his mother."

Frost covered Hanson and Stone in potato as he burst into laughter.

"Damn it, Frost, watch where you're spitting that shit."

"My mother's a saint, spear chukka."

"Ooh," the squad responded to Deacon's insult.

Zeus just nodded and grinned. "That's funny man, cause she's a demon under the sheets." The squad laughed.

Deacon gave a defeated smirk and threw an orange at Zeus.

"What's with the sudden knight in shining armour routine anyway, Zeus. They're big boys, don't you think they can look after themselves?"

"Perhaps he's taken a fancy to them," returned Deacon, seizing the opportunity to throw another insult.

"Well, it's understandable, Deacon. They are both prettier than your mother." The squad roared.

"So, fellas, what are we gonna be running into inside that installation?" Williams mumbled with a mouth full of food.

"Well, let's work on the assumption that the security system layout hasn't changed," answered Evans. "For a start we know our codes are no longer accepted, so we're gonna have to blow the main doors. Then there's the lift that takes us down into the installation."

"Providing it still accepts our palm prints," Bradley added.

"Yeah, good point, Thomas. we might have to waste a bit of time hot-wiring it so we'd better take the right equipment. Then there's the pressure door to the complex itself. Now it doesn't have any weapons systems to worry about but it's gonna take some getting through if the code doesn't work."

"You let us worry about that," reassured Stone. "Never seen a door yet that a plasma grenade couldn't open."

"Fair enough. Ok, where was I, ah, yes. Once we get into the main chamber, we'll have two chain cannons to take out. Now they're situated in the roof at either side of the system chamber door."

"Is there anything to use as cover?"

"No, the room is entirely empty for that exact reason. If you wouldn't mind coming over here, please, gentlemen."

The squad all picked up their trays and relocated to Evans' table. Evans took his fork and began to sculpt a clumsy overhead view of the room out of his mashed potato. "Ok, this is the main chamber. This over here is the system chamber and this door leads to the lower levels."

"We're gonna be sitting ducks against chain cannons in a space as open as that."

"What's in the lower levels?"

"The lower levels consist of the machine shops and storage bays."

"Great, so our choices are the chain cannons, or the rooms with the tanks. It's gonna be a long fucking night, that's all I know."

"Are you boys playing nice?" joked Miller who had entered unnoticed and was standing behind Evans.

"We're just going over the installation's security system, Sarge. Trying to get a head start." Hanson pointed at the makeshift mash potato blueprints. "This is the main chamber and these –"

"Yes, I know, roof-mounted chain cannons. I've been standing here for a while."

"Ah, right. So, what do you think?"

"I think we're gonna need a way of taking out both cannons at once."

"We could take something down with us to use as a shield while we hit them. I don't know, maybe one of the lift doors or something."

"No, that isn't going to work," explained Bradley. "The cannons are armed with the same armour-piercing rounds as your personnel carrier."

"Jesus, you really went to town on this system didn't you."

"Well, something as revolutionary as Gatekeeper was always going to be under threat from extremists and thieves. Why the hell do you think we built it in the Alps? There aren't many groups with the equipment to mount an operation against a target in this sort of terrain."

"What about taking out the installation's power source?" questioned Stone. "I mean, you two must know some way of shutting the place down."

Evans sighed, "When I designed the security system, I didn't account for the fact that it would be firing at us. You guys aren't listening to me, there is no easy way into the system chamber. The crystalline reactor is positioned directly under Gatekeeper itself. The only way to get to it is through an access hatch in the floor of the system chamber and the only way to get into the system chamber is through the door with the chain cannons."

"Then we're just going to have to do it the hard way," remarked Miller as he started walking towards the mess hall door.

"And what exactly is the hard way?" questioned Evans.

Miller stopped just long enough to answer the question. "Devastators and a lot of luck."

"What's a devastator?" asked Bradley as Miller walked off through the door.

"It's a hand-held rocket launcher about the size of a plasma rifle," Zeus schooled. "It holds a fully automatic thirty round clip that contains missiles about the size of a nine-millimetre shell casing."

"Damn."

"Oh yeah, it's an ass kicker no doubt."

"Then why do you all look so worried?"

"Cos only a fool or a headcase would use one in a confined space."

Suddenly the room began to rumble and shake followed by a flood of flashing red light, as the ship's warning system kicked in.

"What the hell?" Evans watched his tray as it rattled off the table and crashed to the floor.

"This is the captain," came a loud echoing voice over the ship's speakers. "All hands to battle stations."

Evans and Bradley followed the squad out into the corridor where the carriers crew members were rushing around to get to their posts.

"What the hell's going on?" shouted Evans through the screeching sirens.

"We're under attack."

Having just exited the transport lift that led onto the carrier's bridge, Miller could do nothing but watch as the crew frantically ran around trying to get the situation under control.

"It's the Asteroid Defence Satellites, Captain. They're not responding to our command codes."

"What do you mean they're not responding? Double-check the codes."

"The codes are right, sir, it's the satellites, they're not responding to the shutdown order."

"Divert all emergency power to the shields."

"Aye, sir."

"Tactical, return fire. Helm, hard to port."

"Sir, I'm detecting dozens of objects entering the atmosphere. Many of the satellites have launched missiles towards the surface."

"Neutralise those platforms now damn it."

"Missile launchers are online, commencing assault," the sound of multiple missile launches could be heard through the chaos as the Philadelphia's starboard batteries fired. The lights and monitors on the bridge flickered as the inbound bombardment continued.

"The crystalline reactor has been damaged, Captain. Primary power is fluctuating."

"Bridge to engine rooms, we need that reactor back on form. The shields must stay up."

"Gillian to bridge, the reactor's been damaged by a falling bulkhead, Captain, I'll have to replace the crystals before I can get it back to full power."

"I need every spare kilowatt of power diverting to the shields, Gillian. Now!"

"On it, sir."

Miller fell into one of the bridge's diagnostic consoles as a large explosion shook the ship.

"Hull breach section seven, decks five through eight. Energy seals are holding, Captain, but they won't last long with the shields drinking all the juice."

"Understood." Once again, the sound of firing thrusters could be heard as another bank of missiles were launched at the satellites. "Tactical, report?"

"Forty percent of the platforms have been neutralised, Captain."

"That's not good enough, soldier."

"Aye, sir." Another bank of missiles was launched from the ship as the tactical officer tried to target the dozens of satellites. "Shields are starting to buckle, Captain."

Miller took his communications device out of his pocket and put it back over his ear. "Miller to Davidson."

"Davidson here, what the hell's going on out there, sir?"

"Is the rest of the squad there?"

"Yes, sir, they came back to the hangar when the red alert sounded."

Miller walked into the bridge's lift. "Good, prep the ship for take-off, I'm on my way."

"Aye, sir."

The squad was struggling to carry a number of large missiles up the drop-ship's ramp as Miller entered the landing bay.

"Hurry up, this ship's getting its ass kicked. We need to get airborne and take out some of those defence satellites."

Frost and Stone looked at each other as Miller ran straight past them and up the drop-ship's ramp. Stepping up the pace they hurried to load the missile they were carrying into the ship, before heading for the seating compartment.

"What's the plan, Sarge?" asked Davidson as Miller burst into the cockpit.

"Can you out-manoeuvre missiles from the Asteroid Defence platforms in this thing?"

"Atmospherically maybe, in space I doubt it. That's not what she's built for, Sarge."

"Try Davidson, we need to start taking out those platforms before this ship –"

"This is the captain," interrupted a loud echoing voice through the P.A system. "All hands abandon ship. Repeat. All hands abandon ship."

Davidson and Miller looked at each other.

"Sounds like we're too late. Just get us outta here."

"Err, we might have a problem, sir." Davidson pointed to the empty control room of the landing bay.

"God damn it, don't go anywhere till I get back." Miller exited the cockpit.

"What's happening, Sarge?" questioned Deacon as the sergeant opened the seating area's hatch.

"The asshole in the control booth has left already. I'm going to start the decompression sequence."

"I'll get it, Sarge," offered Williams as he undid his safety harness. "I used to run one of these things."

Miller nodded and stepped aside. "Hurry up."

"Aye, sir." Williams ran down the exit ramp and clumsily crossed the now shaking floor of the landing bay. He closed the pressure door of the control room behind him and began to push buttons on one of the control panels.

"Williams to Davidson, starting depressurisation sequence now." A great hissing sound filled the room as it began to depressurise.

"Williams, what are you doing? Set it on a delayed sequence or you'll never get back here in time."

"The docking computer is offline, Davidson. I'm having to do this manually."

"Then set the damn thing and run."

"Sorry, man, it doesn't work like that. The sequence won't run unless the control room's pressure door is sealed and the door won't open until the sequence is complete."

"But. . ."

"Just get ready to depart."

"What the hell's he doing?" asked Miller as he re-entered the cockpit."

"He says we can't get outta here without leaving him behind."

Miller pushed the button on his earpiece. "Williams, stop fucking around and get back here soldier."

"Sorry, sir, but it's not possible to get out of this room while the depressurisation sequence is running."

"Damn it, Williams, I'm not leaving you here." The huge pressure doors of the landing bay began to open, revealing the flashing lights from the surrounding explosions.

"You don't have a choice, Sarge. I'll find a life-pod or something when the room re-pressurises. Now go."

Miller punched the wall of the cockpit. "Get us outta here Davidson."

"Aye, sir, engaging manoeuvring thrusters."

"It's been an honour serving with you, sir."

"Don't give me that shit, Williams. I'd better be receiving your life-pod's location beacon in less than ten minutes or you're in deep shit."

Williams chuckled. "Aye sir."

"Sarge, if you're staying up here you might want to take a seat."

Miller sat down and strapped himself in.

"See you on the ground, Williams."

"Catch you later, Davidson. Give Gatekeeper one from me."

"Consider it done, marine. Ok, hold onto your asses, we're going in."

Williams watched as the drop-ship shifted position over the now fully open door of the landing bay. Raising the tail of the ship until it was perched at a ninety-degree angle with the cockpit now facing the open door, Miller tightened the straps on his safety harness as the tail of the ship lightly scraped against the roof of the bay. "Err, Davidson."

"Relax, Sarge, I'm just making sure we get a running start."

Miller sat staring out into the dark expanse of space that filled the window. His head slammed back into the headrest as Davidson hit the engine ignition button and sent them screeching out into space.

"My god," remarked Evans as the command carrier's flank came into view through his porthole. The entire starboard side of the huge ship was in pieces. Large sections of the interior decks could be seen through the craterous holes in the outer hull. Many large plumes of fire reached out into space fuelled by damaged pipelines and ruptured oxygen storage tanks. Small flashes of blue light caused the whole surface of the vessel to twinkle as dozens of life-pods were launched.

"Incoming."

"Yeah, I see it." Davidson strafed the drop-ship from side to side desperately trying to avoid the incoming missiles.

"What's that?" questioned Bradley, pointing at a flickering blue tint around the command carrier.

"The shields are buckling."

"Jesus," Deacon exclaimed. "Sarge, the carrier's shields have failed," he shouted through his communicator.

"Ah shit, Davidson," Miller replied.

"I'm going as fast as I can, sir."

"Are we far enough away?" Zeus questioned.

"I don't think so," Deacon replied.

"What?" questioned Bradley unaware of the new danger.

"If one of those warheads hits that ship with the shields down –" Stone's explanation was cut short by a large blinding flash of light that suddenly filled the compartment.

"Incoming."

The shields of a command carrier are formidable enough to deflect up to 85% of the force from an Asteroid Defence missile. However, with the shields down the enormous blast-yield of the mammoth warheads tore through the vessel with ease.

"Brace for impact."

The drop-ship shook violently as speeding pieces of debris from the exploding carrier bounced off its hull plating. The enormous amounts of power required to form and sustain ablative energy shielding could only be achieved by use of a crystalline reactor. Unfortunately, the Raptor class drop-ships such as the Black Hawk were not large enough to house a power source of that type and instead ran on a number of rechargeable power cells. Without the benefit of energy shielding, the only thing between the squad and the advancing hail of shrapnel was the armoured hull plating.

Miller shielded his face as the console in front of him exploded under a shower of sparks. Davidson struggled to keep the vessel at the required thirty-degree re-entry angle that its hull design required, as they descended through the atmosphere.

"Hanson!" shouted Frost as a large steel beam tore through the hull, skewering the soldier to his seat. Hanson grabbed hold of the beam in shock as blood began to drool from his mouth. A great wind swept into the compartment from the breach in the hull as the drop-ship sped towards the ground.

"I've lost propulsion!" shouted Davidson through the din. "Starting emergency landing procedures."

Miller watched through the window as the ship cut through the cloud layers.

"Hold on." Davidson pulled a lever and a large set of wings deployed from the sides of the ship. Miller almost lost consciousness from the G-force as the pilot quickly pulled out of the dive.

"EMERGENCY GLIDE SURFACES DEPLOYED," enlightened a voice from the cockpit computer.

"The debris that's pierced the hull is causing too much drag," shouted Davidson "I'm having trouble holding her." Davidson radically altered direction and not by choice. He fought to regain control. "I'm gonna have to put her down soon, Sarge. I need you to find me a landing site."

Miller looked over the global positioning map on the charred and smoking console in front of him. "What about one of the coastlines, it should help soften the landing."

"We're coming in too fast. I'll never reduce speed in time to hit the coast."

"Use the breaking thrusters."

"If I use the breaking thrusters while we're in an emergency glide we'll fall like a rock. I need to slow down gradually or we're not going to make it. Pick a site further away."

"What about the British coastline?"

"Well at least their weather makes for plenty of soft ground."

"Bear right four degrees."

"Confirmed, E.T.A. thirty seconds."

"This is Miller, we're going in, brace for impact."

By the time the Asteroid Defence platforms had launched the last of their missiles the earth was in chaos. Washington, London, Moscow, Paris and many more of the world's capital cities were in ruin. Reduced by the brief but devastating bombardment to little more than tombs of burning rubble. The swiftness and ferocity of the assault could not have hit the world harder. No one had anticipated that Gatekeeper would be able to crack the security codes that protected the satellites from outside interference. In the ultimate ironic nightmare, the unprepared leaders and governments of the world were obliterated in a single attack, using their own weapons. A tactically brilliant assault staged from their own defence system that lasted little more than five minutes.

Four miles inland from the port of Dover, in the cornfields surrounding the town of Lydden, a great plume of black smoke rose into the still evening air. A deep scar and trail of devastation that stretched as far as the eye could see betrayed the final resting-place of the battered drop-ship. Miller and his squad stood over the shallow, freshly dug grave of Corporal Hanson, as Zeus and Stone covered his poncho-wrapped body with the last two shovels of dirt.

"We take a moment to honour the fallen. To honour our brothers," Miller offered.

Evans looked on at what he found to be quite a touching scene between men he previously had mistaken to be heartless and superficial. He was suddenly aware that he had been mistaken.

"Williams…Hanson…Thank you for your service and your sacrifice. You will be remembered. Semper fi, marines." All the squad followed Miller in a salute.

"Semper fi," they all responded in unison.

Miller was the first to move. "Talk to me, Frost."

"You want the good news or the bad news, Sarge?" asked Frost.

"Be gentle, Frost, it's been a long day."

"Well, the APC is still in one piece, somehow. So, I guess that's something. The drop-ship however is totally screwed."

Miller nodded. "No shit." Miller rubbed his neck. "Get all the gear you can into the APC and load any surviving Firestorms into the launchers."

"Aye, sir."

"Sarge, you might want to take a look at this!" Deacon gestured as he started to make his way back toward the APC. Miller followed his trooper over to the lift and after waiting for it to retract back into the vehicle, they walked into the drive compartment.

"What is it?"

"We're receiving standard broadband updates from the Hunter."

"Ah, I was wondering whether both of the command carriers had been destroyed. What do they have to say?"

"It's a repeating message, Sarge. It says that all America's strategic operations are being run through Fort Thomas in Nevada," Deacon paused and turned to look at Miller. "Since the destruction of Washington and the Pentagon."

Miller's face dropped.

"Apparently the missile strikes from the defence platforms were more co-ordinated than we thought. The Pentagon, the White House and several major military bases across the continent have been destroyed. It's not conclusive but it appears that the president and the vice-president were killed in the attack."

Miller sat down in the driver's seat beside Deacon. For a few seconds he said nothing and simply sat staring out of the window with a troubled look on his face. "Any news on the rest of the world?"

"The airwaves are flooded with it. Every station, military and civilian are screaming about the fall of one place or another."

"That would explain why it's so quiet out here."

"Sir?" questioned Deacon.

"We came in over Dover like a bat out of hell and our landing was anything but stealthy. We should have British troops all over us by now, or at least a voice on the com system reminding us of the airspace restrictions. I'd say it's a good bet that Britain got hit with the same kind of coordination."

Miller stood up and slapped Deacon on the back. "Call in an evacuation request, I'll inform the men."

"Aye, sir."

Miller called his men over as the APC's lift returned to ground level. Stopping what they were doing, the squad took up position in front of Miller's position and waited.

"Stand easy, guys. Evans, Bradley!" Miller shouted to the distant developers. "You should hear this too."

Evans and Bradley walked over and joined the squad. Miller sighed and started to speak.

"What's the skinny, Sarge?"

"As you already know, the attack from the orbital missile platforms was directed at the surface as well as at the Philadelphia. I've just received intelligence on the effectiveness of the surface damage from the Hunter command carrier, which I'm relieved to say is still in one piece." Miller stopped as he struggled to think of a way to break the news to his men. "Well, there's no easy way of saying this, so I'll just say it. The Pentagon, the White House and most of our military strongholds have been destroyed. Along with the lunar habitats."

The squad's composure broke into a chaotic din of questions and profanity. "Lunar too?"

"What the hell are we gonna do?"

"The White House? Where's the president?"

"Compose yourselves, marines. This is no time to go to pieces." Miller gave the squad a few seconds to calm down. "The president, the vice-president and all the chiefs of staff are presumed dead."

"Jesus Christ."

"What are our orders, Sarge?"

"The message we received was just a recording, as of yet I haven't received any updated orders."

Deacon lowered himself down from inside the APC. "I managed to reach the Hunter, Sarge. Apparently, there are no ships available for an evacuation at this time. We've been ordered to secure our own means of transport if possible and head for Fort Thomas."

"Fuck me." Miller kicked one of the lift struts. "Ok guys, surprise, surprise, we're on our own."

"What's the plan, Sarge?"

"Our best bet is to head for London. Or what's left of it. It's our best chance of securing some form of transport large enough to carry the APC."

"Sergeant Miller?"

"Yes, Mr Evans."

"I wonder if I could have a word with you in private?"

Miller nodded. "Ok marines, move like we got a purpose." The squad quickly returned to their tasks and Miller turned his attention to Evans. "What is it?"

"It's my wife. I want your approval to fetch her and bring her with us. You know as well as I do what the major cities will be like once the population starts panicking. It's gonna be chaos."

Miller sighed and shook his head. "This is a marine squad not a coach trip."

"Damn it I know that, Miller. I also know that the safest place on this continent right now is right behind you."

Miller stood and stared at Evans. "Where from?"

"Hawkhurst, Kent."

"Damn it, Evans, that's in the opposite direction to where we're going."

Evans said nothing and just stared at Miller with a look of uneasy anticipation.

"Stone, Davidson, front and centre."

The soldiers quickly complied. "Yes, sir."

"Take the speeders. Go with Evans to fetch his damn wife."

Stone and Davidson looked at each other.

"Do me a favour and just fucking do it. I have a bad fucking headache."

The marines took the lift up into the APC.

"Thanks, Miller."

"Don't thank me, Evans. I'm just trying to keep you alive so you can fix this shit storm you've created." Miller reached into his pocket and took out an earpiece. "This is Hanson's communicator, push the button if you want to talk, but speak up so the microphone gets a clear signal. It has a built-in locator that I can track from the APC, so don't even think about disappearing."

Evans nodded and put the communications device on his ear. His attention was suddenly drawn to the loud humming sound of motors as the hatch on the rear of the APC slowly opened. Davidson and Stone roared out into the air on two large bike-like machines that circled round and hovered down to the ground with a loud blast from their thrusters.

Evans gave one of the machines a quick look over as they waited. Except for a number of small pistons that controlled the directional flaps, the whole of the machine was a dark green colour. Attached to either side of the main frame just below the handlebars were two large gun barrels. Evans didn't know what type of guns they were, but he decided to hazard a guess.

"Twin machine-guns?"

Stone shook his head. "Devastator cannons," he informed with a rather disturbing grin on his face. Evans nodded and climbed on the back of the machine.

"Ever been on a hover sled before?"

"No, I've seen them but they always seemed a little too dangerous for my liking. Although, those models didn't carry warheads."

Stone handed Evans a helmet and smiled. After slipping on his helmet, he nodded at Davidson and began to rev the engine. Evans' feet left the floor as the sled ascended into the air.

"It's not the warhead you need to worry about." With a twist of the throttles, the sleds screeched into action and tore off into the distance.

Miller watched as they disappeared over the horizon. "Ok marines, get a damn move on, I didn't call a break."

CHAPTER 10
When all else fails. Blow a hole in it

"Assault squadron to command, come in. Pearson to command, please respond?" Colonel Pearson shook his head. "Where the hell are those guys? Command, if you can hear me, be advised, we have arrived at the battle zone. The Gatekeeper complex will be within firing range in approximately two minutes." Again, Pearson got no response. "This is Colonel Pearson. All squads stand ready."

"Area is quiet, sir, no sign of any hostiles."

"Keep your eyes open, Private."

"Yes, sir."

"Artillery batteries report armed and ready, Colonel."

"Second wing, move in when ready."

"Copy that, sir, we're going in."

"All scopes still report no movement or traceable power sources of any kind. Second wing is closing on the installations entrance."

"Second wing, be advised, all perimeter defence systems have been reported as neutralised, but keep your eyes open anyway."

"My thoughts exactly, Colonel."

"Sergeant Naylor to Colonel Pearson, first wing is ready to advance at your discretion."

"Negative, Sergeant, hold position till the area has been secured."

"Second wing has reached the installations entrance, sir. Still no response from Gatekeeper."

"Second wing here, requesting permission to see who's home."

"Confirmed wing two, knock when ready."

The sound of a large explosion filled the air as the second wing's lead hover tank fired on the main doors of the complex. The doors were blown apart with ease, exposing the empty interior of the ground level chamber.

"Door is open, Colonel, chamber is clear, there is no one home.

"First wing, spread out and secure the surrounding area. Remember to watch out for the machine shop doors."

"Affirmative, Colonel."

"Sergeant Kelly, is the rapid response squadron ready for deployment?"

"All hover sleds, ready and willing, sir."

"Intelligence states that there are only three surface-to-air missile launchers and that they should have already been neutralised. Keep a lookout for any additional platforms while you're out there."

"Copy that, sir."

"All remaining vehicles stand ready. This is a little too easy."

The sound of hover sled engines briefly filled the main chamber of the mobile command vehicle as the squad left the safety of their APC and sped past. As Sergeant Kelly and his squad rocketed over the site he glanced around for any sign of hostile vehicles. Except for a few frozen bodies and the twisted remains of the Allied vehicles from the first engagement with the system, there was nothing to be seen but snow-covered mountains and ridges.

Suddenly the sounds of multiple explosions filled the area. "Shots fired, shots fired, the Artillery batteries are under attack."

"What, where the hell is it coming from?"

"I don't know, sir, everywhere."

"Damn it, Private, where?"

"From the surrounding ridge-lines, the scopes say there's nothing there."

"All units to battle stations. Sergeant Kelly, do you have a visual on the enemy targets?"

"Negative, Colonel I don't see –." The sound of static replaced the Sergeant's voice.

"Rapid Response squadron is under missile fire."

"Damn it, can anyone see what's firing at us?"

The mobile command vehicle shook as an adjacent hover tank exploded.

"All units, open fire on the surrounding ridge-line," the dozens of tanks raised their turrets and opened fire. As the first wave of shells hit, the snow-covered ridge-line began to flicker like the faltering picture on a television set with bad reception. As the second wave of shells hit the illusion shattered.

"The ridge-lines are false, sir, it's some sort of holographic projection."

The projection of the long surrounding ridgelines gave way to reveal menacing lines of waiting vehicles. Enemy battle tanks that spread out in several positions, waiting in ambush and totally surrounding the squadrons. Colonel Pearson felt a sudden cold shudder of fear as he realised the reality of their situation. "My god."

The surrounding aggressors fired, indiscriminately targeting the Allied vehicles with deadly accuracy and no sign of mercy. It took Pearson a few seconds to pull himself together, as he witnessed the slaughter of his battle force through the command vehicle's view screen.

"All units break formation, fall back to grid forty-six-mark-three-two-five."

In the hellish noise and confusion of the constant onslaught, the disorientated squadrons did their best to obey. Hover tank after hover tank the squads engaged their afterburners and retreated away from the ambush area. Relentlessly the attack continued as the enemy battle tanks pursued.

"Pearson to command, Pearson to command, we are under heavy attack. At least thirty percent of the battle force has been destroyed. Attempting to fall back to a neutral position."

Unit after unit the retreating battle force grew smaller and smaller, as the enemy targeted them from behind with ruthless efficiency. The frenzied attempts to fire back by the fleeing troops were hasty and panicked. Lacking any real accuracy or co-ordination they did little to alter their collective situation as it unravelled before them.

"We are clear on three sides, sir. All hostiles are on our six."

"Pearson to squadrons, hold and attack."

The raging afterburners of the hover tanks silenced as they began to slow and turn.

"Destroy them! All units, fire at will."

The fast-approaching enemy vehicles broke formation with pinpoint co-ordination and scattered, as a hail of Firestorm missiles filled the air. A great cloud of snow and dirt cloaked the aggressors as the hover tanks turrets fired shell after shell into their ranks.

"Yes!" shouted Pearson as the Firestorms arced back downwards and laid waste to the entire area causing the cloud of debris to swell in size. "All units hold fire." Pearson grinned and whispered, "Take that you bastards."

Meanwhile on the outskirts of Hawkhurst, the growing sound of approaching engines had begun to draw a crowd.

"Where?"

"Over there, the third street on the left."

Several people quickly moved out of the way as the two hover-sleds swung round the corner and sped along the street.

"Jesus, look at this place," Evans made reference to the long row of buildings surrounded by glass from their smashed windows. "Here, stop."

The sleds swung round and came to a halt outside the entrance to the large apartment complex. Evans quickly jumped off and ran inside.

"Never fails, man," Stone remarked to Davidson as he glanced around the street.

"Yeah, introduce a little panic into the status quo and everyone thinks they're Robin Hood."

"It don't make any sense to me, man."

"Ooh the worlds ending," mocked Davidson. "Let's go steal some television sets."

Stone laughed. "Pussies."

"You said it."

Evans burst through the door to his apartment. "Jayne! Jayne!" he shouted as he ran from room to room.

"Jake!"

Evans ran into the bedroom where his wife was sitting on the bed. Evans ran over and hugged her. "Thank god."

"What's happening Jake, where have you been?"

"I'm sorry I didn't call after the presentation at the White House. I had to go back to the lab to find out what was wrong with Gatekeeper. They didn't exactly give me time to make a call."

"I've been worried, the attacks started and you didn't call and I wondered what –"

"Shush, stop crying. We don't have time now, there are some people waiting for us outside."

"Who? Where are we going?"

"They're soldiers, American Marines."

"But –"

"Look," he interrupted, "I'll explain everything once we get under way, but we have to go now, ok?"

Jayne nodded.

"Have you been eating like I told you last time I called?"

"Yes, only tinned foods and bottled water that's over a week old."

Evans gave a relieved sigh. "Good girl. Put everything you think you'll need into a rucksack, and hurry."

"What about a suitcase?"

"Trust me there's no room, now go. Oh, and wear some flat shoes." Evans ran back out of the apartment complex's main entrance with his wife directly behind him.

"Wow, nice ass," Stone complimented through the headsets.

"Yeah, I wouldn't mind a couple of hours with that one."

"Hey, assholes."

Stone and Davidson stopped as Evans' voice came through the earpieces.

"You're not the only ones with communicators."

Davidson and Stone grinned at each other.

"Jayne, this is Stone and Davidson. Stone and Davidson, this is Jayne."

"Pleased to meet you ma'am."

"Err, thanks."

"Afraid we're gonna have to cut the introduction short, I'm picking up a large storm-front heading this way."

"Don 't suppose it's heading in from a clear zone?"

"Yeah, you wish. It looks like it formed somewhere into the south-west."

Davidson sighed, "Definitely going to be acidic. Think we can make it back to the APC before it hits? Or do we need to find some shelter?"

"It ain't moving that fast, out-running it shouldn't be a problem."

"Evans, we need to get moving."

Evans reassured his wife as he helped her onto the back of Davidson's sled. The marine handed her a helmet that was clearly too big for her head. He quickly jumped onto the other vehicle behind Stone, put on his own helmet and wrapped his arms around the marine's waist. As he did so, Stone set the machine into motion and sped off through the streets towards the edge of town.

"Dear god." Miller couldn't believe his eyes as he stared out of the APC windscreen. He looked in dread over the broken heaps of flaming debris that occupied the space where the great city of London once stood. "Deac' get me a reading."

"I'm only picking up a few dozen life form readings, Sarge, and most of them are too small to be human. Except for the unstable structures the place should be relatively safe."

"Can you tell if any of the airports are still in one piece?"

"Hold on a second, sir, I'll try to patch into one of the surveillance satellites."

"Surveillance satellites?" repeated Bradley in a questioning tone.

"Yes, Bradley, surveillance satellites."

"Big Brother really is watching you," Deacon boasted wearing a smug grin.

"Ok, I think that's got it." A small screen on the drive room's dashboard crackled into action as Deacon typed on the keyboard in front of him. From what Bradley could make out it appeared to be a view of the planet from orbit.

"Zoom it in."

"Aye, sir, going to twenty times magnification." The picture quickly changed to a tighter view of what was now more obviously the British Isles. "Going to thirty times magnification."

Bradley could now make out the city through the monitor screen. Or at least what was left of it.

"Damn, this place was hit big time. The whole city's been completely levelled."

"Is there anything that resembles a mode of transport?"

"Nothing, sir, the whole place is on its ass. I can't make out an airport let alone any aircraft."

The squad's attention was suddenly drawn to another small monitor screen as it started to beep and scroll line after line of unreadable text.

"Getting a message, Sarge."

"You don't say," replied Miller sarcastically. "What does it say?"

"Bear with me a second, it's encrypted." Deacon pushed a few buttons on the keypad beside the monitor and the still scrolling text suddenly became legible. "It's another message from the Hunter. Apparently, a new offensive has been co-ordinated against the Gatekeeper bunker following the orbital attacks. The United Nations, Korea, Russia, hell, it looks like everyone is invited."

"When?"

"It says the attack is planned for zero-eight-hundred tomorrow morning."

Miller smiled.

"What happened to the European Alliance squadrons that we were supposed to meet? What happened to that assault?" questioned Bradley.

"It doesn't say." Deacon looked across at Frost who slowly shook his head to signal his lack of optimism for the Allied squadron's survival. Deacon continued to read the message, "We have special instructions to get the egg-heads back to the system complex by whatever means necessary."

Miller nodded and thought for a moment. "Open a communications line on broadband. All channels."

"Line open, sir," whispered Deacon.

"This is Sergeant Miller of the United States Marine Corps. Any members of the British military that can hear this message please respond. Repeat, any members of the British military who are hearing this message please respond."

"This is General Savage of Scarab squadron eight, I read you, Sergeant, go ahead."

"I assume you just received the same message I did from the Hunter, sir."

"If you mean the times for the reunion then, yes."

"I need your help, General, me and my boys are currently stuck in London. I have two V.I.P guests that need to get to that party. Trouble is we can't find a cab."

"So, you need a lift, Sergeant?"

"Basically, sir, yes. Do you know anyone that might be close enough to lend a hand, preferably someone capable of carrying a rather large present?"

"Well, it's a little out of the way but I don't see why I can't swing by. I shouldn't have a problem getting clearance to leave a little earlier. I'll have my man send you encrypted co-ordinates where you can find that 'cab'."

"General, I owe you one."

"Don't worry, I get the feeling you'll have a chance to pay me back. Savage out."

"Deac', as soon as you decrypt that message, get on the line to Stone. Make sure he knows where to meet us."

"Message coming through now, sir. Decryption underway."

"Frost, get us to that rendezvous."

"No problem, Sarge." Frost took a look at the readings on his console and veered the APC to the right, flattening a small private transport vehicle as he turned. He pushed forwards on the drive levels and the APC roared into top gear, heading towards its new destination.

Pearson stood in his command vehicle staring at the scope. "Report," he demanded, as he watched the cloud of debris begin to settle around the enemy vehicles.

"Nothing yet, sir, the cloud is still too thick. Sensors show nothing moving out there."

Pearson's suddenly remembered to blink as the burning sensation in his eyes became enough to snap him out of his shock. "Did anyone see that?"

"Sir?"

"Look there, some sort of orange glow."

"Yeah, I see it."

"What is it?"

The crew of the command vehicle watched as the strange orange glow became more and more apparent in the settling cloud of debris.

"My god."

As the cloud dispersed the whole force of battle tanks came back into view, standing motionless and virtually unscathed in one solid line before Pearson's squadrons.

"That's not possible." The command vehicle shook as the enemy vehicles commenced firing, sending parts of an adjacent hover tank crashing into its hull.

"All squadrons fire at will, repeat, fire at will."

The orange aura of the enemy tanks grew brighter and more apparent as Pearson's squadrons opened fire.

"The glow is some sort of energy shielding, sir. Our attack isn't even scratching those things."

"Open me a channel to command."

"Channel open, sir."

"Command, this is Colonel Pearson, come in? Command, sound off damn it." Pearson kicked the communications console in frustration. "Why is no one answering?"

"Sir, the enemy vehicles are starting to advance, eighty percent of the battle fleet is down or destroyed."

"Signal the retreat."

"All exit routes from this valley are on the other side of the enemy forces, sir. We're cut off."

Pearson dropped back into his seat. His eyes fixed on an advancing enemy battle tank through the view screen. He watched calmly as it sped straight towards his command vehicle, its weaponry trained and locked. He felt a feeling shared by many commanders over the centuries. A feeling that he had always hoped to avoid. He took a breath. "Damn!"

A storm had settled over the agreed pick-up site. It had been raging for some hours now with little sign of tiring. A single figure could be seen standing watch, covered from head to toe in green plastic overalls. Standing beneath the hull of the APC offered some protection from the toxins in the rainfall, but in a downpour such as this, the bio-suit was still necessary.

"Miller to Stone, how's it going out there?"

"Peachy, Sarge."

"You've been out there long enough, come back inside, I'll send Zeus out to relieve you."

"You don't have to ask me twice." Stone suddenly became aware of a new noise piercing the sounds of the storm. "Wait a minute here! Deacon, you got anything on the scanners?"

"Yeah, one big ass storm."

"No, there's something else, I hear thrusters."

"There's nothing on the scanners that's small enough to be a ship, Stone. All I got is a shit load of low clouds."

Stone directed his view to the sky as six large ships descended into view through the thick black clouds. "Deac', that ain't clouds you're scanning."

Deacon leaned over and looked up through the windshield. "Sarge, our ride's here. I hope."

Miller walked into the drive room as the drop-ships touched down. "Jesus, I don't think they're gonna have any trouble carrying the APC," Miller watched as a large ramp in the rear of one of the large ships slowly descended to the floor.

"Sergeant Miller, come in."

"This is Miller, nice of you boys to be on time."

"We're guilty of a lot of things, Sergeant, being tardy isn't one of them." The locking mechanism of the APC entry lift drew Davidson's attention as Stone came back inside. "Bring your personnel carrier inside whenever you're ready."

"No problem, Miller out."

Frost powered-up the motors and slowly rolled the APC up the ramp and into the back of the drop-ship. He was surprised at the chaotic set-out of the ship's hold, as he carefully manoeuvred between many protrusive and bulky struts that spanned its walls. Except for a few scattered munitions crates and the half-dozen troops that stood awaiting their arrival, the entire hold was empty.

"What the hell is this thing? It's too big to be a drop-ship," Deacon questioned.

"Beats the hell out of me," Frost replied.

"APC powered-down, Sarge. Stabilisers are locked and holding."

"Deacon, get me a check on all systems." Miller walked out of the drive chamber and headed past the squad before stepping onto the lift.

"Need any company, sir?"

"No, I got it, Zeus. Then again, Evans, you might prove useful." Evans joined Miller on the lift-pad. He smiled reassuringly at his wife as he descended out of view.

Evans steadied himself on the lift's guardrail as the ship took off, its rear hatch closing but still more than halfway open as it began to climb. The sound of the roaring take-off engines was deafening. If the room hadn't been full of hardened soldiers, he would have covered his ears with his hands.

"Sergeant Miller, I presume!" shouted General Savage, his voice barely distinguishable through the din.

"Thanks for the help, General." Miller shook Savage's hand. "We'd have been lost without you."

"Don't thank me till you know what I'm flying you into."

"Do you have any word on the progress of the squadrons your boys sent in?"

Savage shook his head. "The entire Alliance was hit pretty bad by the satellite defences. All our primary command installations were destroyed. By the time we got our shit together the whole of Europe was in chaos. All attempts to reach Colonel Pearson or his battle force have failed. In case that wasn't bad enough, the damn virus has taken more than half my men. Don't get me wrong, their replacements are all worthy soldiers, but they're not exactly trained to use these Scarabs."

Miller frowned. "Scarabs?" Miller followed the general's pointing finger to the roof above him, and suddenly the chaotic layout of the room made sense. The large protrusive support struts that spanned the walls of the chamber were actually legs. Legs that held up the huge bulky chassis of the war machines that loomed above them. It was a few seconds before Miller could make out the full shape of the enormous machines. There were three of them standing tightly packed along the length of the shadowed chamber. True to their name the machines vaguely resembled large beetles that towered above the twenty-two-foot-high APC.

"Jesus Christ." Miller looked at General Savage. "And I thought our intelligence network was up-to-date on Alliance weapons technology."

The general grinned. "Six months ago, these things were just a concept, most of the Alliance countries aren't aware they exist yet."

"Very impressive."

"Wait till you see them in action." The general suddenly diverted his attention to a call that was coming in through his headset. A couple of seconds later Miller also received a call.

"Deacon to Miller, come in."

"What is it, Deac'?"

"We've just received an update from the Hunter, France is under attack on several fronts, sir."

Miller watched General Savage's face drop as he listened to his message.

"Should I forward the message to General Savage's men, sir or do you want to tell him yourself"

"I think he knows, Deac'."

General Savage released the button on his headset and ended his transmission. After a few seconds of contemplation, he looked at Miller. "I'm sorry Sergeant we're gonna have to drop you off a little short. We've been re-directed to France to reinforce the city of Grenoble, apparently they're under heavy fire."

"I heard. We'll help out as much as we can, General but understand, I have orders to get these designers back to the Gatekeeper complex and –"

"I know, Sergeant," interrupted the general. "There's no need to explain, we all have our orders. I'm not sure how much your APC could do against these things anyway. Our intelligence reports that they have energy shielding."

Miller nodded. "We've faced them before. Shields would explain how they managed to withstand a direct hit from one of our cluster missiles."

"All hands to their seats, we're going down in three minutes," the intercom message from the cockpit ended the conversation. Miller and Evans headed back to the APC as the general and his men disappeared through a small door in the wall of the cargo hold.

Miller rushed off the lift as it locked into position inside the APC. Evans took his seat beside his wife and strapped himself in.

"What is it?" she asked as she noticed the look of worry on his face.

"I shouldn't have brought you here. You were safer at home."

"I was scared out of my wits at home. Hundreds of people were rioting in the streets below the apartment and the reports on the news kept getting worse and worse. I want to be here, with you, Jake."

Evans shook his head. "I've put you in more danger than you ever would have been in at home."

"It doesn't matter, at least I'm not alone." She grinned.

"What's so funny?"

"I knew you'd come and get me as soon as you could, I just can't believe you turned up with the army." They both chuckled.

"Don't worry, man," added Zeus, who had been quietly listening in on the couple's conversation. "Anyone who tries to harm this little beauty while I'm around is gonna get a visit from the hurt fairy."

"Thanks, Zeus." Evans frowned. "I think."

Miller had strapped himself into the command seat, which was set back between Deacon's and Frost's control chairs in the drive room.

"General Savage is on the line, sir."

"Patch him through."

"Miller, the local intelligence network shows that the enemy vehicles are trying to secure the west side of the city. That entire area is full of automated construction yards and other industrial buildings."

"Are those construction yards capable of creating military technology?"

"They're top-of-the-range, Miller, they'll build pretty much anything they're programmed to build, and the raw material stores of the yards are reported to be just about full."

"We have to secure or destroy those buildings, General."

"Negative. I've been ordered to preserve the construction yards to aid in the war effort."

"Very well, but I can have our command carrier's arsenal trained on this area within five minutes if you need it."

"Nice to know, Sergeant, get ready, we're touching down."

The Alliance drop-ship landed with a jolt. The large exit ramp opened and under a cloud of burning rubber from the wheels the APC quickly backed out. After a tyre-screeching one hundred and eighty degree turn, Frost hit the power and the team rapidly and noisily accelerated away.

"Miller to Savage, I'm heading towards the west side of the city. With a little luck I can find out what the state of play is before I'm noticed."

"Copy that Miller, we're right behind you. Good hunting, Sergeant."

"And you, General, Miller out."

Suddenly the personnel carrier's auto-drive system kicked in and the bulky machine turned towards the buildings on the side of the road.

"Frost, what the fuck. . ." Miller's question was cut short as the APC smashed through the front of the building, rocking him violently in his seat. "Frost, what the hell are you doing?"

"It's not me, sir, the auto-drive system's kicked in."

"Turn it off for god's sake." Another violent shaking of the compartment silenced Miller.

"I can't, sir."

The APC burst back into the open streets through the opposite side of the building. The demolition continued however, as it continued straight through the wall of the adjacent structure across the street.

"The computer's been hacked, sir. Command codes have been re-directed to an outside source."

"Can you get control back or not damn it?"

"No, sir!" shouted Deacon, frantically pushing buttons.

"Move."

Deacon turned to look at Miller. Noticing the plasma pistol in his hand he quickly ducked out of the way of his console. Miller opened fire and under a shower of sparks and blue plasma the console flickered and shut down, sporting a new smouldering and glowing hole.

"That did it, Sarge, I have control back."

"Then for god's sake, stop."

Frost brought the APC to a halt as it smashed through the exterior wall of the building and back into the open air. "Receiving a message from General Savage, Sarge."

"Patch it through."

"Sergeant Miller, come in."

"This is Miller."

"If your vehicle is equipped with an auto-pilot, disconnect it now. Gatekeeper has figured out how to –"

"Yeah, I know," interrupted Miller. "I've just had to blow out a hole in my cockpit to stop this thing."

"Any major system damage?"

"Standby. Well. Deac', how's it look?"

Deacon shook his head. "It's bad, we still have sensors but the weapon system controls are fried."

"Do we have anything left to engage the enemy?"

"Nothing but insults and bad language."

"Fuck me!" Miller slammed his fist into the armrest of his chair. "Miller to Savage, come in."

"What's the prognosis, Miller?"

"The weapons system control unit is fried. It doesn't look like we're gonna be much help until we can get it fixed."

"Sorry to hear that, we're gonna have to continue to the western industrial zone."

"Understood General, good luck."

"Sarge, I'm picking up three large objects moving in from the north-west."

"Identification?"

"Couldn't say, the sensors can't match them to anything on record."

"Can you tell if they've spotted us?"

"They're heading straight for us."

"Frost, get us out of here."

"Yes, sir." Frost powered-up the motors and headed away from the sensor blips that were slowly closing on their position. He changed roads as many times as he could to prevent the pursuers from getting into visual range.

"They're splitting up, trying to flank us." Deacon relayed the positions of the blips on his sensor screen as they slowly but surely closed in.

The Special Forces armoured personnel carrier was one of the only remaining wheeled vehicles used by the US Army. Since the invention of the anti-gravity platform, wheeled vehicles had been deemed as obsolete. However, anti-gravity platforms required tremendous amounts of power and were unsuitable for lengthy operations. As some Special Forces missions involved weeks, even months in the field, the sturdy and reliable APC became standard equipment.

"Vehicle at three o'clock," warned Deacon as they crossed a large intersection. The APC shook as a large explosion narrowly missed its rear end. "Definitely hostile."

Frost struggled to hold the APC steady under the blast from another explosion, this time on their left side. "Jesus that was close. Hold on." In a desperate attempt to avoid further shots, Frost ploughed the APC into the closest building. The sheer bulk of the vehicle made smashing through the bricks and mortar relatively easy.

"Frost, the building on the other side of this one is made from…" Deacon's warning was cut short as a large decelerating jolt racked the APC. The huge machine suddenly dropped several feet and slammed into the floor as the forward-most wheel supports broke loose. It continued to skid along under its own momentum for a few seconds before coming to rest, still in the centre of the buildings. "…alloy," Deacon sarcastically finished his sentence as he climbed out of his seat.

"Ok, everyone up, we have to move now."

Evans was checking over his wife as the squad leapt from their seats.

"Stone, Zeus, I want Devastators and rocket launchers."

"Yes, sir."

"Davidson, Frost, as many plasma grenades and landmines as you can carry."

"No problem."

"Deacon, get the portable communications up-link. Bradley, give him a hand. Guns people! All the guns you can carry!" Miller and the squad quickly grabbed as much equipment as they could carry and hurried into the rear section of the APC. Davidson and Frost began the hover-sled start-up sequences as Miller tried to give his passengers a fighting chance.

"You three, put these on."

"What is it?" questioned Evans as he looked at the small badge-like piece of equipment.

"They're bio-dampeners. They mask all the traceable signals that your body gives off. They'll help hide you from vehicle sensors." The rear hatch of the APC opened as the sleds powered-up.

"Bradley, Evans, get on the sleds."

"What about my wife?"

"She's only small, sir, I don't think the extra weight will be a problem," Frost reassured.

"Fair enough, just go."

"What about the rest of you?"

"We'll meet you one-mile due east of here. Now go."

Evans and his wife climbed aboard Frost's vehicle and with Davidson and Bradley in tow they sped off through the battered building. Miller and the rest of the weapon-laden squad climbed down from the battered APC and started looking for another way out.

"Over here." Stone directed the squad's attention to a small hole in one of the walls. One by one they started to squeeze through the gap. As they did, the sound of squealing tank tracks grew closer and closer, then suddenly stopped. Miller slowly turned and looked through the gaping hole left by the APC's entry into the building. The turret of a large battle tank loomed over the entrance. It slowly moved until it was pointing straight towards him, then fired.

CHAPTER 11

<u>One-mile due east</u>

The battle in the city's western industrial zone had been raging for almost twenty-six hours now. Over a day and still the sound of distant weapons fire showed no sign of easing. Every so often the sound of terrified screaming could be heard as the patrolling mechanised battle tanks found another cluster of hiding civilians. The machines swept through the all but deserted city in a spiralling search pattern that grew ever wider, guaranteeing that they would cover every inch of the streets in their quest for extermination. When they reached areas too small for them to explore with their massive bulk, the tanks released hordes of blade covered metallic nightmares designed to hunt down any human hiding in the dark. No matter where people hid, no matter which streets or buildings were chosen as sanctuaries, the machines would find them, and the squad knew it.

"Ok Davidson, here it comes."

"Are you sure about this, Frost?"

"Yes, they can't be totally shielded on their undersides or their tracks wouldn't touch the floor. Trust me this will work."

"It'll be hitting the landmines in about ten seconds, are you in position?"

"Yeah, I'm ready. Now keep your damn voice down."

"Come on baby, just a little closer."

Frost and Davidson ducked as an exploding landmine sent dirt and pieces of twisted metal hurtling in all directions.

"Booyah! Score one for the home team," Zeus shouted in delight.

"Told you it would work."

"Damn that felt good. Are you reading any more of those fucking things?"

"I got two more heading this way. We'd better fall back." The pair stealthily retreated back into the battered building behind them and headed up to the roof.

"Well done," congratulated Evans, who had been watching with his wife and Bradley from the rooftops.

"Won't that explosion bring more tanks this way?" questioned Jayne nervously.

"Don't worry, ma'am, we have this whole area rigged with explosives. Nothing's getting through here unless it comes through in pieces." Davidson tapped the bio-dampener on his arm. "Just make sure this stays on you and active, and they can't track us on sensors."

Frost stood looking at the personal sensor panel on his left forearm. "Davidson, the other two tanks are gonna be here in about two minutes. The sneaky bastards are splitting up and coming in from two different sides."

"Where?"

"One's coming in down the main carriageway, the other should be coming in past the shopping precinct. Both routes are rigged, we shouldn't have a problem."

"Confirmation of the tank on the carriageway. It's heading in fast."

"Ok, Evans, be careful not to take those binoculars out of the shade. The sun reflecting off the lenses would give away our position."

"This isn't my first rodeo, brother."

The group's attention was drawn to a large explosion, somewhere off the other side of the rooftop. Bradley ran over and took a look through his binoculars, being careful to keep the lenses out of direct sunlight with his jacket.

"Well?" questioned Frost impatiently.

"Nothing but a smouldering hole in the floor. I think we got it."

Frost took a look at his sensor screen. "Yeah, it's gone."

Another large explosion drew the group's attention back to the tank on the carriageway.

"Did we get it, Evans?"

"I'm not sure."

"What do you mean you're not sure?"

"Here, take a look."

Davidson climbed under the fallen concrete slab that Evans was using as a vantage point and looked through the binoculars. The tank was sitting motionless in the middle of the carriageway with several pieces of its equipment and armour plating surrounding it. The only sign that the vehicle was still functioning at all was an orange aura that surrounded it, flickering like a faulty light-bulb.

"It could still pose a threat."

"Should I take a sled and check it out?"

"No, there's no point giving away our position for one tank. Besides if it's still in one piece it could still be full of those fucking blade spider things. And fuck those things! We'll give the Sarge one more hour, then we'll get moving."

"What if he doesn't show?"

Davidson moved closer to Frost so that the others wouldn't hear him. "We've been waiting here for over a day. If they were able to get here, they would have been here by now."

"What are you saying?"

"You know exactly what I'm saying, Frost."

Frost suddenly looked troubled. "We should break radio silence, try to contact them."

"We can't and you know it. Even the short-range coms are a risk."

"So, what if we're detected. We can outrun these things."

"We can't outrun their energy weapons. Or their hunters. I don't like it any more than you do but you know it makes sense."

The group's attention was drawn to the sleds as their consoles started to make a beeping sound.

"What is it, Frost?"

"An update from Hunter."

"What does it say?"

"Hold on, the translation matrix is still decoding it." The look on Frost's face became more and more troubled as he read through the message on the vehicle's monitor screen. Suddenly his legs gave out from under him and he fell to his knees. He sat motionless with his head down and whispered one single word. "No."

Davidson walked over and started to read the message. The same discomforted look spread across his face as he ingested the passages on the screen.

"What is it?" questioned Bradley in an uneasy tone.

"The States are gone."

"Three hours ago, the entire US nuclear stockpile launched by itself. Russia, China and the whole of North America have been obliterated."

Davidson sat down on the sled beside Frost and stared out into nothingness. "There's nothing left."

Bradley and Jayne walked over to the edge of the roof where Evans was sitting. Jayne sat down and Bradley placed his hand on his shoulder.

"How you doing?"

"My god, Bradley, what have we done?"

"It's not your fault," reassured Jayne.

"Yes. Yes, it is."

"It doesn't make any sense. Nuking continents will kill everything, not just humans. The radiation from those missiles will stop life returning to those continents for years. It's totally against the system's programming to do that."

"Actually, it makes perfect sense."

Everyone turned and looked at Davidson, awaiting any kind of explanation for this madness. "The only two American military sites that survived the orbital attack from the defence platforms, were Fort Thomas and a missile base in the Rocky Mountains. The missile base was supposed to be a closely guarded secret, so we assumed that it was missed because Gatekeeper didn't know it was there." Davidson stood up and walked around as he continued his explanation,

"That complex was constructed to build and house a new type of nuke. The basic warhead and missile housing was the same but the missile also carried something called E24. A bio-engineered chemical that's capable of neutralising radiation."

"How fast?"

"With enough of this stuff accompanying a warhead, the radiation emitted can be neutralised before it even hits the ground. It basically renders fallout a thing of the past."

"Jesus."

"I know."

"What's to stop it nuking the rest of us?"

"It can't nuke the whole planet," interrupted Evans. "Only a small percentage of the surface can be hit at any one time without kick-starting a nuclear winter from the clouds of debris. Besides, its programming won't allow it to wipe out any species entirely. It has to allow for the re-population of the plant and animal life after it's finished."

"If that's true, how can it be trying to wipe us out?"

"I'm not sure."

"The only way it could possibly kill us is if it didn't consider us as plant or animal life," Bradley offered.

"Quite possibly."

"What the hell are you talking about?" shouted Frost angrily. "Any idiot can see that we're a life form."

"Yes, but it's not programmed to protect all forms of life."

Frost gave a confused frown. "I don't understand."

"Gatekeeper was basically told to find ways of destroying certain forms of life as part of its primary objective. Unnecessary, destructive forms of life such as the AIDs virus and malaria for instance."

"So, you're saying that it considers us a virus?" questioned Davidson, seeming a little offended by the accusation.

"It would explain why it's attacking us."

"That's bullshit."

"Is it?" Evans paused to consider the best way of expressing his response. "Define a virus."

"What?"

"Define a virus."

Davidson stood quietly for a few seconds looking thoughtful. "A life form that uses other life forms to survive."

"Yes, a life form that infests something and feeds on it, using it to survive no matter the cost. An infestation that breeds and spreads exponentially, until the sheer scale of its infestation starts to damage or even kill the thing it inhabits. Do you agree with that definition?"

Davidson nodded. "Yes, that sounds about right."

Evans sat and stared at the soldier, wearing an intensely serious look. "Now, consider the earth as the thing that we are inhabiting... ...then define mankind."

The group's conversation was stopped as the distant explosions from the western industrial zone ceased. Evans, Bradley and Jayne stared nervously at the soldiers. The battle for control of the construction yards was over, but who had won? Jayne jumped as Frost's forearm sensor-pad started to beep.

"We got incoming. From the North-West. Airborne. Three small objects, approaching at speed." Frost looked up at Davidson. "They could be missiles."

Davidson ran across the rooftop and jumped on his sled, frantically trying to get it started.

"No time man, they're almost here!" Frost shouted at Davidson as he and the others ran past. Davidson continued to fiddle with the vehicle. "They'll be here in seven seconds damn it, get inside."

Davidson gave out a frustrated roar as he abandoned their only mode of transport and sprinted towards the stairwell door. Frost counted down the seconds till impact, "Four, three, two…"

Davidson dove through the door at the last second. He rolled uncontrollably down the metal stairs as the objects rocketed overhead. He gave out a sigh of relief at the total lack of explosions involved.

"They're some kind of aircraft," explained Frost as he watched the speeding objects fly off into the distance.

"Aircraft? You fucking asshole."

Frost turned at this remark and looked down the stairs. Davidson was laid on his back in a heap on the first landing of the stairwell. At least ten steps down.

"Err, sorry." Frost's quivering lip betrayed his insincerity as he desperately tried not to laugh. "Wait a minute." Frost's expression turned to one of concern. His lack of concentration had caused him to miss another movement confirmation on his forearm sensor pad.

"Multiple targets, several of them heading this way."

"From the industrial zone?"

"No, their course heading suggests that they came from the direction of the Alps."

"What's their E.T.A?"

"Estimated time of arrival for the leading objects is two minutes."

"Can you identify them?"

"Not yet." Frost grabbed Bradley's jacket as he tried to walk out onto the roof for a look. "Stay in here."

"What about the equipment?"

Frost gestured to Davidson and the soldiers ran out of the stairwell and across the roof.

"No, get the water and the food supplies," corrected Frost as Davidson headed straight for the last of the landmines.

"What? Are you crazy? We're screwed without these things."

"We're screwed if we run out of water." Frost pointed to a number of dead bodies laid out in the streets ten stories below. "We can avoid the tanks; we can't avoid the virus if we run out of bottled water."

"We can take the sleds."

"Think about it man, their energy signatures will light us up like a beacon now that the battle's over. Every enemy vehicle in the city will know where we are the second we twist the throttle."

Davidson grunted and picked up a backpack full of supplies.

"I'll get the supplies," offered Evans who had left the relative safety of the stairwell and walked over to lend a hand.

"God damn it, I told you to stay inside." Davidson passed Evans the bag full of landmines and patted him on the back as he walked past towards the stairwell door. "Come on, they'll be here any minute."

Frost and Evans hurried back into the doorway and turned to watch the skies. Several small aircraft sped silently overhead at incredible speed, as they did so Evans warned his wife to cover her ears. She jumped in fright as a deafening noise exploded from nothing all around them, shaking the building beneath their feet.

"They're firing at us!" she screamed.

"Calm down," snapped Evans as he stopped her from running down the stairs. "Calm down, they're not firing at us. That blast is called a sonic boom, it happens when an aircraft is travelling faster than sound."

"They looked like our boys to me," stated Davidson, an obvious air of relief in his tone.

"Not quite," responded Frost as he pushed buttons on his arm pad.

"What do you mean?"

"They were American fighters alright but I didn't detect any life form readings from them."

"Aren't most military aircraft equipped with sensor jamming equipment?"

"I know what you're thinking, Bradley, but this sensor pad is equipped with the codes to neutralise American jamming signals." Frost continued to push buttons on the pad. "Hmm, that would explain it."

"What?"

"All of those jets are missing their ejection-pods." Frost looked at Davidson, "They're being remotely piloted."

"The sneaky bastard must have broken the codes for the remote piloting systems."

"Yeah, probably at the same time as the APC. I wonder how many vehicles it managed to take."

"The crews of any affected ground vehicles could simply smash their auto-navigation computers like we did on the APC," Davidson sighed as he considered the problem further. "Now aircraft, that's a different story. Ejection-pods separate from a ship in something like two-thirds of a second, there's no way any pilot could react fast enough to stop it."

"So, what you're saying is that Gatekeeper could potentially control every aircraft in the area?"

"Worse," interrupted Evans. "We gave the damn thing access to just about every communication up-link that exists. With the exception of certain military frequencies."

Frost looked at Evans, defiantly shaking his head in anticipation of his next sentence.

"Gatekeeper could potentially control every ship in the world that's capable of being remotely piloted." The group covered their ears again as another wave of aircraft shot overhead. Dust fell from the shaking support beams of the ceiling as the sonic boom hit.

"Five more. Two fighters and three British drop-ships, all without pilots."

"This is a fucking nightmare." Davidson rubbed his head and sat down on one of the steps.

"How many aircraft can be remotely piloted?" questioned Jayne nervously.

"About eighty percent."

"Jesus Christ." Bradley sat down beside Davidson and stared blankly down the stairs.

"Definitely every military ship that exists. Plus, probably thirty, forty percent of commercial aircraft and starships."

"Be quiet." The conversation stopped as Frost turned towards the door. "Davidson, can you hear that?"

"Yeah, it sounds like an anti-gravity engine."

"I'm not reading it on the sensors. It must be coming in low behind the buildings."

"It sounds like a hover tank, maybe the Allies won the battle." Davidson stood up and followed Frost out onto the roof.

"Sounds close. Somewhere in the street below us."

Evans, Bradley and Jayne joined the soldiers out on the rooftop.

"What is it?"

"Shut up!" snapped Frost. "Listen."

"It's getting closer."

"It's not that close, it's too quiet."

The group watched as a small metallic object slowly ascended into view over the side of the building. Measuring about two metres in diameter the machine resembled a large rugby ball, hovering on its end in the sky. Except for one counter-sunk pit in its centre, the object was totally smooth and reflected the scenery around it in its shiny surface.

"Don't move," whispered Davidson. The machine quickly turned towards the sound of his voice. As the group silently and motionlessly watched, the sound of another humming anti-gravity engine could be heard approaching. The machine quickly turned its attention to Jayne as she took a step back in panic. The deep pit in its centre began to glow and the machine backed away, further from the rooftop. Under a shower of sparks and dispersing blue plasma, the machine fell from the sky and out of view behind the edge of the rooftop. After checking themselves for holes the confused group turned to Frost and Davidson, who stood casually behind their smoking rifle barrels.

"What..." The marines spun quickly around as another machine rose up the building-side behind them. They quickly took aim and fired. Two speeding, blue plasma bolts smashed into the adjacent building across the street as the object quickly dodged to one side.

"Shit."

"Run." The soldiers ran backwards still firing at the object as they followed the civilians through the roof access door. With a great release of energy, the machine fired, sending the entire upper section of the stairwell and all surrounding walls flying explosively in all directions.

"Go! Go! Go!" shouted Frost as the group ran down the stairwell towards the street, ten floors below. Another explosion sent a hail of debris crashing down around the group from the battered floors above.

"Take the next door into the building." The group exited the stairwell as a section of the roof collapsed and bounced down the shaft, taking large sections of the bolted metal stairway with it. The shape of their fast-moving pursuer almost immediately filled the window beside the group.

"Don't stop, keep moving." Frost slammed into the back wall of the room as the windows blew out, under the force of another assault. The machine quickly disappeared out of sight as Davidson opened fire to cover his team-mate.

"Come on damn it!" he shouted as he dragged Frost to his feet. The soldiers continued to run through the corridors and offices of the building in the direction of the still moving civilians. All the while the pursuing machine continued to lay down fire in their direction. Frost noticed as he ran that the lighting above his head in this section of the building was still working, which gave him a terrible idea.

"Quick, into the lift."

"The lift, but..."

"I know, I know."

The group rushed into the large cylindrical lift and the doors slowly closed behind them. The lift shook violently as it descended through the relentless onslaught towards the ground. Suddenly it began to fall as a shot from the machine's energy weapon severed the cables. The sound of the screeching emergency brakes was second only to Jayne's screams as the lift crashed into the floor of the ground level.

"Is everyone ok?"

"Fuck you, Frost."

"I'll take that as a yes, what about you three?"

"We'll be ok."

"Davidson, help me with these doors." The pair pulled at the now buckled doors as hard as they could but they would not budge.

"Stand back."

The lift door surrendered to the force of Davidson's plasma rifle. After only a few carefully placed shots and a big kick, there was now a smouldering circular hole in the two-inch thick metal alloy doors, allowing the team to carefully squeeze out between its glowing hot edges.

"How the hell is this thing tracking us, I thought these armbands masked our bio-signs?"

"They just block our life form readings from sensors. The damn thing can still see us."

"Frost!" Davidson shouted as the machine descended into view in front of the building's main entrance. Frost turned just in time to see the glowing energy build-up from its priming weapon. "Get down!" he screamed.

The ceiling of the large reception area collapsed as the machine fired a shot through the door. Darkness and disorientation gripped Frost as the entire area filled with thick dust from the shattered structure. It suddenly became very hard to breath.

"Frost, Frost, where are you?" shouted Davidson as he struggled to work out which way he was facing. In the distance through the rumbling of the still falling rubble, he could hear the weapon of the machine as it began to charge. He quickly made his way towards the sound, stumbling on the scattered rubble as he tried to get a clear view of his target. As he finally reached the clear air of the main entrance, a screaming Frost ran past him carrying what appeared to be an emergency fire axe. He ran unwaveringly at the machine and as it turned to intercept this unexpected onslaught from the murk, he swung the axe as hard as he could and jammed it into the attacker's side.

"Fucking die!" he screamed, spitting with rage as he shouted. The machine made a loud crackling sound before dropping from the air and rolling to a silent halt.

Davidson, looking rather shocked, lowered his rifle and slowly turned to look at Frost.

Frost just raised an eyebrow and shrugged his shoulders. "I lost my rifle in the blast. I was improvising."

Davidson nodded approvingly. "Fair enough." The pair walked calmly back into the building. The dust was starting to settle now and they could just about make out the floor of the room.

"Where are you guys? Hey, Evans, Bradley, Jayne."

"Help!" A shaking hand rose from beneath a pile of rubble across the room.

Davidson ran over to lend a hand. "Damn, Bradley, are you ok, man?"

"How is he?"

"Not sure. He passed out."

"That's probably a good thing. He doesn't want to see this."

Davidson turned and looked at Frost. "Both of them?"

Frost nodded.

"Fuck. Now we're really screwed." The pair suddenly noticed the distant humming of another anti-gravity engine.

"Ah shit. Come on, we'd better get outta here." The pair both grabbed one of Bradley's arms and quickly dragged him out of the building.

"How close is it?"

Frost looked at his armband. "Close. We need to find cover fast." The soldiers dragged Bradley out of the building and headed as fast as they could down the street.

"Over there, in the apartment complex." Frost tried the keypad on the large metal door of the building. "Amazing, there's a fucking mass evacuation to escape the killer robots, and the bastards still manage to find time to lock their doors." Frost took out his knife and pried the keypad off the wall.

"Frost."

"Just a minute, there's not a door in the world I can't hotwire."

"Tell that to them."

Frost looked up at the two rugby-ball shaped machines that were speeding towards them along the street.

"Shit."

"Come on."

"Shit, shit, shit."

"Hurry up."

"I know, I know."

"Damn it." Davidson picked up his plasma rifle and walked out into the middle of the street. He took aim at the closest machine and began to fire.

"Hold 'em off for a few more seconds."

"A few more seconds and they'll be close enough to spit on us."

Strafing from left to right across each other's paths the drones dodged his plasma bolts with relative ease. Closer and closer they drew, speeding straight towards him, their now glowing energy weapon pits signalling their readiness to fire.

Davidson couldn't help wondering how painful the next few moments were going to be. His attempts to hit the fast-moving machines were futile at this range and he knew it. Maybe he would have a better chance of hitting them if he waited awhile. Maybe they would have a harder time dodging his shots at close range. Maybe he should have picked up more power cells from the rooftop instead of rations. "Oh shit, Frost, I'm out of ammo, throw me another power cell."

"I don't have the power cells, they're in the bag with the landmines."

"Oh, fucking beautiful. Evans was carrying the landmines."

"Fucking priceless." The pair jumped and fixed their attention on the middle of the road as the lead machine exploded.

"What the..." As the second machine altered direction to avoid the force of the blast, it too exploded. The pair stood silently wearing frowns of confusion as they watched pieces of the machines raining down to the ground. Walking down the street behind the blast, clutching their smoking Devastator cannons were the large shadowed forms of Zeus and Stone. Frost shook his head and began to laugh.

"Now that's what I call timing!" Davidson shouted as the pair approached. "We thought you were dead."

"Nah, just got detained slightly."

"Slightly, you guys should have been here hours ago. Where the hell have you been, and where's Deacon and the Sarge?"

"We've been pinned down in the sewers, trying to avoid the tanks. I guess we got a little lost. We found a small ore freighter at the ship yards near the docks a few miles from here. It looks like it was left behind in the evacuation because of engine damage. The Sarge and Deac' are working on it now. It isn't much but maybe it can get us up to the Hunter." Zeus looked around. "Where are the other two?"

Davidson shook his head. "They didn't make it."

Zeus sighed and nodded that he understood.

"One of those fucking hovering things chased us through a building down the street. The roof collapsed on Evans and his wife. Bradley isn't gonna last much longer if we don't get him out of here."

Zeus stood silent for a moment. "The Sarge isn't gonna like this. Come on, we'd better get going."

Back at the freighter, Miller and Deacon had finished the repairs and were attempting to disarm a large docking clamp.

"I can't crack the security code on this thing. We're gonna have to do it the hard way."

"Fair enough, Deac', keep out of the way." Miller removed two plasma grenades from one of the many bags they had brought with them. After removing the safety covers on the tops of the grenades, he pushed the small red buttons, placed them under the docking clamp and retreated at speed. The clamp blew into several pieces as the grenades went off, sending large pieces of metal bouncing noisily across the concrete floor of the ship yard. Miller stepped back as the ship's forward landing strut, which had been attached to the security clamp, groaned and collapsed. He winced as the nose of the vessel slammed heavily and noisily into the floor.

"Maybe one grenade next time, Sarge."

"Kiss my ass, Deac'."

Deacon grinned as he climbed in through the now slanting door of the ship.

"Any fresh damage?"

"No, I don't think so, Sarge. All systems seem to be operating within tolerances." Deacon stuck his head back around the door. "Except for the landing gear."

Miller took a second look at the ship's new position. "Take-off should be interesting." He raised an eyebrow and grimaced again.

"At least it's only a tractor unit," offered Deacon. "If it had still been coupled to a freight container, that would have been significantly louder."

Miller quickly fixed his attention on his forearm sensor pad as it began to beep. Several small yellow circles on the pad's screen were slowly moving towards their position. He turned himself to face in the direction of the incoming objects, attempting to work out where they were in relation to the surrounding structures. "You'd better get out here."

Deacon quickly jumped down from inside the ship. "What is it?"

"I got movement, somewhere behind that scraper."

"Could it be our guys?"

"Quite possibly. Whatever they are, they're moving slowly and keeping close to cover. Get behind something."

The pair picked up their plasma rifles and quickly moved off. Deacon took cover behind the fallen front end of the ship and Miller crouched himself behind a stack of metal crates. Deacon lay on his belly and watched the adjacent building-line from under the ship's hull, his rifle aimed and ready. He nodded at Miller as the objects reached the edge of the building that concealed them. Miller stood up and rested his rifle on the top of the metal crates. Looking through the rifle's scope, he trained the cross-hairs on the edge of the building and waited for a target to present itself.

"Deac' hold your fire!" Miller shouted as Davidson and Stone came into view.

Deacon relaxed his grip on his rifle and stood up. "Have they found the others?"

Miller's answer came in the form of a frowning look as he started to jog over to the returning team. "What the hell happened to him?" Miller questioned pointing to the still unconscious body of Bradley, which was slumped over Zeus' shoulder.

"We were attacked by some kind of small hovering cannons, sir. Bradley was hurt by a collapsing roof." Frost paused for a second. "Evans and his wife didn't –"

"Don't say it, Frost," Miller interrupted. "Don't tell me he's dead or I'm gonna fucking shoot you."

"I'm sorry, sir." Frost hung his head in shame. "I…."

"Sorry!" Miller bellowed. "Fuck me!" He stood silently for a moment and rubbed his eyes, taking long deep breaths as he contemplated their options. "Zeus, put him in the ship."

"Yes, sir."

"Davidson."

"Sarge?"

"Do you think that thing will take off in that position?"

"Shouldn't be a problem, sir."

"Good, prep it for launch."

"Yes, sir."

"Frost."

"Sir?"

"I want a tally on all remaining supplies and equipment."

"Yes, sir.

"The rest of you set up a perimeter, keep your eyes open." Miller walked back over to the freighter and climbed onboard. He opened the large box containing the communications up-link, flicked a couple of switches and with a calming sigh, began to speak. Outside, Deacon and Stone talked as they patrolled the area.

"This mission is fubar, man."

"I hear that. How the hell are we supposed to get into the Gatekeeper installation now?"

"No idea. They'll probably expect us to blast our way in."

"Screw that noise. I didn't sign up for no suicide mission."

"We'll be ok."

"Ok my ass. Did you sleep through the briefing on that place? The lift shaft is two miles long and that's the fucking easy part. After that there's chain cannons and god knows what to get past."

"Not going soft on me are you, Stone?"

"Everybody, listen up!" The conversation was halted by Miller's bellowed order from the freighter's doorway. The squad closed in for the briefing.

"What is it Sarge?"

"We can't get into the Gatekeeper complex without both of the designers. So, unless anyone has a plan to resurrect Mr Evans, this mission is scrubbed."

"It's about fucking time."

"Shut up, Deac', I'm not fucking laughing."

"Aye, sir."

"Why don't we try knocking, Sarge?" offered Zeus as he cocked his Devastator cannon suggestively.

"Zeus, right now we don't have enough ammo to successfully assault a schoolgirl. I've been given clearance to take Bradley directly to the medical centre on the Hunter, we'll replace our equipment and supplies when we're there. Any questions?" Miller paused to allow for a response. "Ok, get everything into the ship, we lift off in ten minutes."

CHAPTER 12

Hunter

The nose of the freighter crashed clumsily into the metal floor, as the docking bay's artificial gravity-field was re-established. After the spinning yellow warning lights, which spanned the walls of the large rectangular bay, ceased to flash, the ship's door slowly hissed open, and Miller stepped out.

"Ok, guys, break's over, get out here and secure me some supplies. Deac', clear it with the load master, he's expecting us."

"Yes, sir."

"Sarge?" Davidson and Frost followed Miller across the bay.

"What is it, Frost?"

"We want to come with you, sir. It's our fault that the mission was compromised, it's not fair that you should take the flack."

Miller nodded. "Thanks, but it's not your fault. When you're under fire shit happens." Miller turned and continued across the bay, pointing out the ship to two medics as they ran towards him.

"But, Sarge."

"Damn it, get over there and help the others. I want everybody fully tooled-up by the time I get back." Miller continued across the bay to its main exit, where two guards stopped him.

"Hold on please, sir, no one can exit the docking bay until they've been scanned for the virus."

"I don't have time for this, Corporal. I have orders to report to the bridge."

One of the guards placed himself in the doorway as Miller tried to exit. "You will comply, sir."

Miller stared at the guard for a moment, then stood down and took a step back.

"Thank you, sir." The guard ran a small cylindrical device up and down Miller's body, creating a rather detailed medical diagram of him on a nearby wall monitor.

"Won't take long now, sir." They all watched the monitor as it ran its search cycle.

After a few seconds a light female voice replied with an answer, "Biological contamination negative. Subject clearance granted."

The guard stepped aside. "Thank you, sir"

"No problem."

The command carriers were the largest vehicles ever built by man. Measuring in at just over two miles in length these mammoth vessels dwarfed even the Dreadnought class mining ships. The weight of the vessels easily exceeded several hundred million tons and as a result they were totally space-bound, incapable of atmospheric flight. Equipped with a crystalline reactor and many hydroponics bays for onboard food growth, the command carriers were capable of actively sustaining themselves and their crews for years at a time. The ships were also equipped with a record-breaking amount of cryogenic stasis chambers to enable them to carry large amounts of troops into deep space.

"Captain Shepherd, sir, a Sergeant Miller is here to see you."

"Send him in."

Miller walked into the captain's ready-room and saluted. "Sergeant Miller of the Arch Angels reporting, Captain."

The captain was stood staring out into space through a large porthole. He answered without turning around, "Sit down, Miller."

Miller sat quietly awaiting some sort of response.

"You realise how many men are going to die trying to force their way into that complex."

"Sir, I request permission to handle that personally. The designers have already briefed my team on the complex's security systems and –"

"I've already sent a team in," the captain interrupted. "In fact, they should be arriving in a few minutes."

"What about my team, Captain?"

"I'm sending you back to Grenoble. The western industrial zone has fallen to the Gatekeeper's forces and we can't afford to let them keep control of those construction yards. I don't have the troops to rally for another large-scale attack right now, and neither can the Alliance. We're engaged elsewhere. I need you to use your talents to sneak in and level the place."

"Just give me access to a ship and point me towards the armoury." Miller paused for a second. "Thank you for the second chance, sir"

The captain sighed, "I've been kept up to speed on your movements over the last few days Miller. Personally, considering what you've been up against, I think you've done one hell of a job. The fact that you managed to keep any of your team alive against those odds is exceptional. Many other squadrons have fallen under far more favourable circumstances."

"Thank you, Captain. That means a lot."

"Your re-entry window is in three hours, make sure you're ready. Dismissed, Sergeant."

Miller stood up and headed towards the door. As it hissed open, he stopped and turned back towards the captain, who was once again staring out through the porthole. "Sir?"

"Yes, Miller?"

"There really was nothing we could do. I hope your team manage to infiltrate that bunker without too many losses, sir."

"I know, Sergeant. So do I."

Miller steadied himself on the doorframe as the ship suddenly shook.

"Shepherd to bridge, report."

"We've lost helm control, sir, the ship..." the voice through the communications system turned into static as the transmission was cut off.

"Shepherd to bridge, say again. Come in bridge." The captain looked at Miller.

"What is it?"

"I don't know." Captain Shepherd grabbed his desk as the shaking intensified. "It feels like we're descending."

"Can this ship be remotely piloted?"

"There's no way Gatekeeper could crack the command codes for this ship, the system is state of the art."

"Even for a super-computer?"

The look on the captain's face was one of uncertainty. "Get your team ready, you might be leaving sooner than planned."

Miller nodded and headed out of the door as Shepherd hurried to the bridge of his ship.

Crewmen were running frantically from console to console when he entered.

"Report."

"Helm control is not responding, Captain. The navigational computer has started a descent towards the planet."

"Bypass it."

"Already tried, sir, the engineering stations won't respond either."

"Shepherd to engineering, engineering come in."

"The communications system is offline too, sir."

"God damn it. You there, get down to engineering and shut down the navigational computer. By whatever means necessary."

"It can't be shut down, sir, the safety overrides won't –"

"Find a way."

"But, Captain?"

"Shoot the fucking thing if you have to."

"Aye, sir."

"Helm, do we have anything?"

"I still have control of the emergency thrusters, sir, but they aren't helping."

Miller tore back through the door of the docking bay and ran over to the badly leaning freighter. "Davidson, Deac', get the ship prepped, this thing could be going down."

Deacon looked gobsmacked. "What, again, what is it with these things?"

Suddenly the warning sirens in the bay sounded and the yellow lights began to flash. "Warning, warning," came the echoing female voice of the computer as the communication system came back online. "All hands to battle stations."

"Helm, full thrust on all engines, maximum power," ordered Shepherd

"Aye, Captain, all engines full ahead."

"Engineering, come in."

"Engineering, here."

"Finally! I need all emergency power diverting to the engines."

"Way ahead of you, sir, the engines are already at one hundred and ten percent of safety limits."

"Increase it to a hundred and twenty percent."

"But, sir."

"Now damn it."

Miller and the squad hastily walked back out of the freighter ship behind Davidson. The sergeant grilled his pilot as they headed for the docking bays exit door. The floor of the bay was now vibrating noticeably. "What the hell do you mean we can't leave?"

"You're right, Sarge, it's going down. But we're already too deep into the atmosphere." Davidson pointed at one of the windows, which glowed bright yellow from the heat and friction of the re-entry.

"So?"

"Anything trying to leave this ship under re-entry conditions, without a calculated entry vector, would be toast in about two-thirds of a second. I couldn't get us out of here in the Black Hawk now, let alone that fucking junker."

"But –"

"Trust me, sir."

"Sarge, what's the plan?"

"Find an escape-pod?" Miller shrugged, showing how ridiculous he was beginning to find his options.

"Same result, sir."

"God damn it, Davidson!" The group all stopped walking. The vibration in the deck still increasing in ferocity. Miller looked around. "I'm open to suggestions." The squad's attention was drawn to the Hunter's communications system as Captain Shepherd's voice began to echo through the ship.

"All hands abandon ship. Repeat, all hands abandon ship."

"Again!" Deacon shouted. "Davidson, where's the best place to go on a crashing command carrier?"

"How the fuck would I know, Deacon?"

"You're a pilot," replied Deacon as he grabbed Davidson by the shoulders.

"I'm a pilot, not a fucking tour guide."

While the squad argued, Frost typed away on the keyboard of a wall monitor beside them. "What about this?" The squad looked at the internal map that now filled the monitor's screen.

"What is it?"

"A hell of a lot of Cryo-Stasis chambers."

"Jesus, there must be a hundred of them in there."

"One hundred and fifty to be exact," informed Frost as he looked over at Miller. "All equipped with independent inertial dampening systems. Only two corridors over."

"Frost, you're a fucking genius. Which way?"

Back on the bridge the crew's composure was starting to break.

"Where do you think you're going, crewman? Get back to your station. You're bridge crew, we stay till everyone else is safe."

"Hull stress has exceeded tolerance, Captain. Bulkheads on decks twelve through twenty-two are starting to buckle."

"Hull breach detected in cargo bay two, sealing section now."

"Engineering to bridge, the engines aren't gonna last much longer at this output level."

"Keep those engines burning or we're all dead."

"Descending through upper atmosphere. We're in free fall, sir.

"We're gonna die!"

"Get him outta here. Helm, level off our descent as much as possible, target sector seven for crash landing."

"Please confirm, sir, sector seven reads as the Atlantic Ocean."

"I know where sector seven is damn it."

"Aye, sir."

"Sir, at this speed –"

"I know. We need to level off. Give me everything you can from the bow thrusters. We need to get the nose up."

"Aye, sir. Bow thrusters to maximum."

"Burn them till they melt. Do not let off."

"It's working, Captain, our pitch is starting to change."

"Sir, we could create more drag if we open all the underside bays."

"Good thinking, son. You heard him, open all the doors on our belly. Be ready to compensate for shear."

"Aye, sir."

"Ten seconds till impact, Captain."

"What's our angle of descent?"

"Forty-three degrees, Captain."

"Not good enough, our angle needs to be shallower. Engineering, all power to bow thrusters, now."

"Hail Mary, full of grace…"

"All hands, brace for impact."

The cloud layers parted as the Hunter hurtled toward the ground. The massive ship cast an immense shadow across the waters beneath it. A darkness that heralded its calamitous and inevitable fate. As it descended, it slowly altered its angle of decent, still glowing from the friction induced heat of its poorly controlled angle of entry into the atmosphere. The carrier streaked across the sky like the harbinger of doom itself as it did its best to level out of its fall into more horizontal flight before it hit the ocean. The burning underbelly of the behemoth, friction scorched, with melting thruster assemblies still raging, suddenly lost its fire-like glow as it met the water. The sound was deafening, like some biblical thunder clap. Accompanied by an impact wave that fired out from all sides of the vessel as it tore through the waters. Sections of the ship simply exploded into debris under the force of the impact, and for a moment all was chaos. Noise and light and tsunami level seas and metal raining from a smoke-filled sky and then…silence. Peace returned as the ocean claimed the biggest ship it had ever claimed. As it dragged it to its indifferent depths.

Miller climbed out of the cryo-chamber and lowered himself down onto the now sloping floor of the room. Zeus and Stone were already up and were attempting to open the room's large and only door.

"Everybody ok?"

"Yeah, nice call, Frost, didn't feel a thing."

"Inertial dampening fields, the best thing since the invention of airbags."

"Nine thousand points to the inventor of stasis pods."

"The door's jammed, Sarge. Looks like something's hit it from the outside, twisting it into the bulkhead."

"Can you move it, Zeus?"

"Not a chance. Maybe if I had my rifle, I could blast us out, but this thing ain't going anywhere." Zeus shook his head.

"Great."

"Sarge?"

Miller turned.

"The air vents aren't working."

Miller sighed, "Better by the minute."

"Guys, listen a minute." The squad fell silent. "Do you hear that?" A barely audible tapping sound could be heard through the floor of the room.

"Someone's down there."

"Shut up a minute."

"What are they saying, Deac'?"

"Nothing." Deacon shook his head. "It's just tapping."

"Well, someone's obviously down there."

"Where the hell are we?"

"I think we're back on the ground."

"Deac', see if that wall monitor still works."

"Yes, sir."

"We can't be on the ground. There's no way this ship would still be in one piece if we'd hit."

"How do you know it is in one piece? There could be a field on the other side of that door."

"Nah, the Captain must have managed to escape the planet's gravity."

"Then how do you explain the fun-house floor?"

"Maybe the Artificial Gravity generator is damaged."

"Bullshit, this is real gravity, can't you tell the difference?"

"He's right."

The squad turned to Deacon, who was sitting on the floor in front of the wall monitor shaking his head.

"What is it, Deac'?"

"Take a look."

Miller walked over and looked at the screen. "Shit on me!"

"What is it, Sarge?"

Miller stepped back to allow the squad a look at the screen. "We're under water," he explained. "Over three hundred feet down, if this information is correct. Shepherd must have put us down into the ocean." Miller stood for a few seconds in the silence that followed and stared at the floor. "This is some bullshit!"

"What about the ship? It should be in one piece, right? The water would have made for a soft landing, right? Davidson?"

Davidson shook his head. "I don't know, Stone. I really don't know."

"Deac', can you find out what state the ship's in?"

"Already tried, my man. I can't get a damn thing."

"Can you tell us where we went down, send a distress call or something."

"No, this monitor is jammed on the external sensors. It won't show you anything you can't see now. All I can tell you is what you already know. Unless you'd like to know the pressure at this depth."

"We're screwed, man."

"He's right, game over."

"Stow that shit!" snapped Miller. "We're not dead yet. We know there's at least one person still alive out there, and on a ship this size there are bound to be more. This thing is the size of a small moon for god's sake. We'll signal through the hull like our friend down there until someone hears us."

"All due respect, Sarge, but I don't think that's gonna work."

"What do you mean, Davidson?"

"Well, this is a big room, sir and that'll work in our favour. Trouble is, with the ventilation system not working we're gonna be running out of air real soon."

"Any idea how soon?"

"I'd say a day, tops."

"Jesus, Sarge, it could take a week to get us outta here. We don't even know if anyone's close enough to hear us."

"There's at least one person close enough, if we can hear him tapping then he can hear us."

"He's trapped too, why else would he be banging on the hull."

Miller quietly paced back and forth while the squad bickered, trying to think of a logical solution to their problem. "We get back in the pods."

Everyone stopped talking and looked at Miller. "They still have power. The lights are still on in here. Clearly the reactor is still working," Miller looked around the faces of his men. "We rig some kind of makeshift distress beacon and we get back in the pods until someone comes and saves our asses."

After a long silence Frost spoke, "What if the rest of the crew are dead, Sarge? What if there are no rescue teams coming?"

"If anyone has a better idea I'm listening."

The squad remained silent.

"Then it's agreed. Prep the pods. Deacon, Frost, we're going to need a distress beacon." Miller gestured around the cavernous chamber with all its high tec stasis pods. "Plenty of parts to choose from."

CHAPTER 13
Revenant

The humming motors of the cryo-chambers lid woke Miller as it slowly opened. The sensation of awakening from extended Cryo-Stasis was new to him and it took him a few seconds to overcome the unexpected feeling of nausea. As his awareness slowly returned to him, he realised that the room was still in darkness. All except for the strafing beams of light from what appeared to be two torches.

"Who's there?"

"Swan, they're waking up."

He shielded his eyes as one of the torch beams shone directly into his face. "I said who's there?"

"My name's Sykes. How are you feeling?"

"Like hammered shit," Miller replied as he pulled himself out of the stasis pod. He stumbled and held the side of the pod as he unexpectedly struggled to stand. It took him a few moments to steady himself and he stretched his uncooperative legs.

"You've been in deep-freeze for a long time, it'll take your body a while to re-adjust."

"Get that fucking light out of my face," came a barked demand on Miller's right. He looked out into the darkness of the room towards the shouting. It sounded like Deacon, who was now obviously awake and less than impressed by the brightness of Swan's torch, "Who the fuck are you?"

"Deac', stand down."

"That you, Sarge?" Deacon replied, his tone immediately more at ease.

"Yeah, do me a favour and wake the others." Miller turned his attention back to the man in front of him. He was wearing a scraggy, torn pair of overalls and carrying nothing but his torch. The only other piece of equipment on him was a communicator device that was fixed to a band on his left arm. "Well, you're obviously not military. What are you doing here?"

"We're part of a salvage team. We were just checking this room for anything that we could use, you guys are lucky we found you."

"Salvage team?" Miller's look turned to one of confusion.

"Yes, err, Sergeant, was it?"

"That's right. Did anyone else make it? Any of the crew?" he queried.

"I'm sorry, Sergeant. I couldn't tell you what happened to the rest of the crew. I can tell you that you're the only life signs aboard this wreck."

Miller took another look around the darkened room and shook his head. He thought about whoever had been trapped and banging on the hull on the decks beneath them.

"This ship was the last US stronghold. Carrying over five thousand American troops," he sighed. "Now my country is truly dead." He looked at Sykes. "I'm gonna need to speak to someone in your military. I still have orders to carry out. I'm in need of equipment and transport."

Sykes had a very strange look on his face. "Orders?" Sykes repeated.

"What is it?" Miller questioned as the look on Sykes' face filled him with unease. "What did we miss?"

"I don't know how to tell you this, Sergeant, but the war as you know it is over."

"Then we won?"

Sykes shook his head. "We were slaughtered."

"What? But you –"

"With the exception of your team, Sergeant, every human that couldn't escape the planet was killed. Over ninety-nine percent of the population was lost."

Miller sunk back against the stasis pod to steady himself as he ingested the news.

"As far as we can tell, this ship has been down here for almost a hundred years."

Miller's heart imploded in his chest. He stood silently, his eyes betraying his confusion and anguish as he struggled with the news. "A hundred years?" He shook his head. "That's…not…possible."

"I'm sorry, Sergeant. This must be very difficult."

"Difficult?" Miller replied with a slight air of aggression in his voice. "This doesn't make any sense. If the Gatekeeper has control of the planet, how did you get down here?"

The rest of the squad was awake now and attempting to move around, which drew Sykes' attention. He looked over their faces and uniforms with his torch light before returning his gaze to Miller.

"Are all of you soldiers?"

"We're Special Forces. US Marines. Arch Angel squadron."

Sykes smiled and nodded.

"Old Iron-hand is gonna love this!" shouted Swan from across the room.

"Iron-hand?" questioned Miller.

"Iron-hand is what we call our leader. Just a nickname. Look, we'd better get you and your squad back to the sanctuary, Sergeant. I'll fill you in on what you've missed once we're aboard our ship."

Miller nodded.

"Sarge."

"What is it, Frost?"

"Bradley didn't make it, sir."

The squad fell silent for a moment. Miller sighed and looked at Sykes. "Get me out of this tomb please, Mr Sykes."

The squad followed the two men through the twisted and buckled corridors of the command carrier. Miller had a hard time believing his eyes as he looked around. Long corridors of the ship that he had previously walked through now ended abruptly due to their collapsed and crushed bulkheads. Dripping seawater from hairline fractures in the hull had rusted and eroded the walls and floors of the corridors. Small dribbles no greater than those from a leaky tap had over time formed impassable water barriers that filled entire decks of the ship. The salvage crew had obviously spent quite some time cutting doorways and routes through the bulkheads from corridor to corridor in order to reach his team. Miller felt a swell of gratitude for the effort.

After making their way to the outer corridors of the ship, close to the outer hull, they entered a rusty airlock. Through one of the airlock's two small viewing windows, which were positioned at either side of the outer pressure door, Miller could make out what seemed to be a relatively large ship.

"Is that a starship?"

"The Polaris. She's a science vessel."

"What the hell is a starship doing down here?"

"Granted, she's clumsy underwater, but she's rated for the pressure at this depth and she certainly beats swimming."

The airlock's rust-covered outer door squealed open awkwardly. Powered by a large portable battery pack the salvage team must have brought with them. The group walked through the airtight retractable access corridor that led onto the Polaris. The clear air of the ship was welcoming after breathing the old, stale air of the command carrier. Miller was happy to be back under working lighting and not stumbling around following flashlights in the dark.

"So, where is this sanctuary? Let me guess, the lunar shipyards?"

"No, they were destroyed as well."

Miller raised an eyebrow as he tried to think of another place. "Pluto's Duridium mines?"

"No, the sanctuary is much closer than that."

"Then where?"

"You'll see."

Over three hours later the newly informed and updated squad were called out of the mess hall and up to the bridge. Miller looked out through the view port, straining to make out the shapes through the dark murky water. He could see a glow coming from the seabed in front of him. He couldn't tell what it was but it was definitely a light-source. He had been surprised to see a whole starship under water when they had been rescued, instead of a smaller transport. He had been even more surprised when after they had been rescued, the large vessel had not headed for the surface.

"Helm, slow to approach speed," ordered Dillan, the Polaris' captain.

"Aye, sir."

The sandy seabed in view of the ship's lights gave way to a large sea-shelf. The squad gazed in awe as the scattered lights and domes of the sanctuary came into view below them.

"Damn Sykes, you weren't kidding. This place is huge," Stone vocalised his thoughts.

"Size is relative, Mr Stone. Compared to the amount of people it holds, this place is a shoebox."

"You say they built this in under six months?"

"Some of it. The repair drones are still building domes now. I think there are three under construction at the moment."

"Impressive."

"I suppose so. Trouble is the construction of the new sections is taking up just about all the repair drones we have." Sykes sniggered. "Nothing much works around here."

"Sanctuary to Polaris. I'm not going to keep telling you Dillan, transmit your damn code before you cross the ridgeline."

"Sarah, honey, you have to learn to relax. All that negative energy can 't be good for you," the captain replied light-heartedly.

"One of these days, Dillan, I'm gonna follow procedure and activate the cannons. Let's see how relaxed you are after I cut your ship in half."

Dillan grinned. "Transmitting code now."

"Use docking port six. The gantry on port four is flooded again, and stop calling me honey." The speakers fell silent as the controller ended the transmission.

"Oh yeah, she likes you," Zeus mocked.

The captain shrugged his indifference. Miller and the squad continued to gaze out at the surrounding structures as the ship made its final approach towards the airlock.

"Look at that."

Davidson looked out into the water, towards the area indicated by Stone's pointing finger. He could just make out five small craft as they sped by below them.

"They look like sub-orbital attack fighters. Mark six if I'm not mistaken," Davidson chanced a guess.

"Very good," praised Swan from behind his console. "Are you a pilot?"

"Class six clearance," Davidson replied.

"If it has an engine, Davidson can fly it," Miller praised his pilot.

"Yeah, he's crashed more ships than most people will ever fly," Deacon added sarcastically. The squad started to laugh.

"Well, I wouldn't have to risk my ships extracting you assholes, if you could shoot straight Deac', you cross-eyed fuck." The squad chuckled again.

"I spend my days co-ordinating APC mounted missile launchers to fire at multiple targets," Deacon responded. "Moving targets might I add! All you have to do is avoid hitting the ground. I believe the technical term is flying."

Davidson grinned and replied with an eloquently placed middle finger.

The deep and meaningful conversation continued until the ship had successfully docked with the sanctuary. After locking down the ship, Sykes and Swan led the squad into the relevant airlock. After the brief pressure equalisation cycle had finished the airlock hissed open and the group walked out.

"This is dome three, it houses most of our machine shops!" Swan shouted to be heard over the dozens of busy repair drones that all but filled the large chamber.

"What are they doing?"

"They're upgrading the roof supports. The engineers have just finished converting the level above this into a dry dock for the starships. We need to start treating the hulls before the rust from this damn salt water eats the whole fleet."

Two fast approaching guards with plasma rifles halted the group's conversation. "Do you have clearance to be in this dome, sir?"

"Yes, we're going to see Iron-hand. I forwarded a message hours ago, he's expecting us."

"Who are you, sir?" questioned one of the guards as he pulled a small computerised pad from its belt pouch.

Sykes sighed, "First Officer Sykes of the Polaris. This is crewman Swan and these are honoured guests."

The guard checked the information on his pad. "Ok, that checks out. You're free to go."

"Thank you." The team walked on.

"Why do you call him Iron-hand?"

Sykes grinned. "You'll see."

Swan and Sykes led the group through several corridors of the dome and into a transport lift. After Sykes gave the command, the lift began to move, taking them all the way to the very top of the dome. The lift doors opened into what was obviously an operations centre.

"Captain Hawkins, sir, these are the soldiers I told you about. Sergeant Miller and his squad."

"Don't salute me, Sykes, you know I hate that shit." Hawkins stood at the far side of the circular room stubbing out a cigarette into an ashtray on a large console.

Miller couldn't help but notice the shiny metallic limb that hung in the place of his left hand and forearm.

"And tell Dillan to supply his damned access code on approach. If I have to read one more complaint from perimeter control, he's gonna to be trying to shit this." Hawkins raised his prosthetic hand and balled a metal fist.

"Sorry, sir. I'll pass on the message, sir."

"Sergeant Miller?" Hawkins asked as he scanned the new faces.

"That would be me, sir."

Miller saluted.

Hawkins rolled his eyes. "Don't you start, he's bad enough."

Miller grinned. "Very well, sir."

Hawkins noticed Miller's attention still on his prosthetic arm. He raised his hand and wiggled his fingers. "Old war wound, Sergeant," he explained. "Spent months trying to save it and in the end, I got tired of the grafts not holding." He shrugged. "Sometimes you just have to cut your losses."

"Indeed, sir," Miller responded. "If you don't mind me saying so, sir, I don't recognise the tech."

"One of the many things we took back from our adversary," Hawkins answered dryly.

Miller's eyes narrowed and he nodded in approval.

"I trust you and your squad have been properly briefed on our current situation?"

"Yes, sir. Might I say that from what I've heard, your ingenuity during the battle with Gatekeeper's attack fleet, was worthy of a US Marine."

Hawkins laughed. "Well thanks Sergeant, but as I'm sure you'll agree, a commander is only as good as the men he commands."

Miller nodded. "Too true sir."

The doors of the lift hissed open again and a young man stood nervously in the doorway. Clutching a stack of computerised pads.

"What is it, Jacobs?"

"Progress reports from sector three, Captain."

Hawkins sighed. "Put them on the desk."

The young man deposited the stack of pads on top of the virtual mountain of pads that already graced the desk. In his rush to leave he accidentally knocked the desk as he turned and sent the entire pile clattering to the floor. "I'm sorry, sir." The boy's voice trembled as he began to scoop up the pads, his face displaying a look as though he was about to be flogged.

Hawkins sighed and closed his eyes. "Just leave it."

"Yes, sir." The boy stood up and quickly made his exit into the transport-lift.

"Jacobs."

The boy turned. "Yes. Yes sir?"

"Relax."

"Yes, sir, thank you, sir." The young man replied, easily as rigidly as before. Zeus grinned as the lift doors closed.

"Good lad but he's too damn timid. You'd think growing up in this environment would have hardened him to it but…" Hawkins shrugged.

"Exactly how long have you all been down here, Captain?" questioned Miller as he gazed out through one of the room's many large windows.

"We've been down here for almost eighteen months."

"How long have you been back on the planet?" asked Frost. "Sykes and Swan mentioned something about living on the surface for a while. Peru wasn't it?"

Hawkins nodded. "Yes, that's where we decided to settle after we destroyed the mothership," he sighed and shook his head, turning to look out of a window into the backlit waters beyond. "We thought it was over. We returned to Earth and began to build ourselves a new home. Our great city in the highlands of Peru, overlooking the great rainforest. I don't know why Gatekeeper waited so long to mount its attack. Maybe it was waiting for us to drop our guard, who knows, but attack it did.

"One morning, gateways opened above the planet. Through them came half a dozen arrowhead fighters that headed straight for orbit. Destroying any ship in their path. By a stroke of luck, the city's defences had been completed before they showed up." Hawkins smiled. "How I love those cannons," he sniggered. "We cut every last one of those bastards in half before they even cleared the atmosphere."

"Strange that something as logical as Gatekeeper would underestimate your defences," Miller queried. "It may be a psychotic murdering bastard, but from what we've experienced it's tactically adept."

"We don't think it was aware of the cannons at that point. We only ever used those weapons against a mothership in the Vega system. At the time we thought that ship was Gatekeeper, but it's obvious now that even the motherships are simply autonomous constructs of the system. During that encounter the mothership was trying to destabilise the system's star. The effect was creating a lot of emissions from the star and disrupting the fleets long range communications. Maybe that works both ways. Maybe it couldn't send long range communications either, who knows. All I can tell you for sure is that we caught the fighters off-guard when they attacked."

"I see."

"At that point it was obvious that the city's location was no longer adequate. The site was chosen for its abundant resources and its aesthetic properties, not its tactical positioning. We all knew that the element of surprise was the only thing that saved us that day. We wouldn't have lasted five minutes against an all-out attack without it." Hawkins lit up another cigarette and took a long drag. "The only place we could go that gave us a chance of survival was deep under water."

"To hide yourselves from sensor scans?"

"Exactly. We already had huge stockpiles of raw materials at our disposal that were going to be used on the city. We relocated the materials and a veritable army of repair drones to the coast. We recalled the ore mining vessels from the asteroid belts in the system and we hid. Most of the colonists spent weeks living out of submerged ships until enough of the new sanctuary had been built to sustain them. Me, my crew and a few others stayed at the Peru site to keep up the appearance that someone was home."

"What happened to the Peru site?"

"We managed to fend off a couple more attacks. Every time they came it got harder and harder to stop them. Their attack patterns changed. Their tactics altered. They even changed the active frequencies of their shielding to stop the lasers passing through. Gatekeeper learns fast." Hawkins took a drag on his cigarette. "One of my engineers had the foresight to see the shield remodulation problem coming. He really saved our asses on that one. He came up with a computer programme that allows a laser to find and match the frequencies of the enemy shields, while it is firing. The way I understand it, the programme cycles a laser through its possible frequencies, as it is being fired. It then monitors the resistance the beam is coming up against. When it registers a drop in the resistance the laser must be passing through whatever it is hitting and therefore if it is hitting a shield, it must be operating at the correct sympathetic frequency to pass through it." Hawkins shook his head. "Clever son of a bitch." He smiled proudly. "We kept moving the cannons between attacks to keep the bastards guessing. We fired them remotely from a small camp outside of the city, so we weren't in the line of fire. We did everything but throw our shoes at the damned things. One evening it sent another contingent of fighter ships. This time they were accompanied by a new mothership." Hawkins shrugged. "I guess those things take time to replace." He shook his head. "The complex was destroyed in minutes. We were lucky to escape the blast zone in one piece."

"Gatekeeper must know that you're down here, under the water somewhere. If that mothership's still in orbit, it will be searching for this place."

"Oh, it's still up there alright. The fucking thing started sending drop-pods into the oceans about three months ago."

"Drop-pods?"

"Yeah, full of strange sea-bound machines. Its technology is getting better and better all the time. At first, they were clumsy and slow, but it learns real quick. Every time it sends another wave the machines get better, faster, harder to stop."

"So, you hunt the machines down and destroy them before they get a chance to start searching for the sanctuary?"

"Yes, there are always at least two full sub-fighter squadrons on patrol around the clock."

"Where did you get those fighters? We saw some on the way in here. They appeared to be standard military issue."

"Well actually, we got the fighters from the command carrier you were found on. There was a flight bay full of hundreds of them. Although, with the force of the crash-landing only twenty were salvageable. Still, the crew of that thing made one hell of a landing considering it was never designed for atmospheric flight."

"How did you manage to get them to operate under water?"

"That I have no idea about. The engineers get the credit for the technical shit, I just co-ordinate this circus."

"So, what do you intend to do, Captain? I mean it's only a matter of time until Gatekeeper finds this place."

"We're very aware of that. The trouble is we don't have a target to attack."

"Sorry, Captain?"

"We don't have the technology to trace the origin of the jump-gates. The anomalies that allow Gatekeeper to travel so fast."

"So, they could be coming from anywhere?"

"Exactly, the only thing we can do is have a ship ready and waiting in space the next time Gatekeeper opens a jump-gate."

"So, you're gonna let the enemy vessel exit then send a ship back through the anomaly before it closes. Does it work both ways? Can you send a ship back through an incoming gateway?"

"Yes."

"With all due respect, Captain, how can you be sure?"

"Because we've been doing tests with our jump-drive system."

"You have jump-drive technology?"

"Not exactly, we have an Anomaly Drive generator that we took from the first arrowhead fighter we destroyed. We managed to connect it to our ship but we haven't been successful in duplicating the technology. The engineers have tried to reverse engineer it, but we just can't seem to get any of the copies to work."

"So, let's say that we can get a ship through one of Gatekeeper's jump-gates, what then?"

"Then the ship would have to relay its co-ordinates and any useful info back to the sanctuary before it was destroyed. It would be costly but at least we'd have a strike point. It's about time we got back on the offensive in this war." Hawkins returned his gaze to the window and stared out into the darkness of the deep ocean. "We could use my ship, then at least there would be a chance of getting back without being killed but..." Hawkins stopped to find a reasonable way of putting the next sentence. Before he had chance Miller began to speak.

"But your Anomaly Drive generator is too important to risk."

Hawkins turned and looked at Miller, who continued to speak.

"I understand how hard it is to justify sending men to their deaths, Captain. God knows

I've done it more times than I care to remember, but if you intend to attack Gatekeeper itself, you're gonna need that piece of technology."

Hawkins nodded. "I know Sergeant, but I'm not a soldier. Logical or not it still seems wrong."

"What if I offered you another solution, sir?"

"I'm open to suggestions."

"What if it wasn't your only Anomaly Drive generator?

Inside one of the other domes of the sanctuary, Kane was busy training a group of would-be engineers. A job he did not particularly enjoy. "Yes Johnson, it is faster to adapt a type three sensor node for underwater use. But the type fours have a far superior effective range."

"Sorry, sir."

"Don't apologise. A good engineer should always be trying to make things more efficient, well done."

"Hawkins to Kane."

Kane raised his hand. "Hang on guys. Kane here, what can I do for you, Captain?"

"I need you to find Clarke and Blaine and meet me in the command chamber."

"Problems, Captain?"

"Time to test the Laser Sword. Hawkins out."

"What is it Kane?" questioned one of the trainees as he noticed the concerned look on Kane's face.

"Not sure, I'll see you guys later." Kane walked off through the long dark passageway of the corridor away from the puzzled trainees. His boots splashed in the thin layer of water that always covered the floor down here on the lower levels under the domes. No matter how many times the repair drones swept the area for cracks and loose seals the water still managed to seep in. Still, he thought, with the speed this place was built it was a miracle that it held the water out at all.

Clarke was flicking through pages of information on an enormous monitor screen as Kane entered the computer core room.

"Yo, Clarke. How's it going?"

"Slow, real slow. Where the hell have you been? I haven't seen you in weeks."

"Ah you know, here and there. I've been spending so much time in the tunnels under the domes that the trainees have started calling me tunnel rat."

Clarke chuckled. "Well, if the shoe fits."

"How's the data-logging going?"

"I'm starting to think we've got all we're gonna get out of this enemy databank. The rest of this stuff is either incomplete or too complicated for the computer to translate. Anyway, I doubt you came here to discuss my progress. Is there something I can do for you?"

"Hawkins wants to see us in his office."

"Any idea why?"

"Not really, but he did say it was time to test the Laser Sword system."

Clarke's face dropped. "Oh shit."

"Funny, that's just what I was thinking," Kane replied.

Clarke typed the security code into the keypad on the door as they left, locking down the whole chamber. "I just know I'm gonna hate this."

As the pair walked through the corridors Kane tried to reach Blaine on his communicator. "Kane to Blaine come in please? Blaine, sound off. Where the hell is he?"

"He'll be in the flight bay with the pilots." Clarke looked at his watch. "If I'm not mistaken it's time for the weekly match."

The doors of the flight bay opened to reveal a fight. Just about every chair and table in the hangar's seating area had been knocked over and cards were spread across the floor. A large group had gathered in the far comer of the bay and Kane and Clarke quickly made their way over.

"I'm telling you, I had a straight flush," choked Blaine, who was being held up against the wall by a rather large and muscular man, his feet not quite touching the floor.

"Kiss my ass Blaine, you're a fucking cheat."

"Hey!"

The crowd turned as Clarke shouted, he and Kane pushing their way towards Blaine. Taking advantage of the distraction, Blaine punched the large man as hard as he could in the face. His feet suddenly returned to the floor as the man dropped him. As Kane reached the pair, Blaine quickly ripped a wrench out of the engineer's utility belt pouch and swung it as hard as he could before the man had a chance to retaliate. The room fell silent as the muscular form hit the floor.

"I've told you before Rosa," Blaine boasted as he looked down at the now unconscious giant. "You bring the ass, I'll bring the whupin'."

Blaine, Kane and Clarke waded back through the group and headed towards the door.

"Nice timing, guys."

"No problem," replied Clarke.

"Does he need a medic?" Kane queried, looking back at Rosa who was just starting to regain consciousness and was being looked over by a couple of concerned members of the crowd.

"He is the medic," Blaine replied.

Kane, Clarke and Blaine exited the transport-lift and glanced around the room at the camo-clad soldiers. Clarke had no idea what was happening yet, but he knew he wasn't going to like it. "You called, Captain."

"Thanks for coming, guys. This is Sergeant Miller and his squad. Sergeant, this is Kane, Clarke and Blaine, my crew." The squad and the Dark Star crew exchanged nods.

"You're the guys from the command carrier, aren't you?" Blaine blurted.

Miller looked surprised. "That's right. Does everyone know we're here already?"

"Small colony, news travels fast. Besides, it's not every day we find survivors from the massacre."

Miller nodded.

"Should we get down to business?" Hawkins suggested.

"By all means, Captain."

Hawkins looked at his crew. He couldn't think of a way to ease his boys into the plan gently, so he decided not to try. "We're going to attack the mothership in orbit."

The Dark Star crew grimaced in unison.

"I knew I wasn't going to like this," remarked Clarke sarcastically.

"We're gonna attempt to take its Jump-drive generator. We're gonna be handling the attack personally, so I need our jump-drive generator disconnecting and leaving here, just in case."

Kane nodded.

"Sergeant Miller has volunteered to infiltrate the ship if we can disable it. If any of you don't want to do this tell me now, I won't hold it against you." Hawkins got no response. "Ok, this is the plan. We're working on the assumption that the shield generators in this mothership are in the same place as those in the one we destroyed. If they are, the first thing we need to do is take one out with the Dark Star's cannons."

"What if they're not?"

"You get to prove your skills at dodging incoming fire."

Blaine sighed.

"We'll take two fighter squadrons with us to deal with any arrowhead fighters that might be up there." Hawkins pressed a few keys on his command console and the blueprints of the Dark Star flashed up on the monitor. "Kane, we're gonna need a cargo bay converting into a launch deck."

"No problem," replied the engineer.

Hawkins brought up a copy of the arrowhead mothership blueprints on a separate monitor screen. He looked at Miller. "Our scanners are unable to penetrate the hulls of Gatekeeper's ships. We have this blueprint we acquired that proved to be accurate enough when used against the mothership in the Vega star system. If the mothership in orbit over our heads shares the same design, then its jump-drive generator should be positioned here." Hawkins pointed at the screen and Miller nodded his understanding. "We'll keep the Dark Star docked with the mothership for as long as we can, but you're gonna have to hurry."

"Your team will have to do this in spacesuits, Sergeant," enlightened Clarke. "From what we've experienced previously, those ships have no breathable atmosphere."

"That's gonna slow us down, Sarge," Stone complained.

"I know, Stone, but how long can you hold your breath?" Miller turned to Hawkins. "Let's say everything goes to plan. We get up there, disable that mothership and destroy any escorts it might have with it. It still only takes backup to arrive while the Dark Star is docked and you're gonna be sitting ducks. I suggest we come up with another way to get my team onto that ship that doesn't rely on a hard dock."

Deacon looked at Miller and pulled a face that clearly indicated his contempt at the suggestion.

"We still have the breaching-pod that the last mothership hit us with," Clarke offered, "It's still in pretty good shape."

"Good idea, Clarke, but no human could survive that kind impact."

"We could equip it with an inertial dampening system easy enough," Kane offered. "The fastest way to do it would be to strip a couple of cryo-pods for the generators."

Miller nodded. "You know, that just might work. Just like back on the Hunter."

"We'd have to cut a hole in the mothership before we launched it. That pod would bounce straight of that hull plating."

"Shouldn't be too much of a problem, all going well."

"What's the plan for extraction?" Clarke questioned. The room fell silent. Everyone looked around waiting for someone to offer an answer.

"Let us worry about that," offered Miller. "Extraction plans tend to alter real quick. Just be ready to pick us up when we call."

"Anything else?" Hawkins questioned.

"Yes, Captain."

Hawkins turned his attention to Davidson. "Go ahead."

"No disrespect intended, but how good are your fighter pilots?"

"As good as can be expected considering we don't have any fighter pilots. What we have are a lot of commercial pilots that have only been flying military craft for a short time." Hawkins shrugged. "That's the no bullshit answer."

"If you'd like I can put them through their paces. Give them a bit of training."

Hawkins nodded then looked at Miller. "What do you think Sergeant?" he asked, mostly out of respect.

"It's a good idea. In fact, Davidson's piloting skills would be invaluable on the mission. I'll miss the backup inside the mothership, but if I'm honest, I'd feel a lot better with him watching my ass from a cockpit."

Hawkins looked at Davidson. "That good huh?"

"Class six rating, sir." Davidson smiled. Deacon rolled his eyes.

"Then I'll give you command of all twenty fighters. Can you handle co-ordinating both wings?"

"Not a problem, sir."

"Clarke, make sure the pilots get that message."

"Aye, sir."

"Ok then, if there's nothing further." Hawkins paused, "Let's get to it."

The next few days were extremely gruelling for the whole colony. Kane and his hand-picked team of engineers worked around the clock to complete the changes to the Dark Star and the other tasks set for them. Cargo bay three was painstakingly converted into a hangar for the Sub-orbital fighters.

"Murphy, get those rails straight before you attach them. If they're not perfect when the fighters launch, we could lose half the bay."

"No problem, Kane, it's under control."

"Thompson, bring me a laser torch. This bulkhead's gonna have to learn the hard way."

In between border patrols, Davidson trained the pilots ruthlessly. Leaving no manoeuvres untried, no scenarios unexplored. Slowly but surely the group of fighters became a squadron. Two combat ready wings forming one solid group. Everyone was painfully aware that drilling manoeuvres under water was nothing close to handling a fighter in space, but choices of training ground are limited when you're being hunted.

"That was the best run yet," congratulated Davidson as two of the squadrons climbed out of their ships. "If you can perform those manoeuvres under water with all that drag, you'll be untouchable in space." Davidson nodded approvingly.

"Davidson, how goes the training?" shouted Miller, as he and Hawkins strolled into the hangar.

"Squad, fall in." The pilots quickly obeyed Davidson's bellowing and grouped up. "Who are we?"

"We have no name!" shouted the squad in unison. "You will know us by the trail of dead!"

Davidson grinned smugly. Miller looked noticeably embarrassed in-front of Hawkins.

"Well, you've clearly taught them how to bullshit well enough, but can they fly?"

"They could fly a cargo ship backwards through an asteroid belt," replied Davison. Miller gave him a stern look that Davidson recognised as universal command code for cut the bullshit. "Well, they're not setting off each-others proximity alarms anymore. What do you want from me, Sarge? They're mostly freighter pilots."

Hawkins looked uncomfortable. "Thank you for the assistance, Mr Davidson. Any improvement is better than none."

The day of the launch finally arrived and the atmosphere in the Sanctuary was chaotic. Equipment loaded and teams strapped in, the Dark Star, for the first time in months, lit up her engines. The wake from the Dreadnought rocked patrol vessels and towers as it slowly left the sanctuary. Huddled together to find a view through the windows of the domes, the colonists watched and cheered. All that stood between the Dark Star and the mothership now was a few hours' worth of undersea travel. Necessary to not give away the colonies position when the ship exited the ocean.

"Ok, Blaine, I think we're far enough away from the sanctuary."

"Copy that, sir, prepping ion engines for ignition."

"Sir, before we get started. Do you think we should send Reeva with the soldiers?"

Hawkins raised an eyebrow. "You know I'd completely forgotten about that thing." Hawkins activated his communicator. "Hawkins to Miller, how do you feel about a little extra manpower over there?"

"No disrespect, sir, I know your crew is capable, but I think a civilian would just get in the way."

"Well, I was thinking of a crew member, but something a little more impressive than the ones you've already met."

"That hurts my feelings!" offered Blaine.

"Sorry, Captain?" replied Miller.

"I'll send her down. You can decide when you see her."

"Her?" questioned Miller in a rather startled tone.

"Trust me, Sergeant." Hawkins stopped before disconnecting the transmission, "Oh, and Miller."

"Yes, Captain?"

"Don't shoot her, that's an order."

"Err, yes, sir."

Hawkins grinned as he ended the transmission and looked over at Clarke. "Go for it."

Clarke nodded and began typing on his keyboard. "Reeva is back online, sir." Clarke pushed the communications button on his armband, "Reeva, report to cargo bay one."

Miller and the squad were waiting in the cargo bay for the captain's last-minute addition to their team. No one knew what to expect as the cargo bay door opened, but the sleek metallic cat was the last thing they had imagined.

"What the fuck?"

Miller grabbed the front of Deacon's plasma rifle as he raised it.

"Hold your fire. That goes for all of you."

"What the fuck is it?" Stone questioned nervously.

"I don't know, Stone, but I hope to god it's friendly."

Reeva slowly crossed the cargo bay, the blades on her metal paws clanging on the grid metal floor as she walked.

"Miller to Hawkins, what the hell is this thing?"

"It's a hunter drone. Courtesy of Gatekeeper. We acquired it a couple of years ago in Scotland. Don't worry we reprogrammed her, she's on our side.

"Where the hell was this thing? I'm pretty sure I would have noticed it running around the ship by now."

"We keep her powered-down when we don't need her. She has a habit of chewing things when she's bored."

Miller and Deacon looked at each other. "When she's bored? You mean this thing can think?"

"Very much so. We've discovered that most of Gatekeeper's drones have a rudimentary intelligence. In Reeva's case, roughly equal to that of a dog. But it only kicks in when she doesn't have an order to follow."

"So, this thing can do whatever it wants to do?"

Hawkins grinned. "Don't sound so worried, Sergeant, we'll keep her on a leash from up here. You might want to go strap yourselves in. We're about to break for orbit. Hawkins out." Hawkins turned to Clarke. "Her programming prevents her from harming them, right?"

"Her programming prevents her from harming the four of us." Clarke shrugged.

Now Hawkins looked a little worried. "Keep an eye on her."

"Yes, Captain."

Hawkins sat back down and strapped himself in. "Blaine, whenever you're ready."

"Aye, sir, ignition sequence engaged," the bridge began to rumble as the engines built up power.

"Hawkins to all hands. Anyone not strapped in is gonna be a stain on the back wall in exactly ten seconds. Confirm that, Blaine?"

"Ignition in eight seconds," Blaine confirmed.

"There's gonna be a burst of acceleration as we break free of the water."

"Thanks, Clarke."

"Here goes nothing."

The force pushed everyone back against their seats as Blaine hit the power. Zeus was a little slower than the other marines at taking his seat and Frost was forced to hold onto him as he wrestled to close his harness catch, fighting against the increasing g force. The Dark Star swayed from side to side as it forced its way through the water.

"Breaking the surface now."

A sudden jolt of acceleration forced back Blaine's cheeks, as they broke free from the resistance of the water. Clarke dialled up the ships inertial dampening field intensity and the forces involved in the acceleration lessened slightly as they were counteracted by the opposing forces of the device. The relief from all four crew members on the bridge was obvious.

"Clarke, I need a course heading."

"Hold on a second, Blaine. The damned sea water is draining off the sensor arrays. Ok, course heading two-thirty-six-mark-four-five."

"Two-thirty-six-mark-four-five confirmed. Coming about."

"What do you see up there, Clarke?"

"I'm still getting some interference from the water on the sensors, sir, but it looks like an arrowhead mothership and two arrowhead fighters. Correction, three."

Hawkins looked at the small tactical display screen on his console as Clarke patched the information through. "Correct course heading to bring us up behind the mothership."

"Aye, sir. Blaine, new course heading zero-two-five-mark-four-eight."

"No problem."

"We should be breaking orbit in about twenty seconds, Captain."

"Let me know the second it's safe to open the pressure doors on cargo bay three."

"Aye, sir."

"This is Hawkins, all fighters prepare for launch."

"We've been detected, sir. All three arrowhead fighters are on the move."

"Activate the Laser Sword system."

"Aye, sir, system activated."

"Shields raised and holding, sir."

"Thanks, Kane."

"All cannons are raised and locked," Clarke updated. "Breaking orbit now. It's safe to open the bay doors."

"Do it. Ok, here we go. Hawkins to cargo bay three, all fighters launch."

Led by Davidson, all twenty fighters screamed out of the Dark Star as she sped past the arrowhead mothership. "Davidson to first wing, engage the first two ships to your port side. Second wing, follow me."

The arrowhead fighters split up as Davidson's squadrons fired their plasma missiles.

"Davidson to Hawkins, we have the fighters under control. The mothership's all yours."

"Well done, Davidson, keep 'em off us for as long as you can." Hawkins took a deep breath. "Ok, same attack plan as last time, get me a lock on that shield generator."

"Cannons charged and ready, frequency modulator is online."

"Coming about, we'll be in position in ten seconds." Once again Clarke brought up the internal deck plan of the arrowhead mothership. He superimposed it over the image of the actual ship on his targeting screen and locked all four cannons on the superimposed picture of the generator. "Target locked."

"Fire."

Through the main view port, the crew watched as the mothership's shielding failed to stop the sympathetically modulated energy beams from the lasers. The beams cut into the hull causing it to glow.

"It didn't work," shouted Kane. "The shields are still up."

"Fucking sensor scrambling hull plating!" Clarke raged as he re-aimed for another shot.

"The mothership is turning towards us."

"Come on, Clarke, come on."

"Firing."

The orange glow of the shield faltered and dispersed as the lasers passed through it and cut into the hull once again. This time finding their target.

"Got it, the generator is toast, sir. The mothership's shields are dropping."

"Blaine, back us off. Hawkins to Miller, get ready."

"Full-yield torpedoes prepped and ready, Captain."

"Fire."

"Torpedoes away."

"The ship will be facing us in about twelve seconds, sir. I'm detecting an energy build-up."

The light from the blast caused Hawkins to squint as the torpedoes hit.

"Shock wave incoming." The ship rocked as the shock wave passed.

"Direct hit to the mothership's port mid-section. I'm detecting a hull breach with a rough diameter of about ten metres."

"Widen that hole, Clarke."

"Now that the hull plating's damaged that shouldn't be a problem." Clarke locked the Dark Star's targeting sensors onto the gap in the mothership's hull plating. "Firing torpedoes."

The bridge crew listened to the beeping of the range finder on Clarke's tactical console, as the torpedoes closed in and found their mark.

"Direct hit." Another shockwave rattled through the Dark Star's bridge.

"Davidson to Hawkins."

"Received, Davidson. Go ahead."

"The fighters have realised we are no threat, Captain. We're just bouncing shots off their shields. I think this little distraction is over."

"He's right, sir, they're coming this way. Reading energy build ups from all three ships."

"Is that hole deep enough, Clarke?"

"Only one way to find out, sir."

"Do it!"

Clarke looked at the closing enemy fighters on his tactical console and grimaced. "I hope this works." Clarke reached for a particular button on his console. With a press of the button Keymaster was activated. The Dark Star emitted the radio wave out in all directions and continued to do so. The energy shielding on the three enemy fighter craft flickered and failed and the energy signatures of all four hostile vessels disappeared off Clarke's tactical console as they lost power. "Yes!" Clarke shouted. "Surprise you metallic bastards!"

Davidson's fighters, now co-ordinating all their firepower on one of Gatekeeper's fighters, began to tear through its hull plating. Several explosions went off in sequence along the vessel's length and the friendly fighters pulled out to a safe distance as it exploded. Clarke watched his hazy sensors scans of the two remaining enemy fighters as they drifted closer and closer to the Dark Star they had been approaching. The two fighters sailed past silently and drifted onward towards the planet's atmosphere.

"Keep that wave up, Clarke," Hawkins demanded as he rose from his seat.

"Don't you worry, sir, that wave isn't going anywhere."

Hawkins looked at Clarke as he realised something. "Hawkins to Davidson, stand down attack."

"Davidson here, message received, Captain."

"Clarke, we should change targets."

"Sir?"

"We have two immobilised fighters to take jump-drives from. We don't need to send Miller's team into that mothership. The smaller ships are surely safer to board."

Clarke looked thoughtful for a moment and then returned his attention to his console. His enthusiasm waned quickly. "I'm sorry sir, those ships are drifting toward the atmosphere. In ten minutes, they'll be starting to heat up." He shook his head. "They're a comparable size to the Star, sir. The only way we'd stop one is to push it to alter its course."

Hawkins thought back to how much damage he'd caused the Dark Star when he ordered Blaine to use the ship to push the small asteroid. He also remembered how little effect it had.

"The mothership is in a stable orbit, sir," Clarke continued, "It's in no immediate danger."

Hawkins shook his head. "Ok, Blaine, dial it back. Just be ready to move if there are any surprises.

"Aye, sir." Blaine reduced power to the engines and brought the Dark Star into a slow patrol circle around the area.

"Hawkins to Miller."

"Miller here."

"I was hoping to give you a smaller ship to board, Sergeant, but it appears the remaining enemy fighters are drifting into Earth's atmosphere without power. I'm afraid our plans have not become any less complicated."

"I'll take more hostiles over a tight window and a fiery death any day, Captain."

Hawkins nodded. "Ok Sergeant. Brace for launch."

"Good to go."

"Good luck, Sergeant." Hawkins nodded at Clarke.

"Launching pod now," Clarke responded. The tracking monitor on Clarke's console began to beep as the breaching-pod rocketed out of the cargo bay and made its way at speed toward the mothership. As the small and heavily armoured pod impacted with the gaping hole in the mothership's hull plating the beeping stopped.

"What's the status of the team, Clarke? Did the pod stay together?"

"The pod hit its target perfectly, sir. It showed no signs of breakup. The open coms line has been severed however. Must be interference from that damn hull plating. I am still getting a strong signal from Reeva. I can see that the squad is up and moving. All present and accounted for."

"Put the cat on point in front of the squad. Tell her to protect them. Everyone, keep your eyes on your scopes. There's a hundred ways this could go south."

Thanks to the damage the structure of the mothership had already sustained from the Dark Star's weapons. The breaching pod had crashed through several internal bulkheads with ease, burying itself deeply into the vessel and coming to rest with its nose protruding out into a long and very wide corridor. Miller and the squad had survived the initial impact from the pod's landing and were attempting to get their bearings. Thanks to the success of Keymaster, the area was very quiet and reasonably dark. There was some emergency lighting active but not enough to render the lights of the team's pressure suits unnecessary. Having already exited the breaching pod with Reeva in tow, the squad was now stood, failing to realise how much trouble this unexpectedly deep impact was causing to their navigator.

"Speak to me, Deac'."

"Hold on, sir." Deacon was still attempting to get his bearings, as he looked over the blueprints for the mothership on the screen of his forearm sensor device.

"Don't tell me to hold on, marine. Tell me where the fuck I am."

Deacon continued to study the blueprints.

"Zeus, Stone, Frost, secure the area."

"Yes, sir."

"Damn this thing's big."

"Can you get us to that generator or not?"

"I'm doing my best, Sarge. It doesn't exactly have a 'you are here' arrow."

"Sarge, we're not alone in here."

"What is it, Stone?"

"Not sure, sir." Stone stood looking at his forearm sensor pad. "There's a lot of movement about a mile down this corridor and it's heading this way."

"You hear that, Deac'?"

"Almost got it."

"How fast is it moving, Stone?"

"Not that fast, but fast enough to catch us while we're in these pressure-suits."

"There we are," Deacon celebrated. "Ah shit."

"What is it?"

"We're nowhere near were we expected to be. The reactor is in a large chamber about three quarters of a mile from here."

Miller sighed, "You know, I'm starting to think I'm being punished for something I did in a previous life."

"With the luck we're having lately, you must have been a real asshole, Sarge."

"Stone, do you think we can keep ahead of whatever's heading this way?"

Stone shook his head. "I don't think so."

"Contact the Dark Star. Make sure they know where we are."

"Dark Star, come in please? Come in, Dark Star." Frost waited for a response. "Dark Star, respond?" Frost shook his head "The transmission's not getting through, it must be this thing's hull plating." The floor of the corridor suddenly began to rumble and the emergency lights flickered.

"What the hell was that?"

"It must be the Dark Star."

"They couldn't have heard us, the message never got through the hull."

Miller jumped as Reeva rubbed her nose on his leg. "What the hell is this thing doing?" Miller looked thoughtfully at her as she stood in front of him. "I wonder." He knelt down and looked into Reeva's eyes. "If you guys can hear me, make this cat sit down." Sure enough, Reeva sat down on the floor of the corridor. Miller smiled. "Not perfect but I'll take it."

"Ok, guys, we can contact the ship by talking to the cat."

"This shit gets stranger by the minute, man."

The ship rumbled again and this time the lights failed completely.

"The power's offline."

"No shit, Frost," replied Miller sarcastically as he floated around in the dark.

"No, Sarge. I don't think you're following my train of thought."

Miller looked at Frost. Frost deactivated his magnetic boots and slowly lifted off the floor. He gave himself a little push with his pressure suit's thruster pack and drifted around Miller and the team. "I mean the power's down."

Zeus smiled.

Clarke typed away on his console as Hawkins stood looking out of the bridge's main view port at the crippled mothership. He was painfully aware of the metal nightmares those ships held. The small fighter ship that his crew had boarded was bad enough and that was nowhere near the size of the floating labyrinth that

Miller's team now navigated. Worry profits a man nothing. Hawkins knew this saying and he agreed with it. But whoever came up with that line was clearly never hunted by Gatekeeper's bladed abominations.

"Booyah! This is the only way to travel," shouted Zeus. The squad was travelling through the zero-gravity environment of the corridors at speed now. Their pressure-suit thrusters propelling them forwards through the zero-gravity environment.

"How long, Deac'?"

"At this speed, we'll be there in under a minute." Deacon followed the internal map he had downloaded from the computer up-link.

"How's the trail look, Stone?"

"Whatever I'm detecting is still behind us. Although we seem to be gaining ground on it."

"How the hell is that thing staying on the floor?" questioned Frost, in reference to Reeva, who was running along in front of them.

"I don't know man, but if that one can do it, you can bet your ass the rest can too."

"Oh shit. I hadn't thought of that."

"Sarge, I'm picking up a lot of movement in the section ahead of us."

"How far?"

"The closest signal is about eight hundred metres ahead."

Miller cocked his plasma rifle.

"Coming up on the generator's co-ordinates, Sarge." Deacon fired the opposing thrusters on his pressure suit and began to slow down. The rest of the squad followed his lead.

"What about the movement?"

"The closest signal is coming from the same location."

"Of course it is. What about the movement behind us?"

"Still with us, Sarge."

As they came to a halt, they engaged their magnetic gravity boots and returned to the solid metal floor of the corridor.

"Are you sure these are the right co-ordinates, Deac'?"

Deacon checked the deck plan. "Yep, right behind that wall."

"So, no door?"

"Not that I can identify, sir."

Miller shook his head. "Ok, let's do it the hard way, for a change. The centre of that panel on my mark." The squad took aim with their rifles. "Fire."

The soldiers all opened fire at the same spot on the wall. The intense heat from the superheated plasma emitted by their rifles easily melted the metal alloy. When he was satisfied that they had created a large enough hole Miller ordered the team to stop, "Hold your fire!" he shouted over the racket from the discharging weapons. The shiny smooth wall now gave way to the glowing edges of its freshly installed and smouldering door, "Ok, two by two, left and right, move, move, move," the squad carefully made their way into the adjacent chamber, their rifles raised in readiness. Reeva headed straight ahead as the team checked their flanks.

"Left side clear."

"Right side clear."

Miller looked around the room. "I thought you said something was moving around in here, Stone?"

Frost's face suddenly disappeared as he spat blood over the inside of his helmet visor. Zeus looked up to the roof above Frost, where a large spherical object was clung to the ceiling. One of its many limbs stretched out, skewering Frost through the back.

"No!" He raised his rifle and fired at the machine, blowing it loose of the roof. The rest of the squad opened fire as Miller made his way over to Frost. The machine stopped moving and drifted, smouldering through the chamber. The marines aimed their attention and their rifles on the ceiling and the walls.

"Frost, speak to me man."

Frost clutched Miller's arm tightly, his eyes flicked around the room in a state of shock and panic.

"Hold on, I'll get you outta here."

Frost managed to compose himself slightly as he drew his face closer to Miller's. His words were barely audible as he choked on his own blood. "Anything you want me to tell Williams and Hanson?"

"Stop talking shit, marine, you're gonna be fine." Miller could feel Frost's grip on his arm loosening. "Don't you fucking die on me, Frost, that's an order."

Frost released his grip as his body went limp. Miller screwed his eyes up and hung his head.

"Sarge, the movement in this section is getting awfully close."

Miller took a deep breath and stood up. Frost's body hung almost upright on the spot, his magnetic boots not allowing him to drift.

"Stone, Zeus, go and stand over by the door with the cat. Keep your eyes open."

"Yes, sir.

"Deacon, give me a hand with this generator."

The bridge of the Dark Star was calm and quiet. Hawkins stood at the main view port in front of Blaine's station, still looking out at the mothership with a concerned frown on his face.

"Davidson is requesting permission to bring his squadrons in, sir.

Hawkins shook his head. "Tell him to hold position for now."

"Aye, sir."

"The signal from Reeva is coming back online. The squad must be moving back towards the hull breach."

"Do they have the generator?"

"Bear with me, sir. The transmission is still very faint."

"Blaine, be ready."

"Aye, sir."

"Miller's team appears to have the generator and..." Clarke stopped. "One of the squad is down, sir. The big man is dragging him."

"Where are they?"

"They're about six hundred yards from the breach."

"Blaine."

"On it, sir." Blaine started to move the Dark Star into position.

"There's something else, sir, Reeva's sensors are going ballistic."

"What is it?"

"Hold on. Reeva, identify movement ahead." The picture on Clarke's overhead monitor started to zoom in as Reeva altered her view. Her optical sensors adjusted allowing him to see what she was detecting further along the corridor. "Jesus."

"What is it?"

"There's a whole group of machines waiting by the breach."

"Could they be some kind of repair drones?"

"They're not repairing the breach, sir. They're just standing there." Clarke looked at Hawkins. "The personal sensor devices the marines are using are little more than biological sensors and motion trackers. If those machines don't move, the squad won 't be able to detect them."

"Smart, very fucking smart." Hawkins thought for a moment. "Can we clear them out with the laser cannons?"

"There's no time, sir, the squad's almost there."

"Open me a channel."

"Aye, sir, but I don't think they're close enough to the breach to receive it."

"Hawkins to Miller. Miller, come in? Miller, come in god damn it."

Miller and the squad continued to follow Reeva along the corridor. Unable to receive the transmission from Hawkins they drifted along blindly towards their doom.

"Are you sure, Stone?"

"Certain, sir, I'm no longer detecting any movement down here."

"I thought we were being tailed?" Miller engaged his pressure-suit's reverse thrusters. "Hold on, something isn't right here." The squad halted.

"Stone, your rifle please."

Stone was the squad's best marksman. His rifle was equipped with a long-range targeting scope for sniping. Miller looked through the rifle scope and zoomed in along the corridor. "Dirty metal bastards."

"What is it, Sarge?"

"There are about twelve machines standing around near the hull breach. The sneaky bastards were just waiting for us to fly into them."

"What now, sir?"

"Now, Deac', I'm gonna give this rifle back to Stone and smile while he clears us a path." Miller handed Stone the rifle.

"They look like big spiders or something," Stone described what he was seeing through his scope. "Like those damned hunter things in Grenoble. They must be five feet tall."

"Can you hit 'em from here?"

"No problem." Stone locked his magnetic boots back onto the floor plating and the squad followed suit. He took aim on the closest machine and pulled the trigger. The blue tint of the plasma bolt disappeared out of Miller's view as it flew down the corridor. "Damn." Stone knelt down on one knee to steady his aim before firing off multiple shots towards the machines. He watched through the rifle's scope as the bolts of plasma hit the machines and dispersed.

"No effect, sir. I didn't even scratch 'em. It's like shooting at a tank."

"Ok, everybody aim along the corridor." The squad obeyed. "Fire at will."

Shot after shot the squad sent speeding balls of super-hot plasma crashing into the machines. Stone watched through his scope as he fired.

"Hold your fire. Did we get 'em, Stone?"

"We hit 'em, but all we did is piss 'em off." Stone looked up at Miller. "They're coming this way, sir."

"Deacon, are there any other ways off this ship?"

"Not unless you want to take a three-mile trek to the closest cargo bay."

"God damn it! Which way?"

"Straight down below us, Sarge."

"Fuck me!"

"Sarge, I'm detecting movement closing from behind us"

"How far?"

"Maybe two thousand yards."

Miller looked back down the corridor towards the now, barely visible machines. "We're gonna have to go for it."

"Sarge?"

"Let's find out how fast you can dodge in a spacesuit."

"Sarge, this is crazy."

"Do you have a better idea?" Miller shouted. "Now come on, everybody behind me. Zeus get the generator."

"What about Frost, sir?"

"Leave him, Zeus."

"But, sir."

"You're not slowing yourself down for a body, Zeus, now get the fucking generator,"

With a look of shame on his face Zeus released his grip on Frost's body. He watched as it slowly drifted away from him. "I'm sorry, brother."

"Ok, let's move." Miller deactivated his magnetic boots, held down the buttons for his suit's thrusters, and accelerated towards the approaching machines. "Spread out. No matter what happens, get that generator out of here. Do you all hear me?"

"Yes, sir."

Reeva sped off in front of the squad along the floor at speed.

"What the hell is that thing doing now?"

With no sign of slowing and no fear, Reeva smashed into the foremost machine skittling it and several others backwards and causing them to lose their attachment to the floor plating. Miller watched as the remaining machines closed in and tore her apart.

"Come on."

The machines rammed by Reeva were drifting around, thrashing their limbs wildly as they floated. Miller saw his opening as one of the machines drifted upside down, partially shielding an area from the other nightmares. He couldn't help but tense up as he reached the blade-covered arachnids.

"Don't stop!" shouted Deacon as one of the machines stopped him in his tracks. Stone could hear nothing but the sound of motors and blades slicing through the air.

"Bring it on!" shouted Zeus as he watched his gap through the machines disappear. He pushed the generator as hard as he could and sent it flying clear as he smashed into the moving barrier. He grabbed the flailing mandibles of the machine looming over Deacon and wrestled with it, muscle against motor.

"Deac', get outta here."

"Come on." Deacon hesitated, waiting for his team mate.

"I can't hold this thing for..." Zeus exhaled heavily as another of the drones forced a limb through his torso. Still, he held the machine off Deacon.

"Zeus, no!" Deacon discharged his rifle at the machine. Another set of bladed limbs cut Zeus down from his right-hand side, sending the machine he was trying to hold, crashing down on top of his friend. After placing the generator by the hull breach, Miller went back for his team. He grabbed the strap of Stone's chest rig and pulled him off of the blade that had passed through his shoulder. Stone fired at the attackers as Miller dragged him away.

"Miller to Hawkins, come in?" Miller looked out through the breach, trying to locate the ship. "Come in damn it."

"Hawkins here, hold on we're coming."

"Sarge!"

Miller turned to see the machines almost upon them again. He took a couple of deep breaths and kicked off. Dragging Stone and the generator out into open space.

"Captain, I could use a little help here." His suit's thrusters out of fuel, Miller could do nothing but drift and wait. He looked back at the still thrashing machines. His team decimated and his heart breaking as the Dark Star moved gently into range behind them. The massive cargo bay door opened and they drifted inside. Miller watched the door slowly close behind them and then fell to the floor as the artificial gravity was restored. Stone and the refrigerator sized jump-drive generator clattering to the deck along with him. He felt the atmosphere being pumped back into the room as the pressure pressed against his suit. Hawkins and Kane rushed into the bay. Stone and Miller had removed their helmets now and were lying on their backs panting.

"Are you two, ok?"

Miller looked up at Hawkins. "No Captain, we're pretty fucking far from ok."

"Kane, get Stone to the medical bay."

"Aye, sir." Kane helped Stone up off the floor and walked him out of the cargo bay. Miller stood up and started to remove his pressure-suit.

"I'm sorry about your squad, Miller. They were all brave men."

"They were the bravest men I've ever met."

Hawkins nodded solemnly. "Hawkins to Clarke." Hawkins opened a channel without breaking eye contact with Miller.

"Go ahead, Captain."

"Have Blaine take us out to a safe distance. Then decimate that fucking ship."

"My pleasure, sir. Clarke out."

"Let's make sure they didn't die for nothing.

CHAPTER 14

A rock and a hard place

Hawkins sat in his office with the lights out. His ashtray was full now and the bottom of his bottle of colony home brew was within reach. Even as he stared out into the blackness of the uninviting ocean, he couldn't help but think that they had been lucky. Sure, he was sitting in the only quiet place in the sanctuary and yes, due to the overcrowding he would be sleeping here too. The constant daily struggle to keep the water out of the hastily constructed domes had been the mental end for two engineers already and the fight to keep the colonists fed was a never-ending issue. Yet in his inebriated state it still amused him when he thought that these people were, technically, the lucky ones.

"Clarke to Hawkins."

"Yes, Clarke."

"The jump-drive generator has been reinstalled in the Star, Captain."

"Copy that, Clarke. I'd like you to find Miller and the boys and bring them all up here as soon as possible."

"Everything ok, sir?"

"You can draw your own conclusions when you've heard what I have to say."

"Yes, sir. I'm on it, sir."

"Oh yeah, and make sure Kane brings a supply inventory with him. I need an up-to-date list of every spare component we have."

"No problem, sir."

"Thanks, Clarke, Hawkins out."

Three weeks later Hawkins called a meeting of the entire colony. Every man, woman and child were ordered to attend. A gathering such as this had not taken place since the abandonment of the Peru sanctuary. No one knew why the meeting had been called but everyone knew something was terribly wrong.

"Quieten down everyone!" Clarke shouted down from the gantry above the crowd, where he and his shipmates stood. "I want order, now." Sure enough, the chattering roar of the crowd gradually subsided. Hawkins stepped forward and leant on the cold metal safety rail that surrounded the platform. He took a slow sweeping glance around the packed storage chamber and began to speak.

"Good evening. Thank you all for coming." Hawkins paused and took a deep breath, "As you all probably know by now, Sergeant Miller and his squad managed, at great personal cost, to obtain a second jump-drive generator during the attack on the new mothership." Hawkins held up his hand to silence the crowd as they began to clap. "What you're probably not aware of is that the drive we already had was from a fighter. A fighter that was deployed from a mothership that was already in Earth space, and as such may never have been used. The drive retrieved by Sergeant Miller's squad however, was from a mothership that had jumped itself into our system." Hawkins leaned over the railing a little. "The new drive contains a set of co-ordinates, that are outside the Sol system. Co-ordinates that we believe to be its point of origin." Again, Hawkins held up his hand. This time to stop the chatter. "Tonight, an attack force will be launched to those co-ordinates to determine whether or not Gatekeeper is there."

"What if it is?" came a voice from the crowd.

"Then we send it straight to hell."

Kane pushed a button on a small pad he was holding and a large three-dimensional, holographic picture appeared in the air above the crowd. The looming cylindrical projection slowly turned on its axis to provide a full view from anywhere in the room.

"What you are seeing!" Hawkins shouted to be heard above the ever-increasing din. "Is the design schematic for a crystalline explosive device. Kane and Sergeant Miller have been developing it over the last three weeks. This device is basically a Matrillion reactor that has been modified to continue to operate despite the build-up of resonance caused by the Keymaster radio frequency. The way I understand it, the device's failure to shut down or burn out will result in an energy build up and subsequent explosion that I don't have the words to describe."

"How do you know that will be enough?" came another question from somewhere in the crowd.

Hawkins smiled. "My friend, we'll be lucky if this explosion doesn't wake the devil himself."

The crowd was divided now between faces displaying excitement and faces that displayed an obvious look of worry. This made Hawkins' next statement even more difficult.

"Gatekeeper's latest attack force had plenty of time to send a distress call when we attacked it. As such, there's a good chance that Gatekeeper is now aware of the Keymaster frequency. There's also a chance that the wave shut those vessels down swiftly and effectively enough to stop that information from being relayed back, but we can't afford to take that chance. That means that the element of surprise we have been so desperately exploiting is now gone. A simple remodulation of an energy shield's frequencies is already enough to stop our weapons from passing through it for a short time. The simple addition of a faraday cage to a reactor room can already easily stop Keymaster from having any effect against a crystalline reactor. It's only a matter of time until our tactics become ineffective. Make no mistake people, it's now or never. We dare not wait any longer.

"It is only a matter of time before Gatekeeper replenishes and returns and we aren't going to give it that chance. The next attack will be ours." Hawkins paused for a moment to think. "Only the Dark Star and the Polaris will attempt this assault. We only have two jump-drive generators and therefore we have only made two Matrillion explosive devices. Any ship that followed us through those gateways would have no way to jump itself to safety before the bombs explode and therefore would be at the mercy of the explosions."

"Who will be commanding the Dark Star, Captain?" Hawkins scanned the crowd for the familiar female voice.

"Ah, Commander Redmond." Hawkins smiled. "The only person that leads my ship into battle is me."

The crowd's mood turned to one of chaos.

"But surely someone else should take command of the ship? Your place is here"

Hawkins raised his hand again and the crowd slowly quietened down. "Let's not kid ourselves, this mission is more than likely a one-way trip. I will not and cannot allow anyone to take my chair just in the interest of saving my own ass. However, I realise that a commander's place is here with the colony." Hawkins paused for a moment, "I would therefore like to name First Officer Eugene Clarke of the Dark Star as my successor."

Clarke's face dropped as Hawkins turned to face him and gave a salute. The crowd looked almost as shocked as he did and stood in total silence.

"What the hell are you doing?" Clarke whispered as he tried to keep his composure.

"Eugene Clarke, your bravery and strength of character have been proven time and time again whilst serving at my side. I have no doubt that you are more than worthy to serve this colony as leader and protector and I ask that the colony respects my final wishes as its leader." Hawkins smirked, still holding his salute.

"Oh, you dirty bastard!"

"Do you except the responsibility that has been charged to you and promise to defend this colony and its people with your very life?" Hawkins leaned a little closer to Clarke and whispered, "You'd probably better say something, they're not going to stand there forever."

"But I'm not, I mean…"

"Stop babbling, Clarke, if I didn't think you could handle it, I wouldn't be offering. You said you'd like your own command."

"I meant a starship not the whole colony!"

"In at the deep end, as they say." Hawkins took a deep breath and shouted, "Do you accept?"

"On my honour and my life, I accept." The sound of thousands of boots hitting the floor made Clarke jump as the entire room saluted. He looked out over the sea of faces and smiled. "Thank you, Captain. Thank you all. Well, we have a lot of work to do. So, I suppose we'd better get moving," Clarke looked at Hawkins who smiled and nodded his head. Clarke shook his head and grinned in disbelief as he turned back to the crowd and shouted, "Dismissed!"

The preparations for the launch kept the colony busy for the rest of the day. The sudden change in leadership lead to many mixed opinions, but everybody that knew Clarke had no doubt that he was worthy of his new position. The Dark Star and the Polaris eventually got underway. Sent off by the cheers of the colonists as they departed. Now sat in orbit, high above the earth, the vessels rested momentarily in the silent void. Awaiting their pilots' next commands.

"So, the explosive devices can be activated with these remotes?"

"They can only be activated with those remotes. I thought it would be safer to have only one triggering mechanism for these things."

"Yeah, probably a good idea. So, once I press this button, how long do we have before it blows?"

"There is almost no time delay, sir. I didn't want to give Gatekeeper the chance to break the encryption code before it blows… I know it's referred to as a power build up, but in real time it's about three seconds."

"So, it's 'press' one, two…"

"Goodbye everything that isn't out of range."

Hawkins nodded. "Fair enough. Did you explain this to Captain Dillan?"

"Captain Dillan and the entire crew of the Polaris have been informed how to use their device."

"Well done, Kane. Bring the weapon systems online."

"No problem, Captain."

"Blaine, how's she look?"

"Ready to rock, sir."

"Hawkins to Polaris, are you ready to fly?"

"Fletcher here, lead the way, Captain."

"Miller, give me a gateway."

Miller, who was manning Clarke's old position at the first mates control console, immediately responded, "Jump-drive generator engaged, Captain. Anomaly forming two thousand metres ahead of the ship."

"Ok, Blaine, let's do it." Hawkins watched through the view port as the ships descended into the whirlpool-like anomaly beneath them. As always, the forces exerted on them by the gravity well disorientated the crew. Momentarily distorting reality, as they perceived it. The immense gravitational forces involved bending the fabric of spacetime around them as they passed through the anomaly. Making everything seem to slow down to a crawl.

"Returning to normal space, sir," Miller informed. Hawkins shook off the disorientation quickly and returned his attention to the view port.

"Good god," exclaimed Blaine as he looked out through the main view port.

It was immediately apparent to the captain, that this side of the gateway had not materialised into open space. But instead had delivered them right onto the very outer edge of a large asteroid field. For a moment he froze, as he stared out through the view port at this distant star system's twin suns. Suns that backlit the asteroid field and what appeared to be a particularly large asteroid, positioned directly before them. This was no ordinary space rock, however. Upon further inspection, Hawkins noticed lights shining from several large structures, which were embedded into its surface. He realised suddenly that he was just sitting there.

"This is it. Miller, give me a reading. Blaine, head for that rock."

"Aye, sir," Blaine responded, easing the engines into life.

"Reading multiple energy signatures," Miller replied, looking at his instruments. "These rocks appear to be made from the same metals as the Gatekeeper vessels. The readings are very similar. There appears to be several small, err, I guess vessels, mining them, Captain."

"Captain, look." Blaine drew Hawkins' attention to a section of the asteroid, as it revolved into view of the main viewport. Momentarily still lit by the system's stars, as the massive rock turned, an enormous skeletal framework became visible. Crawling with repair drones the massive construction project struck immediate fear into the entire crew, before it dropped into the shadow created by the asteroids darker side and was once again out of view.

"Was that what I think it was?" Kane queried. The unease easily registered in his voice.

"A mothership!" Blaine responded, "It's building another mothership!"

"Jesus! All those drones crawling on it. No wonder it can replace the ships we destroy so fast."

"Something's happening!" Miller warned, "I'm detecting multiple power build ups. Lots of movement."

The crew watched through the main view port, as multiple large sections of the structure embedded into the asteroid, started to light up and fall away from it. As if it were shedding its scales into space.

"What the hell is that?" questioned Blaine. He strained to get a better look.

Hawkins' face dropped. "They're ships," his blood ran cold. "They're all ships. Blaine, get us moving."

Blaine powered up the engines and the Dark Star accelerated forwards toward the asteroid, as the waking vessels began to animate and take flight.

"There are energy build-ups everywhere. They're overlapping there are so many." Miller struggled to understand the readings saturating the screen of his tactical console.

"Miller, weapons free, fire at –" Hawkins gripped the armrests on his chair, as a large shockwave shook the ship. "Report."

"The Polaris has been hit, sir," Miller looked up. "She's no longer registering on my screen."

"Fuck. It's down to us, Blaine. Evasive manoeuvres. Keep us in one piece."

"No problem, Captain." Blaine tightened his grip on the manual controls. "Ok assholes! Let's see if you can hit –" Blaine's boasting ceased immediately, as the Dark Star jolted violently. Shaking the crew like rag dolls in their safety harnesses.

"We're hit! We're hit!"

"Propulsion is down," Blaine shouted, "Kane, I got no control."

"Damn it, Miller. Shoot something!" Hawkins barked. "Activate Keymaster!"

Miller wasted no time. The Dark Star became a veritable light show of torpedo launches and laser fire. Explosions rocked the Dreadnought from all sides as her hastily launched torpedoes began to connect with other objects in space around the ship. A couple of them striking the smaller enemy vessels, but most of them impacting the surrounding asteroid in the field.

"Kane, damage report?"

"We took a direct hit. The ventral stern on the starboard side is gone. The lower seventeen decks are open to space. Emergency energy seals are holding."

Hawkins noticed the asteroid base growing closer and closer to the main view port as the momentum of the Dark Star carried them toward it. "Blaine, slow her down. Retro rockets, thrusters, anything!"

"All I have is thrusters." Blaine looked out through the forward view port towards the rapidly closing asteroid.

"It's not enough." Hawkins was still staring out through the view port as one of Gatekeeper's ships attempted to ram the Dark Star in an attempt to change her heading away from its home base. The entire bridge jolted as the vessels collided and bounced off one another. The base in the window appeared to be spinning now, due to the Dark Star's erratic, uncontrolled and spiralling approach.

"Lasers are not penetrating the enemy's shields," warned Miller. "Keymaster has no effect." He looked up at Hawkins. "They've adapted, Captain."

The news would have probably been damning to Hawkins if he wasn't already coming to terms with what was now an unavoidable crash.

"Blaine, get the nose up or the impact will crush the bridge."

Blaine fired every thruster and rocket he had at his disposal and the looming asteroid installation slowly left the view port.

"Close the blast shield. Brace for impact!" Hawkins bellowed as he gripped his console. The blast shield closing in over the main view port as Miller activated it. The crew followed suit and braced in their chairs.

The lights of the bridge were replaced with deafening noise and darkness, as the ship collided, belly first, with the asteroid's surface. The impact tore through Hawkins' lower back like a hammer blow to his spine. Sending great waves of pain through his body. Miller cried out into the darkness, as he felt a tremendous pressure against his stomach. He didn't know what it was, but suddenly he could not move. Everything stopped, becoming silent and still and dark.

Hawkins recovered from semi-consciousness and slowly sat up as best he could. Still harnessed into his chair. He wrestled to free himself from whatever it was that had him pinned down. From the feel of the object, he quickly identified it to be his console, which must have torn free from the deck. He managed to push the weight off of himself and it crashed noisily to the floor. He had no idea where his crewmates were through the all-consuming darkness. He couldn't even see his own hand in-front of his face as he blindly felt around the wall for the emergency support locker.

"Who's that?" he whispered into the darkness as he heard someone cough.

"Miller," the sergeant responded. "Is that you, Captain?"

Hawkins finally managed to find the flush mounted locker door in the wall. He opened it and fumbled around inside it, managing to find what felt like a flashlight. Hawkins shone the light in the direction of Miller's voice. Miller frowned in disbelief as the new light source illuminated the large support strut that had torn free from the roof and was now passing straight through his gut. Pinning him and his collapsed chair to the bridge's back wall. Hawkins panned the torchlight around the room. He closed his eyes and looked away, unable to handle the sight, as he illuminated what remained of his crushed and skewered friends. Large twisted pieces of buckled floor plating and sections of collapsed bulkhead thrust upwards from decks below by the impact of the crash, now filled the bridge's starboard side. A veritable scrap yard of unforgiving metal, dripping with blood, where his fast-talking helmsman and his ingenious engineer should be. Hawkins gathered his strength and ignoring pain from his back he moved over to help Miller. He braced the flashlight between two pieces of debris on the floor, facing upwards. This afforded the room some small amount of light while freeing the captain's hands.

"It's no good," he sighed, as he pulled on the large support strut. Failing entirely to budge it.

Miller coughed and shook his head, a trickle of blood running from the side of his mouth and across his cheek. "It doesn't matter now." Miller coughed again, spraying blood across Hawkins. "Strange, but it doesn't hurt." Miller grinned and dropped his head back against the bridge's wall. "That can't be a good sign."

"I'll go and fetch a laser torch to cut you free."

The whole bridge rocked, as something impacted with the ship.

"Now what?" queried Miller.

"Not sure. It couldn't have been from an energy weapon or we wouldn't be having this conversation." Hawkins winced as a wave of pain shot up his whiplashed back.

"What then?" Miller coughed another load of blood from his lungs.

Hawkins turned to face the pressure door of the bridge's transport lift, as the sound of movement became apparent in the lift shaft beyond it. "Breaching-pod," the captain offered dryly. The smooth flat surface of the door buckled inwards slightly, as something smashed into it with a THUD. Hawkins flinched involuntarily.

"Any ideas, Captain?"

THUD.

This time Hawkins did not flinch. A sudden eerie look of calmness spread across the captain's face. He reached into his pocket and took out the remote detonator for the crystalline explosive device. Miller looked at the device as Hawkins raised it. The pair looked back at each other.

THUD.

"Any famous last words, Sergeant?"

THUD.

Miller took his eyes off Hawkins and stared into the darkness of the room for a moment. He took a deep cleansing breath then began to speak.

"We take a moment to honour the fallen." THUD. "To honour our brothers." THUD. "To all who made this moment possible." THUD. "Thank you for your service and your sacrifice." THUD. "You will be remembered." THUD. "Semper fi."

The pressure door began to peel open. Hawkins stared defiantly at the movement in the shadows beyond the buckling doorway. As the door finally succumbed fully, revealing the beady red lights of whatever cold metal horrors were about to step through. He defiantly raised the detonator up in-front of him.

"Get off my ship!" Hawkins pressed the button.

EPILOGUE

Atop a large hill in the darkness of the clear and steady night, an old man stood alone. Peacefully looking up towards the blanket of star. In the fields below the hills lofty position of solitude, lit only by portable lighting towers and the landing lights from many dormant transport ships, a sea of people had gathered. The sounds of laughter and merriment drifted up to pierce the silence of the hilltop, as the large group drank and enjoyed their music in the open air.

Behind the old man two shadowed figures approached from the darkness. As they approached and came into view one of the pair suddenly ran at the old man and he bent down and picked him up.

"Ahh, there's my favourite future starship captain." The old man smiled at the boy and then at the woman who had brought him.

"Mummy said that I should keep you company, grandpa," the boy announced.

"Did she now. Well, your mummy knows best, I suppose."

The woman smiled at her father. The old man's attention was drawn to the device on his wrist as an alarm started to sound. Then drawn to the party below as the music stopped and all the lights dimmed, almost to nothing. He turned and pointed to the sky. "Watch up there. Right there. And in a moment, maybe there will be a…" The old man stopped, as what appeared to be a bright new star appeared in the sky, right where he was pointing. A small blue/purple spec that persisted.

"Wow!" exclaimed the boy. "Is that a star, grandpa?"

The crowd below erupted into applause.

"It, err."

The woman placed a comforting hand on her father's shoulder, as his voice cracked with emotion. He coughed in an attempt to pull himself together.

"Well." He tried again, "It's the light from an explosion that happened a long time ago. Very far away from here. So far away in-fact, that the light has only just reached us now."

"Wow," the boy repeated, his view fixed on the point of light.

"We weren't sure if it would be there or not. All these people were waiting to see if it came." A tear ran down the old man's cheek.

"Are you sad that it came, grandpa?" the boy asked, as he looked at his grandfather and noticed the tears on his face.

The old man looked at the boy and smiled. "No, I'm not sad. That light is a message from some very brave men. You see they went away a long time ago to make sure we were all safe. We weren't sure what happened to them. That light is them telling us how a story ended."

The boy looked back up at the star. "Who were they grandpa?"

The old man's daughter drew his attention to the crowd in the fields below. A sea of small candle lights now shone like a blanket across the darkness, as they paid their respects and gave their thanks… together. The old man looked back at the star.

"They were my friends," he replied. Again, fighting the emotion.

"Tyron to Commander Clarke, come in please."

The old man looked at his daughter, who shrugged her shoulders with a sigh. She raised her wrist and pushed a button on her communicator.

"The sky better be falling, Tyron," she said as she turned and began to walk away. The old man smiled, tightened his grip on his grandson and looked back at the sky.

"Would you like to hear a story about them?"

The boy nodded giddily. "Yes please, grandpa."

"Ok then. It starts like this… With a groan from its pistons the rusty old hatch opened."

Printed in Great Britain
by Amazon

18469677R00243